JOHN RIVERS

Grimm

First edition

This book was professionally typeset on Reedsy.
Find out more at reedsy.com

Contents

My Name, is Cyrus Grimm

My name is Cyrus Grimm, and I have a very important job. Sometimes, actually, it feels like that's all I do. I don't even really talk to anyone, which makes this a bit of a special occasion. Come to think of it, I can't even remember the last time I sat down and had a real conversation. So why would I stop and take the time now?

Well, I want to tell you a story. It's the story of a girl, someone very special that I met. You could say she changed who I am. Caused a few issues with work and, I'll be honest, it turned a lot of folks' lives upside down.

Now, you're probably asking yourself, *why should I care?* or *why are you telling me?* Quite honestly, I don't really care if you care or not. I just think that it's a story worth telling, and it's important to me that you hear it. As for why I am telling you, well, I've been looking for you for a long time and for just that reason—to tell you this story. Well, that and to grant you my services.

So let me start again.

Nice to meet you. My name is Cyrus Grimm, but you know me better as Death.

This is where I usually tell people to not be afraid. The revelation that you are dead can be a bit jarring. The transition between the two states of existence isn't always clear for people. And hearing the confirmation from me can sometimes be a little bit unsettling.

I understand that I don't look like what you expected. That's totally understandable. But I do try to at least dress for the occasion. In my experience, modern clothes almost always trump the black cloak and scythe. Where humanity came up with that image of me I'll never understand; though it hasn't stopped me from having some fun from time to time if someone required a little bit of convincing.

Anyway, let's get back to it. I think I should probably start at the beginning, give a little character history—always important in a good story. It's also helpful for you to understand the reasons for the choices I've made over my very long stay here.

I can't really say that I was "born," at least not in the traditional way birth happens on this planet. It was kind of like waking up from a long dream, as if I had always been here, just not really *present*. The best way I can describe it is, it was like having cold water thrown on you in the middle of the night. The sensation of being hurled into existence was something I can't really compare to anything else. The planet was still hot, molten from the intense gravity of the sun. In time it cooled, giving me some time to grow accustomed to my existence on Earth. And then it settled. The oceans formed and eventually the first creatures swam in it. That's when things got interesting.

For millions of years I was effectively a garbage man, cleaning up the leftover spiritual energy to be recycled into new and more complex organisms. Plants, animals—they were essentially all the same. That is, until the advent of humanity. I remember people slowly becoming self-aware, building bonds with one another, and becoming more than just individuals struggling to survive. It was truly something special to watch.

But you know what it was, the moment things really changed?

I will never forget it.

It was a nice spring morning. I was there to collect the soul of one of the older members who had moved on during the night. The group called him "Rohg." Until that moment, whenever a member of the tribe expired, he/she would have been left behind. No special treatment would be made. No additional attention paid beyond the brief mourning that all higher creatures show. Just left behind. But this time was different. They had learned over many generations that flesh decays, and its smell attracts animals that eat flesh. And, for the first time, they cared about it.

The group dug a hole in the ground, and in it they put Rohg. I remember him standing next to me, communicating as best he could. He asked why they were doing that. Like him, I was new to this concept and didn't have the answer. But looking back, I can honestly say that that moment was when they went from *animal* to something more. Everything changed after that. The social dynamics that arose from that simple act of burying the dead would forever alter humanity. The primitive language became more refined, and the nomadic tendencies stopped. They began to domesticate animals, grow crops, et cetera. It was a very interesting few millennia.

Then came the working of metal. Tools for hunting became weapons of war, and mankind took on a completely different persona. Man had conquered nature and therefore needed something else to combat. What better opponent than one's self? That was when my job became more important than it ever had been. I had always played cleanup whenever a spirit moved on. Now, however, the things that men did to one another had changed the landscape of how souls transitioned.

Humans have innate psychic tendencies, thoughts, and emotions that transfer with their actions. Cruelty, apathy, jealousy, envy—all these things and many more—leave scars on the souls of men. Good men carry with them their good deeds, and when that energy is brought back, they keep it. Violent men carry their actions with them as well. It made things complicated. If it was just *you carry what you are*, that would not be so bad. But that's not how it works.

Like I said, thoughts and emotions transfer with actions, and powerful emotions imprint onto others. Love, compassion, empathy—these things can heal, and people learned this early on. What they also learned early on was that there were others that could wound—not just bodies, but souls. Some are worse than others. Seven in particular cause very grievous damage to everyone they affect.

You know the list.

Anyway, men used these things to wage war on one another. Not just physical war, but spiritual war. Which is important, but I'll get to that. Many more years passed, and humans continued to evolve. Their need for companionship eventually pushed their carnal desires to the back of their minds. Things have remained much as they are now for the better part of the past two hundred years. This brings me to the present, and the real beginning of our story: the day I met the girl who changed everything.

1

One Fateful Evening

It was a warm summer evening in the suburbs. The day thus far had been relatively uneventful. The worldwide death toll had been the lowest for me in recent memory. This gave me a chance to stop and enjoy the nuances of humanity I found so fascinating. I arrived at the home of one Mrs. Norma Bibby. She was a kind eighty-seven-year-old lady. Her body was still strong despite her age, and she likely would have remained healthy for years to come.

However, that was not my first visit to that house. I had come for her husband, Jerry, about seven months before. His passing changed everything for her. She had become more and more depressed ever since I had come to collect Jerry. Until I had arrived, her whole world had revolved around their wonderful life together. But Jerry was a smoker and his fondness for red meat had raised his cholesterol and blood pressure, which in time took its toll on his heart and earned him a visit from me.

Norma had been a very active woman all her life before losing him. She had deteriorated a great deal since last I had seen her. The loss of her beloved had been more than she could handle, and she had relegated herself to the misery of being alone. Her eating habits had grown worse and she no longer kept active. Their children and grandchildren tried to be supportive, but she couldn't get herself past it. And so it was time for her to have what she wanted: a visit from me and a happy reunion with Jerry on the other side.

I stepped into the living room where Norma was curled up on the couch. I could almost see the shards of her broken heart attached to the wadded-up tissues strewn across the floor by the couch. She was trying desperately to move on, but that strong body of hers fought her every inch of the way, forcing her to live on through her tears and heartache. Then it happened. The best description I can give is, it's like watching a guitar string break. She forced the last ounce of strength out of her body and sank into what would be her last sleep.

I tapped her on the shoulder and she awoke.

"Who are you?" she asked.

"My name is Cyrus," I replied, "and I'm here to take you away."

She wasn't afraid. Maybe a little confused. There was only one thing on her mind. And so, she asked.

"Will Jerry be there?" A look of hope sparkled in her eyes. It was something I didn't see very often. People are usually very shocked and afraid when I take them, but she knew from the moment I said my name that it was finally over.

"Yes, he will," I said. I was telling the truth, in a strange sort of way. "You will be able to see him soon." If spirits could cry, she likely would have as I said those words. I sat with her for a moment, like I usually do, until she was ready to leave. Most people sit in silence, trying to accept the situation they're in.

Some have small breakdowns and I need to help them relax. On occasion, we have those that completely lose it. Those people require a little more aggressive handling. Norma had none of the negative reactions I was accustomed to seeing. She was excited and wanted to know as much as she could about the afterlife.

She asked me what it was like, where she would go next—the standard stuff people think about—but mostly she wanted to know about Jerry and what he had been up to. I usually don't check up on those I collect. However, Jerry had been a special case, and luckily, he had stuck in my memory. I was able to answer some of her questions, and she gave me a hug. It was a rare moment of satisfaction in my job.

When we were done, we stood, and I tried to prepare her for the trip. I travel by means of what I call "impression." I've been here a long time, meaning I know this world inside and out. The best I can explain it is that I can connect with any place on earth and be there. And to a lesser extent I can do the same on the other side. Now, it's not like teleporting; I don't actually leave the area of my primary consciousness. It's more like I'm able to break myself into pieces and be where I imagine myself being. Given the intensity of my job—handling about a hundred and fifty thousand people a day—I am almost always doing it, many times over. It's the only way I can be all around the world at once. I explained this to Norma, and we got ready to go.

I took Norma's hand and told her to be ready for a jolt. I closed my eyes and began to think of where she needed to be. When I begin to do an impression, it is as if time stands still. The wave passed over us and she was gone, across the infinite expanse between our world and that of the spirits. She passed through what I call The Veil, the barrier that separates the physical world and the other. Just her and that sliver of me I had charged with taking her to her beloved. I opened my eyes and looked around the now cold and empty house that used to belong to Norma. It was a peaceful place, but sad; just an empty house.

I prepared to take my leave, giving only one final glance at Norma's now empty remains. Every time I leave someone I think about the person they had been and what they are leaving behind. The impact people have on one another is profound, and many of them don't know how important their connections are until someone is gone, even if they aren't very close. I thought about how Norma being gone would affect those she knew and took a little comfort in the idea that she had been a positive influence in the lives of so many.

When I was done, I walked to the window and looked out across the darkness that blanketed the quiet neighborhood. The next day would bring a change, as one of their own had moved on. Such a small change, creating such a profound reaction. I admire humans for that, how they value one another. Since that moment so many years ago when they buried Rohg, I have always seen it bring out the best in them. And I would like to think that it always will.

I turned to step away and move on with my evening, when I saw it—a shadow against the black. Then another. And another. Something was happening across the street, and it didn't look good. I'm usually not one to be nosy—usually far too busy to for that. But tonight was special—a rare, slow night—so I moved through the wall and out onto the grass of the yard. Across the street, the shadows moved swiftly across the walls of the house and inside. I could see the outlines of the figures and knew what I was seeing.

I see things like this every once in a while, usually just remnants of things that don't accept their own passing and choose to remain in the spirit realm. Humans almost always come to their senses and let me complete my task, but those that don't are allowed to stay behind as ghosts, at least for a time. These, however, are quite different. They aren't creatures or spirits wandering until they are ready for me to take them. These are darker, hungrier. I'm not sure exactly where they come from, but every once in a while, something bleeds through from the other side. These things.

I call them Hexen; not sure why, but it just sounds right. They are, for lack of a better term, soul suckers. I come across them so infrequently that I've never really bothered to find out what they really are. And though I was curious, I was too busy to go looking for them. What I did know about them was that they feed on the vitality of living things. Usually they take something small, a few minutes of one's life. Every once in a while, though, one of them would do some real damage. You hear stories of perfectly healthy people getting cancer or having a heart attack in their early twenties. Any story you can think of resembling that, was a Hexen going a little overboard.

I had been down this road before, watched the Hexen feed. But I had never seen more than one at a time, and never ones this large. My interest was piqued. And so, I moved closer to the house to get a better look.

The home belonged to a young couple, Adrian and Ana Harmond. I passed through the wall and moved into their living room. There were pictures of them throughout the house. I wondered what made them special as I watched the

5

shadowy figures move across the walls of the house. There were even more of them than I had originally thought, perhaps a dozen. Whatever they were doing there, it was something I had never seen before. I had a very bad feeling about it.

Bad feeling or not, I was interested to see what was going to happen. I passed through the bedroom wall and emerged near the foot of the bed. The young couple was lying in it. The flickering blue haze of the television clashed with the orange light from the nightstand lamp. I could see the time on the alarm clock next to it. It was 8:43 and, by all appearances, everything seemed normal. The sound of laughter from the television was met by the same sound from the couple. They were watching the evening news, just as millions of other couples might have been doing that night.

The Hexen moved in through the doorway and crept to the corners of the ceiling. I counted them as they did: thirteen. Like the couple, they began to settle in, and just waited. That behavior was something I had seen before. They would keep their positions and wait until the two were asleep before feeding, which would be quite a sight to see, given the amount of them. I pondered for a moment if I should intervene, as the situation would likely result in a life-altering experience for the couple. But I decided against it; curiosity had won.

The two readied themselves for bed. Adrian went to the bathroom while Ana placed her shoes into the closet along with the thirty other pairs and changed into her nightgown. At 9:13 the lights went out. I waited in anticipation for the couple to sleep so the soul suckers could move in and do what they do. Then came the crash of cracking wood. The bedroom door flew violently off its hinges as the steel battering ram careened into it. Jagged remnants of the frame flew across

6

the room and scattered on the floor.

Men dressed head to toe in black tactical gear and wielding automatic weapons came swiftly through the decimated door frame. The Harmonds had pressed themselves up against the headboard of the bed and stared in shock at the men flooding into their bedroom. Ana was screaming, but it was like there was no sound at all. Adrian reached down toward the top drawer of his nightstand where his .38 revolver was.

One of the men raised his rifle and fired twice, hitting Adrian in the chest with both rounds and knocking him back into the headboard. He slumped over and reached for Ana. The light-colored bedding quickly began to turn crimson as his lifeblood poured onto it. I could see the fear in his eyes as the lights in them slowly went out. Ana became silent as she reached for him, at a loss for what she should do. One of the men grabbed her and pulled her off the bed as she screamed back toward the now lifeless body that used to be her husband.

She struggled against the men, but there was nothing she could do. They bound, gagged, and hooded her before sitting her in the corner. They then proceeded to tear the room apart. She sat lost in her terror and drowning in her own tears under the black cowl.

"It's not here," said one of the men as he touched his earpiece.

"Where is it?" yelled another at Ana as he plucked the bag from her head. She continued to cry. "Point to where it's hidden, or you get to go next," the man said to her as he drew his sidearm and pressed it against her cheek. The look of confusion on her face, along with the sheer horror of what she had just been through, told the man that he would get nothing. "Let's go," he said. "Bag the bitch and bring her."

One of the men grabbed her and tried to lift her. She fought as hard as she could to stop them, but there was nothing she could do. She managed to slip a single hand free of her restraints and dug her nails into the carpet, but it was all for nothing. Then, just as she was about to be dragged from the room, it happened. She looked up at me, her desperation pouring out of her like a river and flowing into me. Her eyes met mine and I knew she could see me. Worse, I could hear her spirit crying out to me: *Help!* It was as if one of the men had just placed another two rounds into my chest.

She could see me. I don't know how, but she could; I was absolutely sure of it. I reached out for her, lost in the moment and in awe of the words she hadn't actually spoken. Then, just as quickly as the men had entered, they were gone. I snapped myself out of it and passed through the wall back into the living room. There was nothing there. It was almost as if they had never been there in the first place. I continued outside and looked around, again, nothing. They were just gone. I turned around and went back into the house. I looked back toward the bedroom where the excitement had just happened. The door that had been torn off its hinges not sixty seconds before, was once again where it had begun the night.

I stood in shock and confusion—at least that's what I thought it was. It had to be, judging by how humans react in similar situations. It was not because of the door's magical reassembly, though that was something that was indeed bothering me, but because the two events were things I had never seen before. Ana Harmond, through some method I did not understand, was able to see me while she was alive. The other, more disturbing thing was that I didn't see any of it coming. Someone had died right in front of me, and I hadn't felt it coming! Never in my entire existence had I not felt someone's death coming and been there waiting for it. Something was very, very wrong here, and I needed to know what.

I stood, unable to move for a moment, and then I remembered the Hexen. I had left them skulking on the roof, waiting for the soul of Adrian Harmond. I rushed through the miraculously reconstructed door. As I moved through it, there was a faint shimmer, I paid it no attention and emerged into the bedroom. The shadows from the walls had descended and were swarming around the corpse. I didn't know what to do; it was all so new to me. Never had I seen the Hexen go after anyone so viciously. All I knew was that that soul was my responsibility. And I needed to make sure he was safe.

I felt a wave of power flood into me. Then, almost as if a second part of me awakened, I felt like the images man had assigned me: the reaper in black. My hands felt like blades and I began to cast the Hexen aside one by one as the soul of the recently departed man flailed beneath the swarm. I had never felt so empowered or helpless at the same time. Then, before I knew it, the shadows were all gone, dispatched by my own hand.

The soul of Adrian Harmond was not in good shape. I felt myself relax and become what I can only describe as my "normal" self. I reached down and took him by the arm and helped him sit up. As he did, I could see the body he had left behind. It was mangled, like it had been attacked by wild animals. The Hexen were here not to feed, but to destroy. Something about Adrian had made him a target. The strangeness just kept escalating, and I was lost inside it.

"Who are you?" Adrian asked weakly.

"I'm Cyrus," I said. "Are you okay?"

"I think so. What were those things?"

"Hexen," I said.

"Uh, okay, and those are . . .?"

I didn't know how to answer. He was already weak, and with the shock of his own death, I was afraid it would be too much. I needed to do this slowly. "I'll tell you later," I replied. "First let's make sure you're all right."

"Cyrus," he interrupted, "I know that I'm dead. I remember getting shot, so just tell me. What the hell were those things?"

I paused for a moment. Like Norma, it was not often someone understood their own death so easily.

"They are remnants," I said.

"Of what?" he asked.

"Not really sure," I replied. "Spirits that wander the world. They feed on the souls of others, and in this case, they wanted yours. Do you know why?"

"I don't, I'm sorry," he said.

"What about the men?" I asked. "Do you know who they are?" He shook his head.

"What about your wife, why could she see me?" No response.

I sat for a moment. The strangeness of the events was grating on me. I had not been this interested in anything in a very long time. It was exciting, and a bit overwhelming all at the same time. But it had pulled me out of myself. I could feel the passing of people around the world. I had neglected my duty and it was something that needed to be done. I didn't want to go, but I had to. The curiosity would have to wait (for the moment at least).

"Adrian, I need you to give me a moment, is that okay?" He nodded, and I proceeded to do what I needed to. I felt the shards of my being leave and imprint to the places I needed to be. I did it as quickly as I could. Each soul was important, but so was this. I needed to be able to focus if it was something that I was going to pursue. I scratched the itch and did what I had to. When I was done, I turned back to him.

Adrian spoke before I had a chance to. "Cyrus, I think I know who you are." It was not what I wanted to hear. What if he lost it?

"And who is that?" I asked, biting my lip.

"You're my guardian angel. God sent you here to watch over me," he said.

I simply smiled, trying not to show my relief. For the moment I was going to be able to avoid an awkward conversation. I decided to move on and let him believe what he wanted to.

"Adrian is there anything you can tell me that might help this make sense?" I asked.

Again, he just shook his head. I wanted to know what had happened to Ana, the girl who had seen me, but there was nothing to follow. As much as I wanted to know what was going on, there was nothing else here for me to go on. There was nothing left for me to do but my job, and Adrian was part of it. And so, I prepared him for his trip, explaining where we would be going and all that it entailed. He acknowledged and understood. I walked him through the house and into the street. I could hear the sounds of sirens in the distance; someone had heard what had happened and called the authorities.

"The police are coming," he said. "That's good; they can find Ana."

He was right that it was a good thing. When I was done, I could come back and use them to find the girl.

"They will find her, Adrian, don't worry. That's their job."

"Aren't you going to help them?" I looked over at him. He was still very weak.

"I'm sorry, that's not what I do," I replied.

He looked at me in disappointment. I would guess that what I was feeling in that moment was guilt. I had every intention of finding her in my own time. Not to save her, but to satisfy my curiosity. She had seen me in life, when I was usually seen only by those that have passed. Her fate was none of my concern. The police would do their thing, and they would find her alive, or they would not, and I would collect her soul. Either way, I would speak to her and get my answers. The only thing that would change was the timetable.

"Why won't you help?" he asked, taking a seat on the curb.

I wanted to tell him the truth. I am death, I don't pick sides. Yet this man, himself ordinary, but at the moment part of something special, was asking me to. I thought about what I would tell him. *My job is too important*, I would say. *I can't sacrifice it for one girl. Who knows what would happen?* But the look on his face was unbearable. And so was the itch to know what had happened. Screw the timetable. How had I been tricked? It was something that I wanted the answer to, sooner rather than later. And, who knew? Putting the countless skills I had developed through my eons on earth might be fun. I looked at him. He was still waiting for an answer, and his fragile state was making him even more convincing. It was enough of an excuse. I agreed and helped him back up before walking him to the corner where we watched as the police arrived.

"Wait here," I said. "I'll be right back."

Adrian nodded and again took a seat beneath the streetlight.

As I walked across the street I began to think about how best to approach this. *What would a detective look like?* I thought. I knew the answer. I had been at many murder scenes. I walked out of sight around the corner. Then I did something I hadn't done in a long time: took on corporeal form. I have to say, I looked sharp. The feel of real clothes on me was different, and the warmth of the blood in my veins and wool of the pin-striped suit on my skin was soothing. I could feel the cool night breeze on my face and took a deep breath. Boy, it felt good to feel alive, even if it was just for a moment.

The officers had already entered the house and found what was left of Adrian's corpse. I walked into sight, an overhead streetlight at the corner punctuating my reveal to those whose job it was to protect the people of this city. The officer stringing the yellow tape marked POLICE LINE DO NOT CROSS gave me a look. I held out my fake badge and he let me pass. I laughed a little as I felt the human persona I had adopted cause me to shake my head at the lack of punctuation on said yellow tape. It was no doubt made that way to reduce the manufacturing cost. Something before that moment I wouldn't have noticed nor should I have, due to its irrelevancy. But I was a detective in this moment; it was my job to notice the little things.

I walked into the house where two other men, in all probability detectives themselves, stood. They were discussing the condition of Adrian's mangled body. I moved closer to them to introduce myself. They stopped me before I could.

"And who the fuck are you?" asked the short, plump one.

I produced my faux credentials and replied, "Detective First Grade Cyrus Grimm, on loan from the NYPD. Who the fuck are you?" The look on the two men's faces told me that they liked my retort.

"I'm Detective Aaron, and this lanky fuck is Detective Marx."

"Who you calling a lanky fuck, Oompa Loompa?" They both laughed under their breath and turned to me.

"So, New York, why are you way the hell out here?" Aaron asked. Here was my chance to test my skills. They both had stubble that was at least a few days' grown, meaning that they were blue-collar chaps, more concerned with catching bad guys than their image. This was confirmed by the fact that neither wore a tie and both had sweat stains on their collars and armpits—and, of course, the colorful language. Neither wore a wedding band; they were married to the jobs and each other. The fingernails on their hands were dirty, completely ungroomed—hell, for all I knew neither of them had showered in days. Which very well may have been the case since they were both drenched in a very intense and terrible cologne. All in all, it gave me a pretty good picture of what I needed: two lazy detectives who wanted the glory, didn't care how they got it, and weren't really willing to do the work.

"Let's just say I dealt with something in a way that the lieutenant didn't exactly care for," I said, knowing that neither of them would bother to vet the story.

"Good to have you, then," Marx said. "Care to see the body?" I nodded and walked into the room, knowing what I would find. I felt like an idiot when I tried to walk through the wall like I had done so many times before.

"You okay?" Aaron asked, giving me a strange look.

"Yeah, I'm fine. Had a little bit to drink before I came out," I lied.

"Nice," he replied. "Hope you saved some for us." We all chuckled and moved into the bedroom, this time through the door. Everything was how I remembered it. The mutilated remains of the man I had left sitting on the street corner outside were bleeding into the bed and the sound of dripping blood where it had soaked through the mattress and come out the bottom churned my stomach—which reminded me that I needed to eat. I needed to steer them toward Ana's abduction and away from the brutality of Adrian's demise.

"Where's the wife?" I asked.

"What wife?" Marx asked.

"The one that was taken," I said. They both looked at me in confusion. "C'mon, guys, seriously? What guy buys thousand-thread-count sheets? Two nightstands, two lamps, two alarm clocks. I bet you in the bathroom you'll find two toothbrushes, feminine care products, and pictures with the two of them in it."

They both nodded as I laid it out in front of them. They were not very good at what they did. The help I hoped to find here was not going to be substantial. Then I felt a twinge. Two clocks. I picked up the clock that had been knocked from the nightstand on Adrian's side. Stopped at 9:13, a shard of wood lodged in it. It was from the door that had been destroyed as the men entered.

I took a second look and couldn't place what was off with how it looked. I dismissed it a second time, more concerned with the woman who had seen me. I did not imagine that part, her seeing me was very real, not an illusion. I placed the clock back down as I refocused on the two men looking about the room.

"Aaron, Marx, come here," I yelled at them. They ran over like puppies to a new owner. "Okay, guys, let the unis deal with the guy. Focus on the girl. It looks like she's still alive;

15

let's try to keep it that way. Got it?"

"Yeah, we got it," Aaron said.

"Good. I'll see what I can dig up to give us more to go on. I'll be in touch."

"How do we contact you?" Marx asked.

"I'll contact you," I replied. "I'm not exactly supposed to be investigating anything right now, if you know what I mean." They looked at each other and nodded like I had just told them the biggest secret in the world. If they only knew.

I left the house and walked back toward the corner where I had left the soul of Adrian Harmond. He wasn't there. He had moved closer and was standing at the edge of the punctuation-free yellow police tape. He was stuck in the habits of his life, knowing he shouldn't pass it. Forgetting no one could see him, and even if they could, they couldn't stop him. I walked past him and gave a gesture to follow, which he did.

"You do realize that no one can see you and that you can walk through solid objects, right?"

"Yeah. I saw you try, through the window," he said with a smile on his face.

"Don't give me that look," I said. When we were out of sight I reverted back to my much less hindered spectral state. It felt good to be light again. I explained to Adrian that I had no new information.

"Now what?" he asked.

"Now I take you to where you need to be, then I will continue doing my job, and do what I can to save Ana," I replied.

"Thank you," he said. I nodded and raised my hand, so he would stop walking. I could feel the buzz again. I needed to get back to the job. I closed my eyes and went to those who

16

had died and were dying, to get them to where they needed to be. I was still in the middle of it when I heard it:

"I'm glad I found you before you disappeared on me," came from down the street.

My eyes sprung open. Before us stood a woman dressed in all black with a wide-brimmed hat. She had medium-length blond hair, and her shirt had a clerical collar. Adrian would have said she was pretty. I stood silent until she spoke again.

"Well? Are neither of you going to say anything?" Adrian and I looked at each other, then back at her.

"You can see us?" I asked.

"Yes, I can," she replied. "And before you ask, my name is Vera Essalte. I am a priest of the Church of Saint Ordanis."

"Never heard of it."

"Few have."

"I'd like to say it's nice to meet you, but it's not," I replied and looked at Adrian, who stood motionless, staring at her.

"Given your experience tonight, I don't blame you," Vera said.

"Why can you see us?" I asked, now very intrigued by this person standing before me.

"Good question to start with," she replied. "I can see you because I am one of a select few that has True Sight. I can see the world beneath the world."

"So, psychic," I said.

"Close enough. I'll explain more later. Right now, we need to go, Mr. Grimm."

If I had a physical spine, a chill would have run down it. "How do you know my name?" I asked.

"I know both of you," she replied. "Adrian, you look well. Well, I guess as well as I could expect you to look." I glanced

17

over at him; a look of disbelief was on his face.

"Do you know her?" I asked him. He didn't answer. "Adrian!" I barked, snapping him out of his trance. "Do you know her?"

"Yeah, I do," he said. I waited for him to continue, but he was once more stuck in a daze. I rolled my eyes and continued to press.

"Focus, Adrian! How?"

"She's my boss. From work."

"Another time, gentlemen. Let's go," Vera said.

"I think now is a good time," I said, trying to show impatience. "What do you want?"

"I want what you want: to find out what happened to Ana."

"Why?"

"Because she is one of us," she said. "One of the chosen."

"Chosen to do what?" I asked.

"Chosen by God to protect the world from the forces of hell."

"This is ridiculous," I replied. "I have walked this world for millions of years, and never once has there ever been anything to show me that God exists. Hell, I was here long before the idea of God even existed. So, don't come in here and tell me that God gave you this. There is no God. There's just me, the garbage man!"

Adrian looked at me, confused, not quite sure what to make of me. I remembered that he said he thought I was an angel. It was not the first time I had seen that mistake. For a moment I felt bad that I had just shattered his belief system. But he was about to find out the truth, anyway. I just hoped he took it well. Then Vera spoke.

"You can choose to believe what you want, but I'm asking

you both for your help," she said.

"Wait," Adrian said. "Who are you?" he asked me. Vera realized in that moment that Adrian didn't know the truth. I looked at her and tilted my head, letting her know it was her decision to make. She looked at him and spoke.

"Adrian, what do you believe he is? An angel maybe?"

"Isn't he?" he asked, his still-weak soul struggling with the emotional roller coaster he had been on this evening. She walked up to him and stood close, then looked at me before speaking.

"Yes, Adrian, he is your guardian angel. He's everyone's guardian angel, left here to guard the earth long before man walked on it; for he is the Angel of Death, the Reaper of Souls. Armies kneel at his feet, and even the mightiest man counts himself lucky to have him standing over him. And you and he are going to help me find your wife, aren't you?"

Adrian fell to his knees, completely exhausted. At least he didn't have the energy to lose it over finding out who I really was. He looked up at me, as if God was real and sitting on my shoulder. As Vera knelt down beside him, she knew she had Adrian's answer. And though it was a lie, I had a small piece of mine. Vera had given me the reason as to why I had been seen. And supposedly it was because a divine being had given her that gift. Not exactly what I had hoped for, but, then again, you don't always like the answers you get.

My curiosity felt strangely satisfied. I had every opportunity to walk away at that very moment, drop Adrian off, and move on with my existence, ignorant to the actions of men. But as I looked down at that broken soul and the priest kneeling with him, I learned something very important about humanity. Hope is never dead. I guess I already knew that. I had seen it earlier that night with Norma. So once again I made the excuse. If the taking of Ana Harmond was indeed going to bring about the end of the world—as highly improbably as that was—then that was a whole lot of work that I really didn't want to deal with. And so, I answered Vera's question.

"How can I help?"

2

How Everything Changed

We walked down the dark, empty alleys of the sleeping city—the priest, the soul, and the reaper. I had somehow allowed myself to be sucked into the completely irrational notion that one person could somehow be the catalyst for some type of doomsday device, and that I was to somehow become a tool on behalf of an organization who was going to try and stop it. I mulled it over as the long walk became even longer, marching silently to wherever the priest was leading us.

The night was still, even more so than most nights. I watched as Adrian walked alongside Vera. He had accepted what she had told him as the truth right from the start. To him, she was the path back to his wife, to peace in the afterlife. A lie that I didn't have the heart to tell him was such. Why? Because I had been lonely and curious. I wanted to tell him the truth, take him to where it all ends and begins. Introduce him to his neighbor, Norma. Give him the chance to do as she had done and be at peace. It was my job, after all. Now, to him, none of it existed because he lingered, and I let it be that way. Curiosity had me, and I was neglecting the soul walking right in front of me for it.

I wanted many times to change my mind along the way, but never did. When we walked past the tall, black iron bars of the gates bearing the sign NO TRESPASSING and into the courtyard of the broken-down church, I gave up the prospect of doing so. The building was noticeably old and run-down. It was likely a church from the late 1800s. At some point in the past hundred and some odd years it had been converted into a law office, a dojo, and something that I couldn't make out due to the terrible handwriting in which it had been written. No one had been here for at least several decades, and it showed.

Vera grunted as she pushed the heavy wooden doors open. Dust fell off the warping wood as they creaked open. The inside was dark and musty. The pews had been pressed up against the walls to make room for the various other dilapidated furniture that was strewn across the space. Dead leaves moved across the twisting floorboards from the wind blowing through a few of the windows that had been broken. The feeling of emptiness was comforting, though I couldn't tell you why. I imagined for a moment that God was real, and he was with me in that room.

"Wait here," Vera said as she moved toward where the altar had once stood. She reached her fingers under the carpet where it met the wood and pulled it up, exposing two metal rings. They were attached to the hidden doors that likely led into the catacombs. Most old churches have them; it was where the rich and powerful were buried in the old days. Another reminder of how people had changed over time. At the beginning it was "honor your dead." Then it became "honor your wealthy dead more." Coffins lined in precious metal, entire tombs dedicated to those of higher monetary gains were revered, while it was holes and dirt for the rest. I was never a fan of the concept.

A loud pop echoed in the room as Vera pulled one of the doors open, revealing the stairs underneath. She motioned us over and we went. We followed her down into the basement, and she closed the door behind us and locked the dead bolt she had likely installed quite recently, evidenced by its bright metallic appearance. The click of her flashlight illuminated the basement room. It was a study filled with texts and manuscripts that appeared to be very old. It was clear that she had done a lot of research down here. I looked at Adrian. He was slack-jawed and lost in wonder at what he saw.

Vera pulled out a chair and sat down. Dust shook off it and hung in the air, made plain by the single light source. Vera grabbed a text off the table and began flipping through the text, not saying a word. We stood for a few minutes watching her turn the pages. Eventually I grew impatient. My curiosity needed to be fed if she wanted my help. She had asked for it, after all, and for the past hour not a word had been said between us. I wanted my answers and I wanted them quickly.

"So, what the hell are we doing here?" I asked, trying to portray my impatience. It came out of my mouth and tasted strange. Infusing emotion into my words was not normal; it seemed a little bit of the detective guise I had worn had stuck with me. I would say it felt good, but I have spent a long-time avoiding emotions, so I can't confidently say what "good" feels like.

Vera's gaze rose from the text and she looked up at us. Like me, she looked impatient, but there was something else behind it. I think she could sense that I was still not sold on her story, and she didn't want to say the wrong thing for fear that I would take Adrian and leave. That was a good thing—it meant I was still in control. I seized the moment and kept going.

"Well?" I asked. I am not sure if she saw through it or if it was a poor performance, but she called me on it.

"Well what?" she replied.

"Well, what are we doing here? You ask for my help, and then don't talk to me; it doesn't seem like you meant it when you asked," I said, trying to leave my face blank. She didn't reply, just looked at me. I decided enough was enough. I either needed answers and evidence to satisfy my selfish craving, or I needed to leave and go back to my work. So, I voiced it.

"Look," I said, "I'm sure you understand that I have a very time-consuming occupation. Waiting in the basement of a broken-down church with a cleric of a church I've never heard of, with the spirit of a man who I should have already escorted past this existence, is not exactly what I should be doing right now. So, this needs to get moving, or I will." It felt convincing. Perhaps I would get the answers I was seeking, and if not, then really that was okay, too. I just needed to not be idle. I could feel the itch of the work I was leaving undone.

"Fine," she said. "I was hoping to avoid any details for as long as I could, but since it seems I don't have a choice, I will share."

"Why would you want to do that?" Adrian said before I had a chance. The fear or reverence—whatever it was he had shown toward her—was gone. He was getting used to the idea of being dead. She was now the person who was going to help him save his wife, and if she wasn't, then she had no power over him. Everyone was on equal footing. "This is important to me," he continued. "I'm dead, my wife is gone, you ask for my help, and now you tell us you are trying to avoid details for as long as you can. What the fuck?!"

I could almost see her heart jump into her throat. Adrian had her; the air of confidence she was cloaked in from the moment she approached us on the street dissipated, as if someone had just run by her with an industrial-strength fan and blew it away. Everything stopped; the flicker from the candle flame was the only thing seemingly alive in the room, and it too was struggling.

"I'm sorry," she said. She was exposed, and she knew it. She had something to say, but it wasn't that load of shit she had fed us on the empty street. The vulnerability was good; she was a human once more. She knew to let the ruse go and stop pretending to be some omniscient being. Adrian calmed down and continued to talk.

"Tell me then, what can we do?" he said. Vera took a deep breath before answering.

"Well, lets start with me," she said. "I am not a priest. There is no church of Saint Ordanis. Well, maybe there is, but I'm not part of it."

"Was any of it real?" asked Adrian.

"Yes, maybe, I don't know," she said. "For the past few months everything that I thought I knew has turned upside down. Think about the work, Adrian."

"How does that tie into this?" he asked.

"Has nothing changed for you?

"No, why?"

"Well, this waveform research is something beyond strange. I got a little too close, and since then I've been seeing things," she said.

"Like what?" I asked.

25

Vera looked at me for a moment, then back at Adrian.

"How well do we know each other Adrian?" she asked.

Adrian shrugged. "Not well, you're the project lead. I don't really communicate with you directly. My team uploads our research into the database and I provide you a report."

"Have I ever met your wife?"

"No."

"Should I even know her name?"

"No."

"Then why do I? Why would I know that she has the same true sight that I do? Why would I know that I would find you, with him? Tonight?"

We both looked at her, stunned.

"I don't know what's happening. Why I can see what I see? I have a theory, and it's fucking crazy. And goddamn it what else am I going to do but follow my visions, premonitions, whatever they are?

I looked at Adrian as his entire spirit sank. The hope he had been holding on to wasn't real. His former boss didn't have the answers he sought, hell she was just as lost as he was. I shook my head. This hour had been a waste of time. Yes, someone had taken Ana Harmond. And as puzzling as that was, in the grand scheme of my existence, it didn't matter. The men would do as they wished, and when they were done they would kill her. I could feel it, and then I would be there and have my chance to talk to her. I knew this. I had gone through it many times. Countless abductions over thousands of years. The only reason this one was bugging me was because she had seen me before her passing. There was nothing special, just two psychics who could see me through strange turn of nature. It would end the same as it had so many times before.

26

I mulled it over before making a final decision. It was time to go.

I told Adrian that it was time to leave. He nodded and began to walk toward me as I turned to head upstairs through the trapdoor. My eyes had just risen above the wood when I felt it. It was as if I had stayed in my corporeal form and someone had thrust a blade into my back. I felt the shock hit my system and recoiled in response. I moved in reaction and felt myself fly down the stairs. My hand moved to Vera's neck and I lifted her, driving her across the room. I pinned her against the wall opposite the stairs. Dust particles gave of tiny shimmers in the candle light as they fell from the ceiling, dislodged by the force I had slammed Vera into the wall with. I could feel my teeth clenching and my sight burning. I regained my composure and realized what I was doing.

I looked at where my hands held the woman up. Her feet were a good six inches off the ground, her entire body suspended in my grasp. If I wanted her dead, it would have taken just a flick of my wrist. My wrist—I looked at it—dark gray, and my hand black. It was like my anger had changed it. It made me think of when I had chased the Hexen away from Adrian earlier. I felt the feeling subside and, as it did, the natural color of flesh returned to it. I released my grip and she fell to the ground, grabbing at her throat that I had almost just crushed and began coughing. I took a half step back. I'm sure that if I had had a real heart it would have been racing in that moment.

I looked down at my side, where I had felt the sting of whatever Vera had done. Protruding from the spot was a dagger. A real one, a corporeal object, lodged within the body of something not from its plane of existence. It was

27

impossible. I moved my hand down to grab it, but just as my head had moved right through the trapdoor, my hand passed right through the handle. Vera reached up, grabbed the blade, and jerked it from my ribs. I felt the same feeling from a moment ago begin to rise. Pain—or whatever it was—erupted from where the blade had just been removed. I looked at where the blade had been. There was a small opening, and for a moment, light poured from it. Then there was nothing, just the sensation remained. A few moments later that had faded too.

Vera stumbled back to her chair and, with much effort, raised herself into it. She dropped the dagger onto the pile of papers and tried to catch her breath.

"What was that?" I asked, still in shock at having just been stabbed.

Vera struggled to speak with the windpipe I had very nearly crushed: "It's called *The Answer.*"

"And what is that?" I asked.

"It's not an object. Well, it is—at least the dagger is—but that's not what I'm referring to," she said. "The best explanation I can give is, it's what primitive cultures would have called a spell. A ritual that gives the object the ability to pass between the planes of existence. It's what I've been working on. That's the research that *We* have been working on. It's why I can see you, and him, and everything else."

"Who the fuck are you?" I demanded as I advanced on her once again.

"I'm no one. I'm only what I have told you. I'm just someone burdened with something I don't understand, looking for answers," she said quickly, and backed away in fear.

"I don't understand," I said, starting to calm down.

"I don't either. That's why I need your help. I have been trying to figure this out, and I'm not the only one. The church, this church of Saint Ordanis. It's in my visions. Anyway, I believe that the followers of this quote unquote church are looking for the same thing I am. Or maybe they want what I have, I don't know."

"This is crazy. I don't have time for this. All of this is your problem, not mine; you take care of it."

"But the dagger, its. . ."

"I don't know how you're doing it, but it's not real. Magic is not possible."

"Clearly it is!" Vera replied. "I know you don't trust me. But it's real. And whatever it is that makes this item special, it's very important to somebody. So much so, that they are willing to kill for it. And he is proof," she said, looking at Adrian. "Something big is going on here. I just need time to figure out what. I need your help, please."

I paused for a moment. Her fear was genuine.

"Why me?" I asked. "Why do you need me?"

"Because I saw it. Because you're special. You're something from beyond our world. God, or, if you don't believe in God, something else, has set things in motion that has led both you and I to this moment. I knew we would stand here. And I know that you're not going to leave. You're going to hear me out." Vera said.

"And after that?" I asked.

"I don't know," she said. "But just like this blade, you have the ability to move freely across the barriers between the physical and the other. And I need to understand how."

"Why?" I asked again.

"Because everything about this dagger is dangerous!" she

said. "You're different—immortal—but this could be used to kill more than just the physical, perhaps a soul, like Adrian. This could kill him. There has to be a reason for that."

I thought for a moment about the seven sins, the scars I had seen them leave on the souls of men. Could that spiritual power have somehow been harnessed into a weapon? If it wasn't that, then what was it? Vera was right: this was very dangerous. But it didn't make sense. Why would you kill a soul? What purpose does it serve to kill a spirit?

"It doesn't matter. What would killing a soul accomplish?" I asked.

"There must be a reason," Vera said, "because whoever took Ana is making things like this. This dagger is not mine; I found it, left behind from the last time they took someone."

"What do you mean the last time they took someone?" Adrian said. "This has happened before?" Vera nodded.

"Yes, I saw it. They took someone, someone I didn't know. I went there. I followed my vision and it led me to where that person had been taken, and dagger had been left. After that, I had more than just visions, I could really see."

Everything was starting to make sense. These *visions* that Vera was having had taken to her so far down the rabbit hole that she was running on blind faith. She likened it to some divine plan no doubt. She really had seen what had happened going into tonight. She may have been blindly chasing her own religious beliefs, but she was also a scientist. She understood the danger it posed to spiritual beings.

This made me ponder the questions: Had anyone else been killed in one of these abductions she has seen? Had I been there, in the aftermath, and not known what happened, just doing my job? It was very possible. I needed to know what she knew. Someone was messing with something more powerful and way outside the realm of their understanding. Or even worse, maybe they *did* understand it. Someone was messing with my work, and I needed to know who. I had been watching mankind for millennia, and quite honestly, I did not trust them with that kind of power. She was right, someone was planning something, and it was big.

"I need to know what you know, Vera, and I need to know it now," I said.

"So, you'll help me, then?"

"Yeah, I'll help you," I replied.

"You, too?" she asked, looking past me at Adrian.

"Of course," he said. "What do you need?"

"Everything you know about your wife, anything that could help us find her. Anything you can possibly think of that could lend additional context to my visions. Oh, and everything you can remember about your research on the dagger."

"Wait a second," I said. "You know about the dagger?"

"No," Adrian said, sounding just as confused as I was.

"I promise, I'll explain in a moment," Vera said. "For now, let him tell me what he knows."

"Fine," I said begrudgingly, feeling out of sorts that I was so far in the dark about this very dangerous item. Adrian answered the question, filling in everything he could think of about Ana. He knew her like he knew himself, everything except her sight, he said. We sat and listened for what must have been hours before he was finished, during which I needed to catch up on my duties of serving the recently deceased. I was behind and had to dispense with the formalities during my imprints. When Adrian was finished it was my turn to get some answers.

"So, tell me how you both know about this dagger." Just as she'd promised, Vera answered the question.

"We both work for ARC Industries, a manufacturing company that makes everything from computer parts to weapons systems, software, and machinery. Adrian is a particle physicist assigned to a team I oversee. He studies the effects of radiation and develops ways to reduce, shield, or absorb the harmful particles to make materials safer. I myself am the head of the experimental projects division. I oversee everything that happens in the research labs across multiple teams."

"'Project Angel'?" Adrian asked.

"Correct," Vera said. "Over the past several months. I have had a team working on the properties of a very specific type of radiation signature. We call the project 'Angel.' Adrian is—was—one of the members of that team. Now, what Adrian doesn't know is that the radiation signature is that of what this dagger gives off."

"So, they weren't after Ana, then. They were after me! They were after my research, *our* research!" Adrian said in shock and anger. He lunged forward and passed right through Vera. He turned and threw some haymakers, each one passing harmlessly through her. Adrian fell to the floor, still exhausted from the long night.

Vera waited a moment for him to calm before speaking. "No," she said, "I thought they were after both of you."

"Why did you think that?" I asked.

"Obviously his research is valuable to them, since they are working on it as well. But I also think they need her ability, to be able to see the other side. Why else would they take her and not kill her? I think they are still in the testing stages of these weapons, and they need people like Ana to see if they work. And obviously any research they could get from Adrian was a bonus."

"Well, we need to find out," I said. She didn't reply immediately. Instead I could hear her grind her teeth before she finally spat it out.

"There's more."

"Great," Adrian replied, rubbing his forehead. Vera reached out and grabbed a rolled-up piece of parchment. She handled it with extreme care. Clearly it was something very old, and keeping it intact required a careful hand.

"What is it?" I asked.

"It's a document from Africa," she replied.

"Looks old. When is it from?" I asked, knowing what the answer was and hoping it wasn't what she was about to say.

"Around 1500 BC, Egypt," Vera said. I closed my eyes and shook my head.

"I know where this is going," I said. "Let me guess: there are five more documents, from five more cultures from all over the world and from all parts of history?"

"How did you know?"

"Because I've seen them before—a long time ago, and several times since. In the old days, death was not as understood as it is now. There was no science, and because of that, people made up explanations. It was the best they had. The nomads of early man had their beliefs, but each tribe was different. It wasn't until the Babylonians that an organized system of deities was set in stone. It was Nebuchadnezzar who attempted to try and make contact with the other side. Others had tried before, but they were the first to come close."

"So, like me and Ana, the Babylonians could see you?" Vera asked.

"Not in the same way. You can see me, and actually *see* me. They could only sense that I was there. They called me 'Nergal.' To them I was the Lord of the Underworld, their god of death. I don't control who dies, how, or when. I just help guide them when it's over."

"You said there were more?" Adrian said.

"Yes." I began recounting my experiences over the past several thousand years. I lost myself in it for a moment. The experiences had been neither pleasant nor fun, just strange. The fascination with death had always been somewhat of a mystery to me. Perhaps because I myself couldn't die, so the idea of loss and wishing to see lost loved ones again was a bit foreign. I understand caring, but love is a bit foreign to me. I understand how it works, the chemical reactions that drive people to protect their mates and offspring, but sometimes there were those who overruled the nature of it. Those who showed something more, who, against all reason, instinct, or any other power, did for others seemed more than possible. It was through those impossible feats that I know love exists. I don't understand it, but I know it is real.

I snapped out of my memories as Adrian continued talking.

"What about the others?" he said.

"The others?"

"Yes, you said six. The Egyptians, the Babylonians—what about the rest?"

"Right," I said. "The others are the Greeks, the Persians, the Hindus, and the Christians." A look of disbelief stretched over both of their faces when I said the last on the list. "What?" I asked.

"The Christians don't have a god of death," Vera said. I stared back for a moment before finally speaking.

"'And I looked and beheld a pale horse, and his name that sat on him was Death, and hell followed with him. And power was given unto them over the fourth part of the Earth, to kill with the sword, and with hunger, and with death, and all the beasts of the Earth.' Revelation 6:8," I said.

The looks on their faces as I recounted the passage from their holy book reminded them that I had been here a very long time and that I knew what I was talking about. More still, I knew them—I knew mankind better than they knew themselves.

"I know humanity," I said. "I have seen heinous acts in the name of gods, demigods, pseudo-gods, and any other made-up reason you can imagine but dare not think about. To these six religions I am one. That doesn't make it true. I am not a god, but that didn't stop them from believing me to be one. Now, these six stand out because they have a very unique ability to know when I was there. True believers can almost sense my presence. It stands out, the kind of thing you remember."

Vera and Adrian looked almost pale; my statement did not sit well with them. That didn't mean it was a lie. They were silent for quite some time as they tried to absorb what I had just said. Adrian finally broke the silence.

"So why these six?" he asked, looking at Vera and then me. "Why can they feel you?"

"I don't know," I said. "I didn't really ever bother to find out, and quite honestly, I lost interest after a while. It was interesting to see them and how they behaved when I was there. But that was short-lived. For me, it then turned into not being alone. It was nice to spend time with those who were living, even if they couldn't see or talk to me. Just knowing I was felt made me feel like part of the world."

35

"You know you're a lot more human than you come off sometimes?" Vera said. I assumed she meant that as a compliment, but mankind reacts from their instincts and not logic. They make rash decisions without thinking of the consequences. Being human was not something that I aspired to; understanding was enough.

"So, all that, and you didn't really pay attention to why they could feel you?" Adrian asked with frustration in his voice.

"To be fair, before tonight there was no reason to have paid attention," I retorted, feeling that bit of defensive human reaction that Vera had just said was a good thing. It wasn't.

"Okay, that's enough," Vera said. "The point is there is a reason they could sense you were there. There's a reason why that dagger behaves the way it does. There's a reason why Ana can see you without having been exposed to the dagger like I was. And there's a reason someone took her and is trying to create these weapons. We need to find out what that connection is."

"And I agree," I said. "So back to square one. What do we do?"

"Let's go through this logically," Adrian said. "Vera, show us everything you have."

Vera nodded and motioned us over to the table. She produced the six documents and their recounting of my visits. They were each in their native tongue.

"Do you have translations for Adrian?" I asked.

"I actually don't know exactly what they say myself," Vera replied.

"Then how do you even know where they are from?"

"I scanned them and determined the language—not that hard with the Internet. But Google translate can only take me so far."

I looked at her, a bit disappointed. She caught me and defended herself before I could say anything.

"Hey, this was a research project for work. I have people who do that stuff for me, okay?" I didn't say a word about it, and just decided to move on.

"Looks like I'm translating, then," I said. I went over the six documents. They were generally similar. They spoke about how to speak to the respective god of death and gave fairly detailed information about doing so. The majority of the info was utterly useless, based on man's limited understanding in those times, but one thing stood out. In each and every culture, a plant was used. Sometimes made into a tea, sometimes burned, sometimes eaten—different plants, but there was always one. I shared my discovery with the other two.

"That's common in many cultures," Vera said. "What makes these six stand out?"

"Hallucinogenic, probably. Increases people's sensitivity to spiritual movement," Adrian said.

"Sounds likely," Vera said. "I'll have to research it more when I get a chance."

"Let's keep going, then," I said. "Any and all theories."

We were all quiet for some time. It was deathly silent except for the breath of the one living being in the room and the creaking of the old building above us. I even stopped a few times to take care of my obligations to the recently deceased around the world. Then it hit me. I had been here so long, watching humanity grow, become more, and build gods from their imaginations along the way. That was it—growth. I should have composed a complete thought, but it just came out.

"It's growth," I said. The other two just looked at me, waiting for me to make the incomplete thought make sense. So, I did my best. "The key is in Christianity," I continued.

"Why?" Vera asked.

"Because of growth." They stared at me, lost in the inadequacy of the information I had given. I steadied the hurricane of information spinning in my head and spoke. "What do you do when you are told a story?"

I watched as the wheels in Adrian's mind turned, then he spoke. "You remember it; it becomes part of you?"

"Exactly. You even retell it, perhaps change it a little to make it better, right?"

"Yeah, so?"

"The story grows. That's what this did. You look at all these cultures and belief systems—all of them are from generally the same part of the world. Not the same place, but around the same place. People traveled, told their stories, those stories grew, and eventually a new way of belief was born."

"Christianity," Vera said, having understood my epiphany.

"Christianity," I said. "Some radical faction of it at least. They took what they had learned from these other cultures, somehow figured out how I move through the world, and they copied it, just like they did with their faith."

"But how can you be sure?" she asked.

"I was there to watch them grow. I know the stories," I replied. Vera began grabbing the religious texts she had acquired and tossed them onto the table. I grabbed them one at a time and placed them alongside the Bible.

"Here, look at the creation story from ancient Babylon." I read the stories side by side; the sequence in which the world was created was almost identical. "And here," I said, grabbing the next text, and doing the same thing with another story. I ran the gamut of the documents, saving the best one for last. "This one, I remember it, but it's been well over a millennium since I've thought about it." I looked down at the Egyptian story of Horus and began to recount the similarities to the man known as Jesus Christ.

"Horus born of a virgin, as was Jesus," I said. "The foster father of Horus was Seph. Jesus was fostered by Joseph, and Horus was of royal descent, like Jesus. Horus's birth was accompanied by three solar deities bearing gifts who followed the morning star of Sirius. The birth of Jesus was accompanied by three wise men bearing gifts who followed a star 'in the east'. Their births were both heralded by angels. Herut tried to murder the infant Horus, while Herod slaughtered every firstborn, in an attempt to kill Jesus."

I continued down the list, one after another, parallel after parallel. My point had been made. The connection wasn't innate; it had been built over time, by man.

"So now we know that the connection isn't really a connection, but a fabrication," Adrian said. "But it doesn't tell us anything about what the people who took Ana want. What does building a weapon that can do what that blade does get you?"

"I know what it gets you," Vera said.

"What?" Adrian asked.

"All of these societies somehow had a way to, even if only slightly, reach in and connect to the spirit realm, right? And that's what the early Christians built their faith on."

"Yeah," I replied, "so what?"

"What's the one thing they all have in common?" she asked.

"What?"

39

"You," she said. "They could all feel when death was in the room. You said they had names for you?"

"Yes," I replied.

"What were they?" I gave Vera a look. I was still lost, but I was sure she had a point, and so I answered her question.

"To the Babylonians I was 'Nergal;' to the Egyptians I was 'Anubis;' the Persians, 'Dahaka;' Hindus, 'Kali;' the Greeks called me 'Hades;' and to the Christians I am the 'Pale Rider.'"

Vera waited for me to finish and looked at Adrian.

"Say one of his names," she commanded him.

"Why?" he asked.

"Just do it."

Adrian shrugged, and then spoke. "Hades," he said.

I can't explain why, but almost as if it was instinct, I turned and looked at him. It took me back all those years to the people I had sat with, the living left behind when I took their loved ones. I thought of sitting with them, feeling not alone. Like I belonged with them.

"There," said Vera, "What was that?"

"I don't know," I said. "Not quite sure why I did that."

"I do," she said. We both looked her, a bit anxious for the answer. "Souls are what? Leftover energy, right?" I nodded. "What are prayers?"

"It's energy," I replied.

"Just like a soul," said Vera. "What happens when someone dies? You come running; it's an urge, a need, something you must do. When someone prays, it's the same thing. And when they pray to their god of death, they are offering up that energy willingly."

"Like a moth to a flame," Adrian said.

They were right. If in that moment I had had a real stomach,

I probably would have felt sick to it. The names were how they connected to me. I come running when a soul is free from its physical prison, and apparently when someone actively tries to make a connection.

"Now," Vera said, "what is the one thing mankind fights against harder than anything else?"

I knew the answer, and I didn't like it.

"What is it?" she asked again.

"Me," I replied. "Death."

Vera picked up the knife, held it out to me, and gestured for me to take it.

"If you had a way to stop death from taking a loved one, would you do it?" she asked me.

I didn't have any loved ones. But I had seen enough of mankind to know the lengths people would go for the ones they love. A man would move a mountain if he could, if it meant saving his love. I looked at the blade. A weapon that could pierce the Veil between the worlds. I was a fool. It was not about Ana and her sight. It was not about Adrian and Vera's research. The entire thing was a ruse. It was about me—that's why they kept taking people: a trap, to draw me out.

"Would you kill Death?" Vera asked.

The words sucked the air out of the room, and everything stood still. Then the building above shifted, if only in the slightest. A few particles of dust fluttered down from the boards overhead, indicating the weight of the boots and men in them doing their best to be silent above us. I looked at the others and whispered the only thing that mattered to me in that moment.

"They're here."

41

3

The Hunt

My senses became heightened as I came to grips with the possibility that the group of men coming for me wielded weapons forged to kill me. The falling particles of dust and wood lit up in the flickers of candlelight and stood in stark contrast to the stillness of the rest of the room. It was like the air itself was living and breathing. I took it all in as I realized that it was something I might never be able to experience again, should the men whose boots loosened them achieve their goal.

The sound of the gentle steps converged on the floor above the trap door that lead down. The movements were subtle. The bolt that held the door closed gave a slight clink as it reached the extent of its movement. The person pulling it set it back down gently, trying to avoid creating any sound. But we knew they were there, and they were coming.

This was it. I had seen it many times in raids all around the world. They would breach hard and fast. Storming the small room and peppering its every corner with gunfire. If the tactics witnessed earlier that evening were anything to go by, there would be no survivors.

I made peace with the idea this might very well be the end of my long existence. I wondered what it would be like to pass on. The humans had figured out long ago that energy could neither be created nor destroyed. Whatever was left of me would dissipate and be recycled by the universe. What would I become? It was mildly exciting, until I felt the panic flood into my chest. I, the oldest consciousness on the planet, was about to meet my end. It was exhilarating yet horrifying.

The explosion of the charge set on the doors above the stairs ripped them from their hinges and cast the broken pieces down into the room. I reacted and felt myself dart back to the opposite side where Vera was now taking cover. Every movement I made felt as if I was a mere spectator, natural and smooth. As I waved my hand, the flickering flames that lit up the suspended particles in the air died, plunging the room into darkness. As the still blackness settled I sank into it like I was one with the shadows. The tactical flashlights at the end of the guns swarmed down the stairs.

The sensation that had washed over me when Vera had plunged the blade into my side poured over me again and took over. The point man fired. I moved to the side of the approaching projectiles like they were standing still, motionless between the now-dark particles of dust hanging in the air. I struck; my hand passed through his upper chest and left arm like a sword. The spray of blood was light. It hit the faces of the other three men and prompted them to fire as well. I retracted my arm and moved to the side of the incoming fire once again. The errant bullets ripped through the room. The muzzle flashes were to my advantage as each one lit up the space for a brief moment. I ducked low and advanced toward my assailants. I swung my hand and caught the leg of one of the men. The sound of my arm cleaving his femur was joined by his scream. The sounds penetrated the blast of the firing bullets and met the ears of the other men.

The first man fell. His hand tightened in reflex and his firearm continued to unload, now toward the ceiling. I dispatched him just as his head hit the ground with a quick swipe of my hand across his neck. He didn't feel it; it was just over. Everything felt so slow. My unity with the darkness of the room was almost surreal. It had been less than three seconds and two of them had been already been removed as threats. I could almost read their minds as they scuffled a few steps back. Their fight-or-flight mechanisms were telling them to get the fuck out of there, but it was too late, they were mine.

I ducked under the incoming gunfire and slid my hand into the third man's gut. He didn't make a sound other than a final exhale. I jerked my arm, separating his torso from his lower half, tossing it to the side. I moved to the side of the last volley from the fourth man before the clicks from the rifle's firing pin striking nothing took its place.

The panic in his eyes was mildly gratifying. His pupils were shrunken and his fear had paralyzed him. I swiped at the gun. The metal was like paper. Its barrel separated and fell to the ground. His shaking hand reached for his sidearm, where I caught it. I clenched my hand and felt the bones in his hand turn to dust.

He unleashed a scream as I shifted my position closer and brought his face to mine.

"What do you want?" I asked through my clenched teeth. The man looked at me, frozen in his own fear. I clenched my fingers around his destroyed hand. The pain surged up his arm and brought his attention back to me. For what appeared like a highly trained soldier, he was not holding his composure very well.

"Focus! Why do you want me dead?" I asked. He began to relax and his lips separated. As they did I felt sharpness in my arm. I turned to where it had come from. Where I had cast him down, the still-living top half of the third man held out a 1911 sidearm, barrel still smoking. I felt the darkness of the room move into me again and, like a bolt of lightning, I flew and struck him down. I turned back toward the fourth. He had drawn his sidearm with the other hand and brandished it toward me.

I caught the man's arm with my left hand and drove my right through his rib cage and into his chest cavity. He began to gasp as the air started to escape his punctured lungs. He would not be able to speak now. In mercy, I gave a twist and severed his spinal column. He choked and his eyes fluttered for a moment. The signals his brain was sending in their final moments of panic. I waited to make sure he was gone before setting him down at the base of the stairs where we stood.

The moonlight shone down the stairs and lit up the four corpses I had just created. I looked at my hands. They were black like the shadow, like when I had held Vera by the neck. I felt myself grow calm, and they returned to normal. I moved into the darkness. With a wave of my hand, the flame of the candle, just as quickly as it had died, sprung back to life.

The men I had just dispatched had not ended well. I pulled them from their mangled bodies. They were lost—the anger and fury I had poured into my defense had damaged them. They would be unable to communicate. And even if they had been able, I don't think they would have said much. I did what I needed to and took the men away to rejoin the life stream.

For thousands of years I had seen men destroy other men. I'd seen them break and defile the souls of their brethren. But never once had I touched a soul in a way that had done it harm. Until that moment.

Souls are very special things. I would even describe them as precious. They're more than just remnants of the departed. They are the proof of the mark that someone had left on the world. They are stories, experiences, and feelings. Not just of the past, but of the future. Now, because of my own hands, there were four fewer of them. Yes, these men wanted to destroy me. And yes, what I did was in defense of my own continued existence. And really, anyone would have done the same in my situation. But that knowledge didn't make me feel any better.

I touched Adrian on the shoulder. "You all right?"

He looked around the room for a moment and saw my handiwork. He did a self-examination, then nodded his head that he was okay. I moved over to Vera, who had taken cover behind the table and chair where the now-tattered remains of her research rested. I feared the worst: that the hail of bullets from the assailants had gone primarily in her direction. I moved around the table to check. Before I could ask, she spoke.

"I'm fine," she said. "Just some scratches from flying crap."

I felt relieved, and extended my hand to help her to her feet. Our hands passed through each other and she gave me a look before grabbing the table and lifting herself up.

"Your arm," she said, pointing to where the .45 round had grazed me.

"It's fine," I replied, and rubbed it. But it was strange: unlike the wound from the knife, it did not vanish but lingered. Vera reached out and touched it. I felt the pressure on my arm and the pain. The pain spread like water flowing over my arm, and everything started to tingle. I felt light-headed and my balance failed. I stumbled and reached out.

Out of instinct, Vera moved to steady me. This time, her hands landed solidly on me and she propped me up until the lightness passed. I looked at her and then up at the wound. It looked different. I looked back to where the knife had been plunged into my side. Same thing—something was very wrong; I could feel it.

"Vera, can you choose to not see me?" I asked.

"No, why?"

"Because I don't think I'm phased anymore." I opened and closed my hands a few times and felt the tendons stretch.

"And that means . . . ?" Adrian asked.

"It means I'm physical," I said. "And I think I'm stuck that way."

They both looked at me, their faces blank. I walked over to one of the corpses and reached for his gun. The metal was cold, and the blood on it was cooling. I felt its weight in my hand as I lifted it from the ground. Vera moved over and took it from my hand, ejecting the magazine from the weapon. The same shine that adorned the dagger shone on the bullets. I had figured that would be the case, or the round would have passed right through me. But something was different.

Vera walked back to the table and grabbed the dagger from it. She brought it over and compared it to the rounds in the magazine. The shine on the bullets was much more vibrant than that of the dagger. I looked at her and then down at my torso. The damage the bullet had done, even as a graze, was much more substantial than the now barely visible stab wound.

"Why are the bullets like that?" Adrian asked as he walked toward us.

"I'm not sure. But whatever it is, it's way more powerful than this is," she said, holding out the knife. "And apparently, that wound has him stuck in our world."

"That tells us something," I said.

"That whoever is researching this is much better at it than my team is."

"Either that or maybe someone on your team is helping them," I said.

"That's not possible," she snapped back.

"And why not?" I asked. "It's either that or their scientists are much, much better than yours." Vera looked at Adrian. He shrugged and told her that it was possible, if not probable. The hurt shone in Vera's eyes as she accepted the prospect that one of her own people had killed Adrian and was trying to do the same to her.

"Any idea who it might be?" she asked Adrian.

He shook his head. "I'm only one guy on one team. I can't speak for anyone else." The silence engulfed everything. No one said a word, but we all knew the next destination: Vera's lab. We stepped over the corpses and moved toward the stairs. I placed my foot on the first stair and began to lift myself. The creek of the old boards was cut by the sound of rustling plants outside. There was someone still here. And from the sound of it, they were finding a better position. I leaned closer to the opening at the top of the stairs and listened. It was faint, but I could hear the grinding of the combat equipment on men's bodies. It had to be a second team.

I shushed as quietly as I could and raised my hand to stop their movement. *There's more outside*, I mouthed, and pointed up. This was not a good scenario. I had had the cover of darkness on my side before. But the moon was out, and its rays shone through the broken windows, keeping the place well lit. As soon as I popped my head out from above the stairs I would likely face an incoming fire.

"Are there any other ways out?" I whispered to Vera. She shook her head. If I'm honest, I didn't have high hopes for us making it out with just one exit and a firing squad waiting for us. So we did the only thing we could: we tried to come up with another idea.

"I know what to do," Adrian said. Vera and I looked at him in anticipation. "I go out first," he said, "draw their fire, give you two an opening to escape."

"We're not gonna do that," Vera said. "Everyone gets out, or no one does."

"That's stupid," he replied. "This is bigger than that. No death means the world ends—maybe not now, but in time. Overpopulation will lead to global hunger, economic crisis, the total collapse of our way of life. We can't let that happen. Now that he can't walk through walls, you're the only one who can get him into that building. You have to figure this out."

"I'm not going to let you do this," Vera said, tears forming for the employee she barely knew.

"It's done," he said. "I'm already dead. There's not much I can do, but I can do this."

I could see Vera trying desperately to think of a better idea. But Adrian was right—there was nothing else. She stared at her former colleague. She was memorizing the features of his face so that he could be remembered. I didn't perceive it as deeply as she did, the feeling of loss. But because of my now physical body, it was much more apparent. The chemical processes taking place inside of me drove emotion; I felt the pain. The loss of this man's soul was going to affect me more than just knowing that I let down a soul in my care. I moved to place my hand on Adrian's shoulder and felt the pain sting me more as my corporeal hand passed right through him. It was also reaffirmation that my existence was now limited. I pushed it to the back of my mind and did what I thought any man being given such a gift would do.

"I will never forget this," I said. The chemical reactions within me ramped up, and in the surge of emotion I felt a lump jump into my throat and my tear ducts fill. "Thank you."

He didn't say anything, just nodded and turned. I followed and moved with him to the bottom of the stairs.

Vera came up behind us as we stood on the stairs, mascara marks lining her face where the tears had run. I reached my hand back toward her, and she took it. Adrian raised his hand and began counting down as we readied to make a break for it. Time seemed to stand still as I watched the countdown on Adrian's hand go from two to one. His index finger folded in and, as it did, he vaulted into the open space of the church above. The sounds of the shots pierced the silence and filled the hollowness of the abandoned building, echoing off the walls and vaulted ceiling. The streaks of light left from the myriad of bullets crossing paths in the darkness were beautiful.

I pressed off the steps and felt the muscles in my shoulder tighten as I pulled on Vera's arm. She followed, and we ducked low and to the side, away from where Adrian had gone. I surveyed the room as I ran and aimed us toward the nearest window. I covered myself as best I could and jumped through the stained glass. The sting of the colored shards on my skin was intense as I moved through them. I turned to help Vera, who was but a half step behind. As I did, I saw Adrian's silhouette collapse. As the movement stopped, so did the gunfire. My insides cried out in anger, frustration, and sadness, but I didn't have time for them right now.

The voices of the men around the outside of the building grew in volume as they entered the church. The sounds of them yelling "Clear!" echoed through the night. Vera and I moved as quickly and silently as we could through the graveyard. Vera kept looking behind us to see if we were being followed. There was no one. By some miracle they had not seen us, and it seemed to be a clean getaway. We made our way into the alley and down a few streets, keeping to the shadows as much as we could to ensure our escape.

After a while, we found ourselves on a familiar street. It was the one we'd been on earlier that night. At the end of the long road we would find the former home of Adrian and Ana. I took one last look back in the direction of the church. We were safe (at least for now).

I had found it a bit surprising we had ended up on this street. But my companion clearly did not. She walked on at a brisk pace down the sidewalk toward the Harmond house. I realized that it wasn't an accident—we were going right where she wanted to.

"Why are we going back?" I asked.

"The research," Vera said, her walk turning into a very determined march.

"Isn't it at your lab?"

"Not all of it." She increased her pace to a near jog.

"What the hell is going on, then?" I asked, getting impatient that she wasn't spilling her guts with as much info as she could. She stopped and turned to me. "The clearance for all project information isn't accessible by any one person, not even me. It's protected by four security passkeys. Each one unlocks a different security platform in the mainframe. Unless all four are entered into the project mainframe encryption unit, the information can't be accessed in its entirety."

"But we don't need the information about the project. We just need to find out who's helping the people after me so we can identify who's behind this."

"I know that," she replied. "But the clearance required for this project is immense. Everything is protected, including the personnel files."

"Great," I said. "So what does that have to do with Adrian?"

"He's one of the four project specialists. As such, he has one of the passkeys."

"And why was this not discussed before we left the church?" I asked, frustrated that the only person who knew the card's location had just sacrificed himself so we could escape. She didn't respond.

"Come on," she said. "Let's just find it and get to ARC labs, so we can find the asshole who's trying to kill you, us."

The blood racing through my now-mortal veins was seething. The responsibility I held over Adrian, as one of the departed, was still grating on me. Maybe I was feeling guilty. Or maybe I was upset that we were now in a position with no certainty we would get what we needed. I wasn't sure. I would like to think that like any other mortal, losing someone close was wearing on me. Whatever it was, it made me feel light-headed, and only made it feel like it was taking even longer to walk down dark streets to where everything I knew about the world fell apart.

The yellow security tape shone brightly in the sliver of light that brought the new day. The bright-yellow barrier acted as an outline of the tragedy that had occurred there. Some sinister entity, bent on the elimination of death, had killed a man and taken his wife, simply to draw me out. They had been carefully chosen so that I would notice. Knowing that I had been manipulated in such a way made me feel dirty. Or maybe it was the sweat on my new skin that made me feel that way. It didn't matter—I felt sickened all the same. Mankind struggled so hard to cling to their fragile lives, and I wanted nothing more than to be free of my mortal bindings.

I ducked under the tape and Vera followed. The creak of the doors surrounded by the silence of the early morning was eerie. I felt my stomach lurch as I walked into the bedroom and smelled the curdled blood that had soaked the mattress where Adrian had bled out. Vera walked in behind me and proceeded to tear through the personals of Adrian and Ana. As she did it brought me back to the night before, and how the men who had killed Adrian had done just that. They, too, were looking for the passkey.

Whatever change that was made to reconstruct the door, that's why they did it. Not to hide the murder, but to hide that they had searched the place. They wanted to keep the cops from thinking there had been something of value hidden somewhere in the house. It was all a diversion, meant for confusion. And it had done its job masterfully.

"It's not here," I said. Vera stopped.

"How do you know?" she asked, puzzled.

"Because the men who killed Adrian—the first time—they already searched the place."

"How do you know?"

"Because I watched them do it." I recounted the events of Adrian's death and Ana's abduction.

"Then if it's not here, where would he have kept it?"

I resisted mentioning again that if we'd asked Adrian before our escape, we would know. I felt the anger well up. I clenched my fist and slammed it into the wall. The drywall collapsed under the force and revealed the emptiness within. The morning light shone into the fractured wall and revealed what looked like a vent that ended in the closet. My gut churned and I threw open the closet doors. Everything in the closet had been moved, which meant someone other than the killers had done it. I moved the shoes out of the way and found the grate of the vent removed. I bent down and looked more closely. I removed the grate and looked within. There was a card. I pulled it out and read it.

Francis T. Aaron
Detective

I flipped it over. Scribbled with a pen that was running out of ink was a message:

Detective Grimm, we found something interesting. When you find this, come see us at the ninth.

Apparently the detectives were not quite as useless as I had originally thought.

"How did they know you would find it?" Vera asked.

"They didn't," I said. "However, I did give them the impression that I was pretty good at figuring this stuff out."

"Looks like you are," she replied.

"Either that, or we're really lucky. Come on, time to go and pretend to be cops."

The walk down to the ninth precinct was about an hour and a half. I rubbed my arm where I had been shot. It hurt. I tried to shift back into the ethereal realm, but it didn't work. It gave me time to think. What could I do and what could I not do? I took the time to find out as we walked along. I didn't lose as much as I thought I had. I shifted my physical form a bit and once again donned my detective persona from the night before.

"Nice trick," Vera said.

"Not so much a trick as it is a tool," I replied. "Being welcoming is a valuable thing when I'm collecting a soul. As shallow as it is, dressing well tends to calm people down."

We still had a way to go. And so we filled the time with talk about my job, and talk about hers. The dagger was of particular interest to me. Vera had stated she'd taken it from the scene. That it had been left behind the last time the organization had acted, which made me wonder where they had gotten it from. The object itself was old, but was the enchantment? Mankind had been playing with things beyond their understanding for almost their entire existence. Fire, chemistry, splitting the atom, and from their meddling they had made leaps and bounds in knowledge. There was an explanation for what she called "The Answer." Digging deep enough to find out what it was, would be the hard part.

We walked up the steps of the ninth precinct and into the foyer. The blast of the broken AC pushing warm, stale air into the small reception area was unpleasant at best—a sign of the building's disrepair. We passed through the second set of doors and into central booking where the drunks and hooligans that had been deposited by the previous night's misdeeds stewed in their own excrement as they sobered. I pushed down my anxiety and walked up to the female officer filling out a report behind the reception desk.

"I'm looking for Detectives Aaron and Marx," I said, trying to be as professional as I could.

Her eyes never lifted from the work she was doing. Instead she raised her hand and pointed to the side, yelling, "Asshole and asshole junior, yous gots a visitor."

As she blurted out the words, the broad, short frame of Detective Aaron rose up and waved us back. We moved through the bustle of the office as half the force tried to work while the other half joked around. Paper airplanes and assorted Nerf toys sailed through the air around us as we closed the distance to the detectives' desks. When we made it through the gauntlet of slipshod, I extended my hand toward Aaron. He gave it a single hardy shake and beckoned us to sit, which we did.

"So what brings you here, Detective?" he asked.

I pulled the card he had left in the vent from my coat pocket and placed it flat on the desk before sliding it to him. His eyes never met the card, but a smug grin spread over his face as it moved toward him.

"I knew you were as good as I said you were," he said.

56

"You doubted me?" I asked, playing into the farce.

"No, but skinny over there did," he replied, pointing his lips where Marx was sitting. "You owe me twenty," he shouted.

Marx returned the statement with a flash of his middle finger and stood up.

"Get the keys and meet me in lockup." Once more Marx flashed the bird as he walked away to retrieve the keys.

"Come with me," Aaron said. "You're gonna like this."

We followed him off the floor and through a series of drab cinder-block halls.

"And we're going where?" I asked.

"Evidence," he replied. "Found something in that vent I think you should get a look at. We also hit a wall in the investigation. Your input would be appreciated."

"I don't mind," I said as we made a turn and ran into a cage door that led to a basement area.

"Good, because I have no idea what the fuck to do next."

We waited a moment before Marx rounded the corner with a thick file and the keys to the evidence lockup. He tossed Aaron the key and then handed me the folder. Aaron turned and unlocked the cage and began walking down the stairs. We all followed.

"Who's the babe?" Marx asked as we neared the bottom. Aaron turned and swung his hand, narrowly missing my face. He pointed his finger at Marx, who was at the back of the line.

"Hit that fuck," he said. I smiled and turned behind me to look at Vera, who was still visibly red even in the dimness of the stairwell. She turned and smacked Marx in the arm, who rubbed it like he had been hit with a bat. "Who she is, is none of our damn business, you nosy fuck. Don't be so rude. She will introduce herself or Cyrus will do it if it suits him. Until

57

that time, they're our guests. We'll treat them as such," Aaron snapped as his feet met the basement floor.

"Yeah, yeah, whatever," Marx replied, still babying his arm.

At the bottom of the stairs waited rows of evidence boxes organized alphabetically by crime. We walked through the dankness into the Homicide section and were greeted promptly by the *A*s. We worked our way down the line to *H*. There were three boxes labeled *Harmond, Adrian J*. Aaron pulled them out, plucked the tops off of them, and dug through the contents until he found a bag with a micro SD card along with Adrian's work badge.

I gave Vera a subtle glance, who nodded that the SD was indeed the passkey.

"Check this out," Aaron said, motioning at me to open the folder I had been given. I flipped it open and looked through the report. Aaron continued talking as I did. "So this Harmond guy, definitely not killed by animals. We found several .223 rounds in the wall behind the headboard—they were what killed him. As for the other wounds, we're stuck; the coroner can't match them to any weapon or animal. Another weird thing: they're completely clean. There's nothing in them—no saliva, no metal shavings, no bone, no dirt, and no solvents or water for cleaning. Just nothing. It's like whatever did it isn't real. Because nothing leaves behind nothing, right?"

"I don't know," I said, knowing exactly why there was no trace. The wounds were made by the Hexen who don't have—or at least I didn't think had—a traditional physical form. There had to be more, so I redirected the conversation. "What about those things?" I asked, pointing to the various evidence bags with assorted contents. "Obviously the coroner's report isn't where the shit hits the fan."

The same smug smile spread across Aaron's face from before. "You're right. Here's where it gets interesting," he said, pulling out the bag with the badge and SD card and flipping it around to reveal the back. "The SD card fits into this slot in the back of the badge." He took them both out and put the SD in the badge. When it was in, it was almost invisible. "Clearly designed to be hidden," he said.

"So the guy works for ARC Industries. Not exactly surprising that he had a hidden SD card," I replied, doing my best downplay the card's significance.

"True," Marx said from the background. "Tell him the rest."

Aaron gave Marx a dirty look, perturbed that Marx had interrupted his story. "Anyway," he said, "here's the good part. Our IT guys can't do shit with it. The security encryption is way beyond military grade. And right now we don't have enough for a warrant. So for the time being, we're not getting in. Whatever this thing is, it's definitely something ARC doesn't want people getting their hands on."

You have no idea, I thought. The ability to kill both body and soul is something a little beyond the realm of "socially acceptable."

"Is there anything else?" I asked. From the corner of my eye I saw Marx move away.

"Yeah," Aaron replied, "the best part. This isn't the only one."

"What do you mean?" I asked.

"The vent," he said. "The badge is what I found hidden there, so Mr. Harmond definitely knew it was important. So much so, that someone killed him for it—him and his buddy."

"His buddy?" I asked. Marx returned with another evidence box. This one read *Crane, Lucas M.* The lid came off and from inside came another bag with a badge in it, but no SD card.

"We found the body of Mr. Crane not two hours after we found Harmond. Whoever killed Harmond in all likelihood killed Crane as well, and took the card. Whatever it is that ARC wants to keep hidden, it's being actively chased by someone or some*ones* who are very, very good. Like Harmond, the crime scene was spotless. Even the manner of death is different, likely to hide the connection."

I felt my heart jump into my throat and looked at Vera; she was like a ghost. Someone else was after the keys, and they already had at least one; which meant that this key was why Adrian had been the killed. Maybe it wasn't a trap to lure me out, but just coincidence. Maybe they weren't after me, but Vera.

"Give me a second, guys," I said, grabbing Vera's arm and walking around the shelf.

"Vera, who has the last two passkeys?"

"I don't know," she said.

"How can you not know? Aren't you the boss?"

"Yes, but the team leadership isn't assigned by me."

"By whom, then?" I asked impatiently.

"Randomly assigned via the mainframe," she replied.

"How did you know Adrian had one, then?"

"We talked. He told me he was one of the team leads on the way to the church, while you sulked in the back."

I rubbed my increasingly aching head; maybe I was getting tired. I hadn't ever slept—never needed to—but I was mortal now, so at some point I would have to. Now was not that time.

"So, now what?" I asked.

"We have the one key, provided we can get it out of here.

That gets us into the personnel files at least. We can see who has the other keys. We have what we need."

"One problem," I said. "If we have one key and they have one key, then they have the same access we do. They may already know who has them. Hell, they may have already killed them and taken them. The only one they might be missing is this one."

"We need more info," she said. I nodded, and we walked back around the corner to where Aaron and Marx were.

"What did ARC say about the murders?" I asked. Both Aaron and Marx looked at me to see if I would spill anything that might help their investigation. But I remained mum. Aaron moved closer to me very calmly, almost like he was going to throw a surprise punch.

"Look," he said, pausing for emphasis. "Detective. We know who you are."

My heart skipped a beat and I felt my eyes widen, but I pushed it back down, rationalizing that they couldn't possibly know who I really was.

"Oh, really?" I replied, taking a step forward to meet the challenge of the shorter man. He took his half step forward and looked up at me before replying.

"Yeah, I do," he said. "We looked into you. Turns out there isn't, nor was there ever, a Cyrus Grimm employed with the NYPD."

I stayed stone. "And?"

"What we did find, however, was one Detective First Grade John Graison, age forty-three, tall, dark hair, medium build, listed as killed in action on December twelfth of last year. Took down three of four bosses in the Artoli crime family. But here's the thing: the department kept it very hush-hush.

No public funeral, no flag awarded to a widow. He was just gone. Which made me think WITSEC."

I thought back at John—he was a good man, a good cop. I didn't stay long enough to find out what happened after the Artolis captured, tortured, and killed him. I did my job and moved on. But if Aaron was going to give me this, I would take it.

"It proves nothing," I said, and took a half step back to truly sell it.

"Look, Detective, I'm not saying you're him, and I'm not saying you're *not*. And I know you just wanna help, or else you wouldn't be here. So here's what I would ask."

"Okay," I replied, convinced that he was certain I was John Graison and my real identity was safe.

"ARC won't talk to us. They are denying employment of both Harmond and Crane. And again, a judge won't sign a court order to enter the facility. But I do have unis on both homes and they say that known ARC security personnel have visited both residences. Yes, I know you were there, too. My guys were doing a pretty good job of hiding."

"So you want me to go into ARC off the books, is that what we're saying here?"

Aaron didn't respond, just shrugged. I paused before pretending to reluctantly accept.

"Fair enough, Francis. Give me the badge and the SD card. I'll get into the building and find out what the hell is going on in there. Sound good?"

"You read my mind," he said. "And don't call me Francis."

"It was his idea," I said, motioning at Marx. Everyone laughed, and he handed me the evidence bag. I reached out to take it, and Aaron pulled it away abruptly.

"This is not being officially signed out of evidence. I better get it back," he said. I nodded and took the bag. It went into my coat pocket and we all returned to the chaos that was the station floor. After a near-death experience with a black-and-orange Nerf football, Vera and I took our leave and walked out of the run-down ninth.

The light of the moon shined brightly off the glass as Vera and I walked right through the front door of the ARC research lab building #10741. The lady at the front desk responded to Vera by name and then produced a visitor's badge for me. We both moved through security unhindered. The tech in the building was state of the art. I had been just about everywhere in the world, but this was different even for me. It seemed like it was something out of a science-fiction novel.

The massive steel composite door reminded me of something from *Star Wars*. Vera walked to the security panel at the side and scanned her palm and retina before putting in a ten-digit security pin. The massive doors lurched and whined at they opened. Her office was centrally located and composed almost entirely of glass. It was raised above the rest so she could see the four teams working below. We moved up the clear polycarbonate stairs and into her office.

"What's in here?" I asked.

"The security blade," she said.

"And that is . . . ?"

"It's what the SD cards go into to turn them into passkeys."

"I thought it was the badge."

"No, that's just where it's stored." She produced an item composed of metal and silicon. It looked like a sci-fi prop.

"This device takes the encryption algorithm and plugs it into the mainframe interface. Then we just enter a password and we're in."

She took the SD card out of the evidence bag and slid it into one of four sockets in the security blade. "Okay, time to get some answers."

We returned to the large metal doors. They opened with the same groan they had before, and outside of them stood the reception lady who had issued me my visitor's badge. She appeared to be out of breath, and her face showed panic.

"What is it, Saundra?" Vera asked.

"Ms. Essalte, we've had a break-in. I . . . I don't know how."

"Slow down," Vera said. "What happened?"

"I don't know." Saundra was almost hyperventilating. "It's gone!"

"What's gone?"

"The mainframe."

"What do you mean, like part of the mainframe is missing?"

No, the whole thing, the whole thing—it's been stolen!"

4

A Date With an Exorcist

I turned and looked at the blank stare that hung on Vera's face. It was like she had just watched someone kill her pet. Her life's work, and at the moment our most important lead, was gone. The blinking of her eyes was almost mechanical, as if she herself was a computer and was about to overload and crash at any moment. I turned back to Saundra and asked her when it had happened, but she, like Vera, was mum.

"Hey!" I snapped, bringing them out of their trances. They jumped as the sharp sound hurled them back to reality. "Focus," I continued. "How's the security?"

"The entire building has a CC system that operates 24/7," Vera replied.

"So, what do the recordings say?" I asked, looking at Saundra. She stared at me like I had just asked for her to give me her underwear. Like most low-level employees, she was useless without direction from the boss, who was standing next to me, and, at the moment, just as useless.

"The recordings!" I exclaimed again, this time at Vera to get her into gear so she could do the same to Saundra. She finally got her bearings for good and began to walk at a brisk pace to where I assumed the recordings were securely stored.

"Saundra, call security and pull the tapes for the past twenty-four hours. I want to know when it was taken and how," Vera said. Saundra nodded and broke into a run to the reception area where she made the requested phone call.

"Glad to have you back with us," I said. Vera gave me a look of disapproval at my comment and sped up like she was trying to leave me behind. She shook her head as she moved, clearly upset. It also indicated that something else was amiss with this situation.

"What is it?" I asked. She paused for a moment before answering.

"This isn't possible."

"What isn't—the theft of a memory core from a world-class engineering firm with state-of-the-art security, or the fact that you are walking through the halls of said engineering firm with the living and now ironically mortal embodiment of death trying to track the aforementioned thieves?" I felt snide after saying it.

The pierce of her stare was palpable, and her lips curled into a distinct frown as she tried to light me on fire with her eyes. My little experiment in humor had not landed where I'd wanted it to. As I thought about it, it was understandable. The gravity of the situation made it clear that it was the wrong time to joke. I pulled back my smirk and let her continue with her thought on the impossible.

"The first one," she said. "Not mentioning the security measures on the system itself, the mainframe for this research branch consists of over forty servers housed in a state-of-the-art server cabinet. Each server stores five hundred petabytes' worth of information and weighs close to a hundred pounds. That's nearly two tons' worth of equipment, just in the data storage."

"I'm guessing there's more?" I said as we arrived at the door to the security monitoring center. Vera's badge came off and moved toward the scanner, which beeped and allowed us entry. Inside were two men; one was sifting through the footage and the other was leaning over the top of him, scouring the images with him. Neither of them lifted their heads, but the man standing motioned us in. He was wearing an all-black suit with the jacket open, exposing a shoulder holster with a Glock 17 in it.

"We're already on it, Doc. Who's the guy?" said the man with the pistol, still not averting his gaze from the monitors.

"This is Cyrus," Vera said. She paused for a moment, not knowing how to proceed further. "He's an, um, engineering consultant," she finished awkwardly. Luckily neither man caught it.

The suit continued. "Nathan Prescott, security chief," he said, pointing at himself. His finger motioned over the other man's head. "Gerald Ramsey, IT security." Ramsey raised his hand in a fake wave for a split second. Neither of them broke their gaze on the monitors.

"What do we have?" Vera asked.

"Nothing yet," Prescott said. "Only problems."

"What do you mean 'problems'?" she asked.

"We have the general time of the theft," Ramsey said. "The problem is someone has altered the feed for the server room."

"Altered how?" I asked.

"Not sure yet," Ramsey said. "They're good. The crack was done remotely, probably started a long time ago. Did it slowly to keep themselves hidden from the system." Ramsey broke his stare and turned toward us. "Real pros. Whoever they are, they really knew what they were doing."

Vera and I looked at each other. It lent more credibility to the idea that it was an inside job. One of the team members had done it. At this point we were almost certain.

"Can you find and seal the breach?" Vera asked.

"It's not that simple," Ramsey replied. "The security firewall severed the connection as soon as they passed barrier A-7. The problem is when it did, it released a worm. The worm crippled our CCTV feeds. The antivirus system did its best to isolate the program and prevent damage, but some damage had already been done. The video files were hit; at best, they will be totally scrambled. I may be able to recover parts of the footage, but there's no telling what's what. The time stamps are toast."

"So how do we know the time the server was taken?" I asked.

"Badge swipe," Prescott said. "Dr. Crane. We found the discarded security badge near loading dock J-23, which is where we're guessing they got the hardware out. My guys are on it, but this would have taken a hell of a lot of manpower to do, and moving a few dozen men through this building without being noticed is not an easy thing to do."

"Which is why they crashed the security system," Vera said. "I just don't understand how no one physically saw them." Vera stopped for a moment. "Maybe they were," she muttered under her breath, and turned to Prescott. "Nathan, when was Crane's badge scanned for entry?"

"Why entry?" he asked, confused.

"Just when was it?" she yelled. Prescott flipped through a

manuscript for the entry time. He tilted his head and spoke as he handed the folder to Vera.

"At 10:42 a.m.," he said. "I don't understand—they were here all day? How did no one see them?"

"Not *them*," Vera said, "*him*, or perhaps *her*." She paused for a moment. "Ramsey, when did they scramble the signal?"

"Don't know yet, not until I've reconstructed the files into the proper order."

"That doesn't matter," she said. "How much total video time was compromised?"

A smile lit up Ramsey's face; he knew where she was going with this. "Nine hours, twelve minutes," he said. We all looked at the clock (*8:54*) and did the math. They didn't just take it, in and out, in the blink of an eye. They had all day to do it. I said what we were all thinking.

"The badge was used to get one person in, and then left it in the loading area on purpose to make it look like they took it out through there. Just a decoy." Everyone looked at me and nodded. Thoughts rushed over me and spilled out of my mouth before I could even comprehend them.

"I need the security schedule for the day," I said. I looked around the room unable to tell left from right for a few moments before seeing it. Mounted on the wall in plastic was a schedule. I moved closer to it. "10:00 a.m. to 7:00 p.m.—Lawrence Kennedy," I said. I turned toward Prescott, who was already on the phone. We waited intently for him to finish the call and tell us more.

"Damn it!" he yelled as he slammed the phone down. We all looked at him, waiting to hear the bad news that was coming. "That was his wife. He never made it home." Prescott rubbed his eyes.

"So where is he, then?" Ramsey asked, regretting his question as he began to check the logs. *11:31 a.m. EST—Larry Kennedy—Camera problems, server room, procedural check before contact to facilities for repair.* There was nothing else in the security log past that. "We need to see that server room," Ramsey said. No sooner had the words come out of his mouth than Prescott jerked the door open and the four of us were running to the server room.

The destruction of the remaining systems was not a pretty sight. The damage was easily in the millions. Not to mention the loss in intellectual property to ARC. Their insurance company was not going to be happy. As we looked closer, it was easy to tell the destruction was controlled. The people who had done this were very smart; nothing they did was by mistake. My instincts told me that, much like the badge, the calculated destruction was all subterfuge. Destruction made to cover up something else.

"Look for anything out of the ordinary," I said. "Blood, cloth, anything." The equipment left the building, but not through the docks, and the answer was in this room somewhere. We combed the entirety of it and were about to start over when we heard Ramsey call out.

"Here!" One of the server towers had been toppled over, and, beneath it, the steel door to one of the circuit grids had been torn off. The light-gray paint on it was in good condition. I looked around the room. The grid it had been removed from was a good ninety feet away, on the other side of the room. It was not there by accident. We all grabbed the thousand-pound server case and pushed as hard as we could. It toppled over and struck the ground, creating a massive metallic bang. The sound was amplified by the enclosed space, and I could feel my ears protest with pain.

Prescott reached down and pulled away the door, exposing a gaping hole in the concrete and the black empty space it led to. Prescott volunteered to go first, since he was the only one armed. Ramsey and I lowered him into the blackness of the hole, which then lit up from the tactical light mounted to the bottom of his sidearm. With the light, it looked to be only about fifteen feet down.

"It's clear!" he yelled back up to us, holstering his weapon. I lowered Ramsey and Vera down next before taking the plunge solo. I felt my feet sting at the vibration of hitting the solid surface below. It was not dirt, but concrete—an old service tunnel, perhaps, or sewers. No, not sewers—the accompanying stench was not present. Service tunnel it was. The old ARC logo from the seventies was on the wall in the landing. This was where they had taken the mainframe servers through.

"Shall we?" I said.

We all began to walk through the tunnel. The service lights were not the best lighting, but our eyes adjusted and we were able to do pretty well considering we were running off lighting forty-plus years old that no one had seen for who knew how long. About two hundred feet into the tunnel I saw something that did not fill me with hope.

"Is that blood?" Ramsey asked.

"Looks like," Prescott said. He reached into his jacket and drew his firearm again. The few drops of coagulated blood revealed that it had been there at least several hours, but I didn't want to disclose that to everyone else and kept my mouth shut. We continued down the tunnel until it came to a fork. The trail of blood led to the right and so we followed it. After several hundred more feet, it became evident that the minor injury that had been leaving a small trail of blood turned into much more. The blood droplets had been replaced by pools that continued to form a trail further in. As we came to the pools I looked around the tunnel. There were no apparent signs of struggle.

The mood heightened as the blood trail became thicker and thicker, and Prescott moved into a jog in its pursuit. I knew what waited at the end, but again I held my tongue. I walked while everyone else ran, taking my time to see if I could find anything useful left behind by the thieves. There was nothing, and eventually I came to the group standing over the remains of Larry Kennedy.

I lamented not being there for him as he passed. Though, given what had already happened, it was probably good that I wasn't; and I didn't like that idea. Vera stood in the corner weeping over the loss of her coworker. I understood why, but I couldn't do that. I needed to work. So I did just that. I bent down over the body and looked closer.

A pool of blood surrounded his head where he had collapsed. His assailant had come over and placed a final round through his temple. My attention moved down. He had taken one round in the hip, likely the first wound that started the trail. It slowed him down, but it wasn't enough to stop his pursuit. There was another in his gut. It would have been fatal no matter what. My gaze moved up and found another round in his upper chest near his right collarbone. It was definitely not the precision shooting that I had seen from the teams that had killed Adrian and were hunting me. This person was not as skilled, but he or she wasn't a novice, either. Every round had hit its target, so some skill was definitely at the disposal of the killer.

Kennedy went down from blood loss. The blood was smeared slightly on the concrete. He had tried to crawl before passing out. It was then that the killer returned for the coup de grâce. His gun had never left the holster on his hip—which was strange, given that his wounds had been inflicted over the course of two shootings. Everything about it seemed wrong. There was no reason he shouldn't have drawn after taking the shot in the hip. There had to be something more to it than I was getting.

I reached down and began to roll him over. Prescott reacted and pushed me off him.

"Do not touch!" he commanded.

Larry was his employee, and respect for the man was something he demanded. Or at least that's how I took it. Or maybe he was trying to preserve the crime scene. It could have been a little bit of both.

"Eight months," he said. "Eight months, and he was out—full pension. What am I going to tell his wife?" I wanted to tell him that he should tell her that he died chasing some people who were going to use the information on the mainframe to alter the world in a very bad way. But as I said it in my head I realized that it would just create more issues. So again, I said nothing. I looked down at the body of the security guard, past the blood. The pride the man had taken in his work was clear. His clothes were immaculately pressed, even now. The buttons were polished, as were the shoes, which glowed in the forty-year-old lighting.

I felt my eyes widen as I thought of the shoes. *Glowing.* I looked at the pool of blood where Larry's head had rested before I rolled him. The bullet had passed clean through. I could see the slug embedded into the concrete. It was soaked in red, but the one thing it wasn't soaked in was a glow. There was nothing different or special about it; it was a normal bullet.

"Vera, we need to go!" My words echoed in the tunnel toward her. She wiped her tears and walked toward me.

"What is it?" she asked.

"We need to go. I know what—"

"It's over!" she yelled back at me. "The mainframe is gone. These tunnels have hundreds of paths. There's no way to know where they went. We don't even know who they are or have any way to find out."

"Yes, we do," I said, making sure she could see the smile on my face as I said it. She paused for a second, almost scared to ask. We walked away from the others and lowered our voices.

"What do you have?" she finally asked.

"Lawrence Kennedy," I said, and gestured toward the pool where the bullet that had taken poor Larry lay. She got it, and her face lit up.

"But how?" she asked. "You're not exactly, well, *you* at the moment."

"I have a way," I said. "But we need to go, like, now." Vera turned back toward the other two.

"Ramsey, I need that video unscrambled as quickly as you can." He nodded. "Nathan . . ." Prescott looked at her. "You gonna be okay?"

"Yeah," he said, standing back up from where he was next to Larry.

"Guys, I need this to stay in-house as long as it can, got it?" They both looked at her, knowing that something huge was going on but scared to ask exactly what. "I understand that the cops need to be brought in at some point, but avoid that as long as you can. When the time comes, call Detectives Aaron and Marx out of the ninth. They are the ones investigating the murder of Dr. Crane. Got it?" The two men gave their best acknowledgment to her.

"I need more than just playing interference, Vera," Prescott said. She turned around and walked toward him.

"I understand that. And I understand this is hard on you, but trust me. Do your job—try and find the bastards. I'll tell you more when I can. Okay?" Prescott sighed and then nodded. Vera walked back toward me and nodded. We began walking toward the hole we'd come in from. After some distance I heard Prescott yell toward us.

"Where are you two going?" Vera looked at me, seeking a more solid answer to how we were going to get in contact with the spirit of Larry Kennedy. I smiled and cocked my head back to get the best projection possible in the tunnel and yelled back to Prescott, "To find an exorcist."

The sound of the closing door on the white Ford Fusion I had just sat in was a new experience for me. I had been in vehicles many times while on the job, but that was the first time I'd physically had to get into one. An unsettling feeling churned in the pit of my stomach as it dawned on me that this trip was going to be different. Should anything happen, there was no sitting in the backseat to whisk us off for a second try.

Vera looked at me, noticing at that moment that I was not comfortable.

"You okay?"

"If you kill me in my first car ride I'm going to be very upset,"

I replied. The smugness rolled over her mouth as the sound of the ignition fired and the engine sprung to life.

"Noted," she said, still smiling as she threw the car into drive and put her foot on the gas.

We left the grounds of ARC Industries and made our way back into the city. The dust and grime of the red-light district sharply contrasted against the pearlescent sheen of the company car we had arrived in. We took a few bad turns and ended up at a few dead ends before finally making our way onto Fence Boulevard. It was just past midnight by the time we got there, and business was in full swing. I directed Vera to pull to the corner under a streetlamp that was constantly flickering from its advanced state of disrepair.

One of the working girls chased away the others before approaching, hoping for a big score given the ARC lettering on the side door. I fiddled with the switch on the door to make the window go down as Vera grinned from ear to ear at my ineptitude. As the window finally lowered, the girl leaned over and the stench of cigarette smoke drowned in cheap perfume made its way to my nose, and it burned.

"My name is Charity," she said. "What can I do you for?"

It had been quite some time since I had been here last. My memory told me that it was a bad place. It was never pretty, the remains of what I left behind when I collected. Some were shot, while others had needles in their arms. None of them were bad people, just bad at making choices. But all of it—every shady deal, every pimp's cut, every dime bag in this area—all came back to Vincent Gianni. In the grand scheme of things, he was a bug compared to other warlords and sadists I had seen in my day, but that didn't mean he was nice, either. Regardless, I needed his attention at the moment. And so I did what I had to.

"I'm looking for Gianni," I replied to the hooker. She leaned back a bit, spooked, but the ARC on the door was like a flame that the moth just couldn't resist.

"What makes you think I know Gianni?" Charity replied, curling her hair around her finger and trying to flirt. I gave her a moment before beckoning her closer. She leaned over the window and smiled, exposing the gray-and-brown teeth she had acquired from her years of doing meth.

The crack of said rotten teeth detaching from her gums as my fist impacted them was loud enough for the whole street to hear. The stream of obscenities attached to the blood coming from her mouth made me cringe, and I felt regret for having to do it. I rolled up my window in case she carried pepper spray. She scooted away from the car and picked herself off the sidewalk before disappearing into the shadows to find her pimp. A few minutes later the stereotypical "Mack" emerged from around the building, cane and all, strutting toward the car.

The illiterate string of f-bombs with filler bombarded me as he did his best to be intimidating. I wanted to laugh at his deep-purple suit as he called me out for smacking his moll. But I kept cool until he lost it. The tiny shards of glass hit me in the face and bounced off as the cane came through the window. That was my cue. I thrust the door open as hard as I could, hitting him with it. He tumbled to the ground and I vaulted out of the car after him, making sure to take his cane. I saw him reach toward his backside where he had his piece. But I was faster than he was, and I cast it to the ground with my boot where Vera quickly scooped it up.

"I need to see Gianni," I said calmly, leaning in close to

the now-terrified pimp. He summoned all his bravery and retaliated.

"Fuck you!" he said before spitting in my face. I felt like I had in the church and a wave of fury rushed out of me. I felt my hand on his neck and my fingers clench down. My fingertips sank into his neck, breaking the skin and letting the now-ruptured capillaries release their cargo. The feeling of his own blood running down his neck caused the man to break, and the panic in his eyes told me that that would be the only resistance I would receive. I wiped away the foul-smelling saliva from my face and released him.

"I need to see Gianni," I said again, exactly as I had before. He didn't speak, just nodded and pointed down the street. "Show me," I said.

We walked in plain view of everyone, to make sure they saw us. I wanted the boss to know we were coming. The extravagance of the club's neon sign shouted "overcompensating" as we walked into the alley that led to the district's hub and Gianni's seat of power, The Velvet Orchid. I remembered being there when Vince pulled the trigger himself for the first time. An older man named Hugo had accidentally run into Gianni's car while leaving the club before he renamed it. The complete and total lack of remorse as he emptied his clip was a rarity even among psychopaths. Then there was the day he returned to the club and emptied another clip into Freddy Sparks, owner at the time. He sat for hours thinking of the name. And his lack of creativity was spelled out now in neon with its half-French/half-Oriental tone.

The bouncer at the steel door opened it for us, and we walked inside. The noise and smoke made it difficult to know where we were going. Luckily the walking wall in front of us made it easy to follow. We arrived at the stairs in the back, which led up to an office with one-way glass above the dance floor. I could feel it in the air—everything was very different. It had been a long time since last I had seen Vince, and the man had come a long way. The sheen of his Armani suit in the black light was striking. He turned around and faked a smile, the shine of his perfect veneers coupled with the platinum crucifix around his neck almost blinding us.

"I never thought I would see you again," he said, motioning the mountain of a man out and inviting us to sit across from his desk. We took our seats and he raised a small remote, which changed the room's lighting to that of a private study before continuing. "Why are you here?" he asked.

"I need your help," I said. Vince just looked at me, sizing me up and trying to determine the sincerity of my statement. I waited for him to respond, but he didn't. I could see Vera start to twitch next to me. I put my hand out as subtly as I could so she would calm down, and she did. Vince shifted his position in his chair a few times, but I remained still. I knew this game; I had seen it many times. First one to talk loses. Was my need for help worth more than his curiosity? My break came when the mountain that escorted us here burst into the room.

Vince turned to the door, his face as stolid as it could be, considering the game had just ended and he had just lost.

"What do you want, Joe? Can't you see I'm busy?" he said, making it very clear he was not happy with the interruption. Joe hesitated, understanding the magnitude of his screw-up. "Spit it out, Joe!" Vince yelled.

"Uh, Terry—Terry wants to know what you're going to do about them."

"Tell Terry that it's handled, and if he disturbs me again it's his ass that's gonna be up here in one my chairs, savvy?"

"Yes, sir," Joe said. The door was half-closed before he poked his head back in. "What about Terry's gun—"

"Joe, get the fuck out! Now!" He turned back to us. "Really hard to find good help these days. And really, he's the best there is. Anyway, where were we?"

I remained stone. Vince tried to pick up where he'd left off, but it was over.

"Fine," he said. "What is it I can do to help you?"

I took off my coat and rolled up my sleeve where the wound from the glowing bullet had left its mark.

"No shit!" Vince said. "How did you do that?" He jumped out of his seat and walked around to us. "I didn't think you could hurt yourself. That's crazy! Too bad it's not real."

I looked at him, and his face went wooden once again. He moved his hand and I felt the sting as his fingers pressed against the wound. He pulled them back quickly and went pale.

"No, no, no, no, this is not possible," he said, pacing around the room and trying his best not to panic. He sat back down in his chair and stared at the bullet wound in my arm. "This is big," he said eventually. "Are we talking mortal here? How?"

"Very carefully," I said, intentionally not letting anything else slip. "You in?"

He didn't speak, just kept shaking his head, his eyes still fixed on my arm.

"I need a real answer, Vince."

"No way. Whatever it is, I want no part of it."

"Think of it as a favor," I said, knowing that this would get his attention. He instantly calmed and you could tell he was thinking long and hard about it.

"Hmmm, a favor from you. Interesting," he said, leaving a big gap before continuing. "That's a maybe. But first, I need something."

"Fair enough," I said. "What?"

"Who's she?" I had almost forgotten about Vera, who had been silent since I had told her the plan.

"My name is Vera Essalte, and I'm the one who started all this," she said in a way that was half-proud and half-ashamed.

"I see," Vince said before looking at me. "You want me to kill her?" I gave him a disapproving look. But Vera had had enough games. She jumped out of her seat and pointed Terry's .45 at Vince.

"I'm in this room only because I trust him, and since you clearly you know him, you know what happens when I pull this trigger. I don't know who you think you are, and quite frankly I don't give a fuck. But this is important, and you're going to help us."

Vince leaned further back in his chair and chuckled to himself, looking at me while pointing at Vera.

"Spicy. I like it. Cyrus, you have good taste. Never took you for that kind of man," Vince said. "All right, Ms. Essalte, have a seat. I want to tell you a story."

Vera lowered the gun and sat back down next to me.

"I'll going to let you in a little bit on who I am," Vince continued. "I'm just sorry I don't have popcorn for you. You're gonna like this. I assume Cyrus has told you about how much of a scumbag I am?" Vera nodded, and Vince nodded with her. "Good. It gives some perspective. Now let's flip that on its head. You see, it's been a long time since I've seen Cyrus, and I'm not exactly the man I once was. It was September 2007—the district had been mine about two years. And I had

81

done a lot of really bad things to make it mine. Back then I didn't care. The business was good. I had money, women, power—everything I wanted. Until I met Gary Flynn. He was a regular. Gave us way more money than he reasonably had to spend, which at that time was good enough for me. But one day Gary comes in upset that his favorite girl, Lila, is no longer here. Drug overdose; very sad. I sent flowers. Anyway, his outburst escalates. So, Joe and Eli, how do I say this . . . *escorted* him off the premises. Should have been the end of the story. But it wasn't. Sometime later, Gary finds out that Lila's dead and blames it on me. We don't see Gary for quite some time. And then he shows up one day while I'm down on the floor entertaining some guests and puts four .38s into my chest."

Vince tore open his shirt, exposing the scars where the bullets had hit him. He bit his lip, his face going somber as he remembered the events before continuing.

"Anyway," he said, "emergency surgery didn't go so well. Officially, I was dead for six minutes. I remember sitting up from my corpse as the doctors tried to revive me and, lo and behold, a very sharply dressed man is standing next to me. Gives me a speech about not being afraid and how jarring the experience can be, but I don't hear nothing until I turn around and see myself flatlined. I'll never forget that emotion. But I calmed down, and he takes my hand, then whoosh, almost like I'm flying through the stars and suddenly I'm at someplace else. I can't really explain it. In this place, time doesn't exist. I asked the suit about reincarnation, sin, forgiveness, God. But I get no divinity in the answer, only 'you are what you do.' I asked many questions, and got many answers, none of which were very comforting when it came to my past deeds. One of those answers was to the question, 'who are you?'. Don't know how long we talked for, but just as quickly as I had moved there I was gone again. Next thing I know, it feels like I have an elephant on my chest and some doctors are holding me down."

Vince looked at me and, without moving his lips, gave me a big thank you.

"I'm assuming you know who the suit is," he said to Vera. "Changed my life, in more ways than one. When I came back, I changed the business. My girls used to get twenty percent—now they get seventy. Of the thirty coming to us, half goes to a fund to put them through college if they ever want out. Guys like Joe, mostly former military, they police the block, looking for muggers, rapists, and so on. You can't shut it down, but you can make it better. This place isn't what it used to be; it's better. Since my encounter with Mr. Grimm, we have had only one homicide. Muggings, rape, murder, all of it is essentially nonexistent here anymore. Now I have to keep the persona, so I have to rough up someone on occasion. But never bad, and never permanent."

"Crime boss gone straight . . . ish. Congratulations," Vera said sarcastically.

"Hey, I do the best with what I got. You don't know me—don't judge me."

"Again," Vera said, "I don't give a shit. We just need the exorcist. Just point us to him and we will be on our way."

"Wait," Vince said, "that's what you're here for?"

I felt my face pucker as I saw his reaction. Not what I had hoped for.

"Just tell us who it is!" Vera yelled.

"You need to go," Vince replied. "That's not gonna happen."

"We're not going anywhere until you tell us!"

"Leave, NOW!"

"Who is it? Damn it, tell us who it is!"

"It's me! Goddamn it! I am."

The room fell silent as Vince's words echoed through the office. A look of shock and confusion adorned Vera's face. She did her best to process it before speaking.

"You?" she asked. "No, we're looking for an exorcist, a holy man. Not some fucking pervert strip club owner."

"Charming," Vince said, calming down and taking a seat. Vera stepped back and sat down again as well. I got out of my chair and walked over to him, touching Vera on the shoulder as I did. I put my shoulder on his and he looked up at me with tears in his eyes.

"Finish the story, Vince," I said. He looked at me through the salt water that had started pooling in his eyes.

"This is not what I thought," he said.

"I know," I replied. "But it's important. Finish the story."

Vince took a deep breath and continued. "After I cleaned up and put myself back together, I started to do the same with the district. And that's when the weird stuff started happening. I began seeing things. Shadows in the dark that moved funny. People's faces, right in front of me, like they were falling off. It wasn't pleasant. At first, I figured since I was dead for six minutes, it was brain damage playing tricks on me. But the more I ignored it, the more I saw . . . things. Doctors, therapists, they all told me that it wasn't real, and I agreed. But the meds didn't do anything, until finally it came to a head.

I was out on the streets making sure the girls were doing well. Leena, one my strippers, had just passed her GED. I had just helped her enroll for her spring semester of college. It had been a good day. So I decided to go for a walk. I remember looking into an alley and seeing some creeper there. The scream came next. I realized that he was trying to rape one of the girls. Joe was with me, and we rushed in. Next thing I knew, I was on the ground and my air was knocked out. It was like getting hit with a ton of bricks. I looked up and saw this guy throw Joe like he was a sack of potatoes. Then he jumped on top of me and pinned me down. His arms were around my neck. I was done, blacked out. I will always remember the next part—this."

Vince reached down and twirled the platinum cross around his neck.

"This little thing here saved me. I remember waking up half-dead and seeing it dangling from his neck in front of me. The cross just hung there. I remember thinking *Stab him in the neck with it*. When I touched it, it was like it was on fire. I grabbed it and felt it melt into my skin. Left me with this."

The cross-shaped scar on his right palm was nearly perfect. He rubbed it with his left hand as he continued.

"I let it go as it burned me. No reason it should have, but it did. So I went to plan B, gouge his eyes. My hands went up and as they did I saw his face. The entire left side looked like it was rotting off, just like I had been seeing for months. I pressed my hand against his face, trying to reach for his eyes, when I heard the most bloodcurdling scream anyone has ever heard. And like steam coming off a pot, the rot evaporated off his face. He collapsed on me and I passed out again. When Joe woke me up the man was dead. Only time anyone had died in this area in a long time."

Vince rubbed his temples. It was clear he hadn't thought about it in a long time. He took a breath and finished.

"After that, anything nasty that I touched with this hand, changed. People began asking me to heal the sick, and, for reasons I still don't understand, I actually could. It started small. I began exorcising whatever it was that made these people look like they were rotting. Made them do bad things that normal people don't do. Before I knew it, it had escalated. The more I did it, the more clearly I could see the things hiding behind the world. Eventually, I began seeing the dead. So I began to read up on it. I learned a lot about a lot, when it comes to that. I even found a way to step to the other side. I wanted to help, but it was too much. It seemed the more good I did, the more bad came looking for me. People got hurt. And so I stopped. I don't do that anymore, understand?"

"I'm sorry," Vera said.

"It's okay, I get it," Vince said. "I'm not a good man; I didn't used to be, at least. I try to be better now, in little ways, when I can. But you're right: at the end of the day I'm just a pervert strip club owner." He turned to me, his eyes filled with the kindness he hoped he had become. "Cyrus, I understand that whatever you need is probably very important. You need money, fine. You need resources, sure. But I can't go back into that world. Only bad things can come from it."

I paused for a moment, thinking of how best to respond.

"And what if the alternative is worse?" I asked.

"Worse how?" he asked. I gave him the same look I always did, and he once more began to rub his temples.

"My turn for story time," I said. I knew that this was not the same man I had seen all those years ago. The vile, ruthless killer was no more. This new man was unpredictable, but I had nowhere else to go. So I committed, and prepared myself to catch him up on the events that had brought me to his door.

The sweet stench of Vince's vomit in his trash can as he tried to process what he had just heard filled the room and made me want to do the same. Another new experience, wanting to vomit when someone else does. I waited for the can to make its way back to the floor from his lap. When it did, it was time to ask again.

"So what do you think? You in?"

Vince gave out a long sigh before answering with a reluctant, "Yes."

"Good," I said, standing up. "For now, I have a simple request. I need to talk to someone among the dead. And since I'm not exactly myself, I need your help to do that."

"We have a name?" he asked.

"Lawrence Kennedy," I said. "Can you do it?"

"I'm sure I can. How long has he been dead?"

"A few hours. Nice and fresh," I replied.

Vince hesitated. "That might be a problem."

"And why is that?"

"You of all people know how unstable souls are at the beginning, and without you there to help him transition, they tend to get lost."

"How often does that happen?" I asked.

"Not very, but even you miss one from time to time, a runner who is gone before you get there."

"Hmmm," I said, making a mental note to be more diligent in the future, provided I had one.

"Let me take a look," Vince said. He sat silent and focused. The air grew heavy and I felt the Veil twist, but that was it. "It's not gonna happen. We're gonna need the crucible."

"Are you sure?" I asked.

"If you're on a time crunch, then, yes," he replied.

"Great. I guess I get to finally understand what it means to say 'go big or go home.'"

"What's the crucible?" Vera asked.

Vince didn't answer, and instead stood up and motioned us toward the door. We walked out of the office and down the stairs to a utility door that led into the basement of the club.

Vera asked again. "What's the crucible?"

"Think of it as a portal," Vince said, "but not just any normal portal. There are some places where the barrier between our world and the spirit world is weak. This is the step up from that. It can be used to actually move between the physical and spirit realms. Thing is, it's not clean, like what he can do. It's more of a hole in the fabric of reality."

"That doesn't sound very safe," she replied.

"It's not," I said as we reached the bottom of the stairs and Vince hit the lights, exposing a giant pentagram on the floor. "But not for the reasons you think."

"I don't follow," Vera said.

"It's dangerous because you can't exactly pick where you cross over," Vince said. "And the universe is pretty big. And there's only a few places that are what I call 'anchored,' meaning you can get in and out reliably."

"So we just use those places, then, right?" she asked.

"Right," I said. "And that's why it's dangerous—location."

"Why? Where does it lead?"

I stepped into the middle of the circle and Vince began to light the candles at each of the points of the star. He spoke in Latin as he did and the words echoed through the small space. I looked at Vera as the last flame became alight on the symbol, ready to make my way through, and waved Vera over. She jumped in quickly and met me at the center. The dark lines of the symbol lit up in a bright blue. They traced slowly at first then sped up as Vince continued to chant.

"Close your eyes," I said to Vera.

"Cyrus, where are we going? Where does the portal come out?"

I didn't want to tell her, but I needed her there to help me. Fear is a powerful motivator, but not in situations like this.

"Do you trust me?" I asked.

"I kind of have to," she replied, her eyes still closed. I was putting her in danger, and because of that she had a right to know. I waited for a moment for the symbol to be almost complete. So that when I spoke, the answer would be too late for it to matter.

She asked again, "Where are we going?"

The last edges of the blue met and I felt the world begin to fold around us, and answered her question.

"Hell."

5

Communion of Souls

The heat of the fire that danced about in the cinder-filled air burned as it touched my now-mortal skin. It was the first time in my long existence that the searing winds of that place did more than just glance off me. I knew where I stood, but it was like someone had taken that painting I knew so well and went over it with a completely new color palate based in red. Everything here was so familiar, but suddenly so different. I had walked upon these lands tens of millions of times, but now they were so foreign. It made me feel like my stomach had been twisted into a knot. Maybe it was the feeling, or maybe it was the smell of sulfur and burning flesh that hung in the air.

I looked out across the desolation to see if there was anything that posed an immediate threat. It was clear, but that did not mean we were out of the woods yet. My friend was here with me, and she, too, would have to brave the unforgiving depths if we were to get what we needed. She was bent over, the contents of her stomach spewing out and drying almost instantly as they hit the scorched ground at her feet. At that point I figured it definitely was the smell.

"You okay?" I asked Vera. The look on her face was not promising. The discomfort of the heat melting away her flesh—only for it to simultaneously reconstruct itself—was something I should have prepared her for. But it had never crossed my mind before that moment. I had never had flesh while in this place. She did her best not to scream as the intense pain eating away at her continued, as it had for so long, for so many.

"Vera! Are you okay?" She turned to me and saw that my skin and muscles had also unraveled from my bone. But I was stoic. It was just physical—nothing compared to the emotional or spiritual torment I had seen throughout the history of this world. And so she grinned, nodded, and accepted the violent destruction of her body knowing that I was there with her.

"Come on!" I yelled over the howling winds. "We need to get to shelter in case anything noticed we're here."

"What do you mean any*thing*?" she asked, doing her best to shield her face from the scorching winds.

"You don't want to know." Now was not the time or the place to share with her why it was called hell.

We moved in the open fields for about a half hour before I spotted a crag jutting from the earth like a large stone blade. We moved toward it, and as we got closer it was exactly what I had hoped it would be. At the base was a crevice that opened up into an old lava tube. We moved inside. It was like an oven, but at least we were out of the burning winds and, more importantly, out of sight. We sat down carefully to try to avoid any unnecessary pain due to the heat of the stone. We caught our breaths, and Vera spoke.

"I don't understand. How can any of this be real? You were very adamant to denounce God as real."

"Just because I said that God isn't real doesn't mean that heaven and hell aren't," I responded.

"You could have warned me before taking me into the deepest pits of a nightmare."

I looked at her for a moment, wanting to give some perspective to what she had just said. But to tell her that we were nowhere near the deepest pits of her nightmares would have been insensitive, and would add to her discomfort. I decided it was not a good idea.

"What about demons?" she asked.

"Real, but not in the way you think of them."

"What do you mean?"

"Everything in the universe is energy, at a base level. When you break it all down, its energy—matter, light—everything. You know the science. It's all just different wavelengths that act differently on everything else. Demons are simply extremes within the emotional spectrum. Anger, sadness, indifference—these things are all just emotional states. But like water, they coalesce, group together, and form the worst incarnations of themselves—rage, despair, apathy. In the physical realm, these things can attach to the weaker versions already in people and create drastic change. A man can go crazy and kill his wife in a fit of rage. People say they were possessed, as if by an evil spirit. Not far from the truth. But that's the physical world. In here, those things have much more power. So much so that they manifest."

"I see. So then angels are real, too?"

"Yes," I replied. "They are the virtues, the good things mankind aspires to be, and, like demons, they give men power to make change, usually for the better. That's how miracles happen."

Vera nodded and looked down at her burning flesh. I knew what she was going to ask, so I answered it preemptively to save us time and satisfy her curiosity so I could figure out our next move from here.

"The reason the heat hasn't killed us is because we're not really here. Our bodies are in the basement of The Velvet Orchid with Vince. He's keeping the link open so we can move freely. Because the link is open, everything that happens here is felt by our physical selves. The mind can't separate the two or we die, and so it doesn't. But that also means we burn. While the link is open, we're at risk. We can only leave from where we came in, so we need to be back here with the information before we do. If the connection is severed before we make it out, then we're cut off from our bodies, and that's the end. At least for the physical part of us. So we need to be quick—Vince can't keep it open forever."

"Again with the not telling me vital information before dragging me into hell, quite literally."

"Spiritually," I said in jest, and got the accompanying dirty look for it.

"So what's the next move?" she said, standing up and clearly in a hurry to get back home.

"First we need to make our way to the Hollow. From there I can try and find out where Larry has run off to, and hopefully find him."

"And what is this 'Hollow'?" she asked. I stood up and headed back toward the crevice where we had entered. I poked my head out to make sure it was clear before answering.

"It's kind of hard to explain," I said as I motioned her to

follow. "It's kind of like the waiting place for souls before they make their way to their next existence."

She stepped up next to me and reached out for me to take her hand, which I did, ready to pull her and make a break for it if the need to do so suddenly arose. "So it's like purgatory, or limbo, then, right?"

"Not exactly. Think of it more like a train station that leads everywhere. It's not itself a real, solid place, but it connects everything. Anywhere you want to be in the nether realm has to pass through it. It's like everything in the universe is folded in on itself into one room, and through it you can pass anywhere. I can move there at will, usually. It's where I imprint, and it's how I am everywhere all the time."

"How you what?" she asked. I had never explained it to her. She knew so much and yet so little about me. I gave a quick rundown and continued as we began moving across the devastated terrain.

"There's so much more to everything than I ever thought."

"Just the tip of the iceberg," I replied.

"So how do we get to the Hollow?"

"There," I replied, pointing to a tower in the distance. "That's our way out."

"That's at least a hundred miles away. There's no way we can make it there, find Larry, and make it back before Vince has to pull the plug. It's going to take a month."

"Time moves differently here," I said. "Perceived time and real time are not the same. Our spirits, like our minds, are not bound within the same constraints. The hour it feels like we've been here is maybe a few minutes for Vince. And different parts of hell have different time dilations. The deeper you go, the slower it gets. Plus, I never said we had to walk that

94

distance (at least not directly). Time accelerates and slows based on will. Whoever is in charge of this place can alter how it works. Because of that, I might very well be able to make us a shortcut, with a little convincing."

"How are you going to do that?"

"Energy coalesces, remember?"

"So?"

"So the part of me that was stripped when I was shot might very well still be around here. If I can find it and link to it, I might be able to pull us right to it."

I took her by the hand and told her to focus on me, to feel what it would be like to be me. Walk among the lives lost and to help them move to their next existence. I joined in with her and then, like a bungee cord going taut, I felt a yank. It was only for a second, and just like that we had moved. I looked down at my hands. I wasn't whole, but it worked. The lost part of me, or at least a small portion of it, was back. I could feel some of the power I had lost coursing within me, and perhaps, she could too.

I looked to my side; Vera was still with me. I surveyed the area. It had worked—the tower was no more than a few miles away. She smiled at me and I reciprocated it before we both covered our faces and began walking. The scorching wind died down as we approached.

The tower, broken and battered through the eons, stood before us, a monolith to the majesty and misery of a realm that's entire purpose was to house and punish the souls of those who had earned its harsh confinement. That was, until it was time for them to take another shot. The doors were comprised of the deepest onyx and they opened without a touch. Inside I saw what I hoped would not be there: one of

95

the demon lords. He stood in the middle of the room, a soul of a man naked and writhing in pain right beside him in the fetal position.

"Grimm," said Azazel, turning his attention away from his victim. "Good to see you again. Bring us anyone worth our hospitality? It's not often you grant us a visit."

"No one today, but, then again, the past few days haven't been the best for me. I just need the chair."

"Don't want to stay and watch? We can bring out some of the oldies but goodies. I think we have a few nasties still in our custody we can play with. It will be fun."

"Thanks—just the chair," I replied. I hoped I would not be recognized for anything less than myself.

Azazel overcame the anger that he was essentially the embodiment of. "Fine, but next time I see you, you stay and enjoy the amenities, yes?"

"I'll think about it," I replied.

"Not good enough, but I'll let you pass," said the demon. "Kindness is in my nature," he continued, his smile revealing his daggerlike teeth. I twisted my face to show anger, and Azazel uncurled his twisted finger and pointed to the spiral staircase that led us up to the second floor, where I hoped the chair waited.

Torn leather straps hung from its armrests, and the pipe from which the crown would have been lowered was bent and twisted. The wood and metal of the execution device's sturdy construction matched the room's decor.

"I'm guessing that that electric chair is our ticket out of here?" Vera asked, cringing as she did.

"One zap and we're off," I said. I sat down in the chair. The feel of the warm wood sticking to the sweat on my skin brought me back to the first time I had seen one of these in action. "Don't worry, Vera, it only hurts for an instant, then we're off to the next stage." She gave a reluctant smile and nodded.

I sat down and grabbed the dangling electrical crown. I placed it on my head and felt the electricity pass through me. My eyes snapped open and I felt myself suspended in the vast emptiness of the Hollow. It took a few minutes, but after that, Vera took the plunge and was with me.

"You okay?" I asked. She nodded and stared off into all the parts of reality interlaced around her.

"Why did we have to do that to get here?"

"This place is special. You only get here in one of two ways—with me or through a gate, like the chair."

"Okay," she replied. Her face said she had more questions, but she didn't ask.

"Ready for the next part?" I continued.

She gave another reluctant acknowledgment. I took her hand and focused, like I had so many times before, and once more with a snap of the bungee cord she and I were at the front door of ARC Industries. This time, however, we were on my side of existence. The gray hue that enveloped everything was once more a new thing to me. I had been doing this for so long that until that moment—having been stuck a mortal—I had forgotten how it looked. I guess this was what it must have felt for those I had collected.

We made our way back through the research lab labeled 10741 and into the server room. We descended into the tunnel and made our way to the kill site. Nathan Prescott was still there, and he had moved the body. He was on one of the maintenance phones attached to what looked like an old circuit panel. I could hear him through the distortion between the realms. He was talking to Detective Aaron. The police would be on their way soon.

"Let's see how much juice I still have," I said, and began to focus on Larry Kennedy. The past came to life and we were able to watch the aftermath of Larry's death. Almost like a movie, we watched as Larry's spirit had gotten up and had his minor emotional breakdown at the sight of his own demise. But he handled it well—better than I expected he would, especially for having been alone during it. He looked around, lost at what to do next, and did the one thing I had hoped he would: continued trying to follow his killers.

Everything moved differently from this side. He made ground and we followed. Eventually he caught up to them, or so it seemed. But how he behaved after that was strange. I looked around at the tunnel. Small pieces of debris were on the ground, like an explosion had taken place. It looked familiar, perhaps too much so. The assailants had done it again. They had blown a hole in the wall and then through the same process at Adrian's, they'd reversed it. Or at least it had looked that way. Like at the Harmond residence, there were slight imperfections, bits of rubble that had not returned to their original place. It must have been a strange experience for poor Larry. Physics gets ingrained into how people move and the idea that he could walk through the wall after they reconstructed it must have been foreign. And so the spirit of Lawrence Kennedy, his prey lost to him, sat down and wept.

Vera and I watched the echo for what seemed like an eternity, lost, stuck in his sorrow. I wasn't there and it was painful to watch the soul of this man crumble in the face of his situation. But that was not my biggest concern. He wasn't here. He had been and remained for some time, but he wasn't here now. He should have been waiting here for us, sitting, but he wasn't. Something had happened, and so we continued to watch. It took another few minutes before we saw it. It was like a beast formed of shadow and ice, creeping in from the shadows.

"What is that?" Vera asked. I felt myself become angry. Why had I not seen it coming?

"It's a demon," I said. The sadness that Larry was stuck in had attracted it, and as he continued it moved closer. Then, like a predator dragging its prey into the water to its doom, it wrapped its grimy tendril around him and a moment later he was gone.

"What just happened?" Vera asked, doing her best to keep calm.

"We missed him," I said. "I know who has him. In fact, we passed him on the way here."

I grabbed her hand and asked her to concentrate. The room shook as the Veil twisted around us, and a few moments later we were back in the Hollow.

"Now, focus on the chair," I said, and we concentrated. Again we moved through the nether. The fire slapped me in the face again as I stood up from the uncomfortable wood and stepped away waiting for Vera to join me. When she did, I rushed down to the first floor and belted at the top of my lungs at the demon lord residing there.

"You son of a bitch! Where is he?"

"Come to play now?" replied Azazel, his smugness filling the room with an air of filthiness.

"This is not a game, Azazel. I want that soul and I want it now!"

"Temper, temper, Grimm. I know you, and I know that right

now you are not you. If you want him, then I want something in return."

"And what is that?" I asked, the anger about to burst through me. The demon's hand, with its long, curly fingers, extended toward Vera.

"Her," he said. "You give me a soul, and I give you a soul. It's only fair."

That was it. The fury in me surged, and, like a flash of darkness, I lunged forward and felt my hand strike the demon. I felt the sliminess of his chest cavity on my forearm as my fingers wrapped around his spine. The look of surprise on his face as I lifted him up was satisfying.

"I will not ask again," I said. "I will literally rip you apart over and over again until I get what I want. You are right, I'm not myself right now, and that is something that anyone who crosses me should be very, very afraid of."

"All right," caved the demon in his agony. I discarded him to the side like the filth he was.

"Kennedy, now!" I demanded.

"Vargaz has him—safekeeping. I didn't know how you would react, and I wasn't going to keep him here. He was to be a plaything for me. I didn't know you had claimed him, I swear."

I walked over to the writhing demon and knelt next to his broken form. "Where?" I asked calmly, making it very clear that any deception would not go unpunished.

"The Necropolis. Vargaz will be there. Maybe a few others."

"Who?" I asked.

"Hexas, Ashtaroth, maybe Serran."

"Will they be expecting me?"

"Yes."

"Then you give them a message for me," I said, the fury in my voice like the hellfire ripping at my flesh. "I get the soul, unharmed, and they get to keep their heads." The wounded demon acknowledged my demand, and in a flash of fire and smoke slithered away to tell the others and likely plot his revenge.

Vera turned to me, cringing once more at the melting skin she was wrapped in. "Do you think they will give us Kennedy?"

"Not a chance," I replied. "They will do anything they can to find leverage over me. That's what they do. They want me on their side, to feed them souls they can use to gain more power. With me in this weakened state they figure this is their chance. Good news is, we know that. And better yet, they know that I know. We can turn that against them."

"And how do we do that?" she asked.

I hesitated for a moment, and then it hit me.

"We're going to bring a little extra firepower," I said.

The trek through the Ashengard Mountains and into the Valley of Terror where the Necropolis lay was not an easy one; and I knew that Vera would be near spent as we began our descent into the putrid waste that surrounded the Underbog. The unrelenting assault of the flames was replaced by the toxic stench of a million rotting souls. The hands of those doomed to suffer here until their next allotment of time on earth struggled to pierce the membrane over the foul liquid that kept them submerged, to drown over and over again in their own filth. There was a time when I had felt some pity for them, but the millennia of dealing with man's more brutal indiscretions had showed me that those here deserved it, and so their fates at the present time were of little consequence. They would get the chance to try again and do better. Vera was not of the same understanding.

"You have to help them," she said.

"They don't need our help," I said as I held her hand and carefully navigated the little bit of muddy land jutting from the vile liquid.

"But they're suffering," she said.

"Let them," I said, trying to keep her focus on getting out of the waste. But she was a good person and couldn't just watch. She released my hand and ran to the edge of the water, jabbing her fist through the thin membrane that was keeping her safe from the vermin beneath. The hands reached up and grabbed her. She let out a scream as the fingernails dug into her forearm and pulled her into the opening she had made. I moved in reaction, grabbing her shirt and pulling her back out of the water, the three souls she was trying to help clawing at her.

I felt myself sink into my anger, and with a flick of my wrist, detached the souls' forearms at the elbows, causing them to sail a good twenty yards before landing on top of the membrane at another point. All three grasped at their stumps with their remaining limbs and sank back into the bog. The membrane sealed itself as they vanished, and once again she was safe.

"Are you okay?" I asked Vera as she spat out the rancid fluid that had sunk into her lungs and took a big gasp of the poison gas. Her face contorted as it burned her lungs, but she calmed and slowly recovered. She nodded, and I knelt next to her for a moment while she sat and did her best to catch her breath in the fetid haze. When she was ready she took my hand and I helped her to her feet, once more asking if she was okay. She gave me a look of apology and then nodded again before we continued.

I told Vera about the Necropolis. It was one of six strongholds within the realm. Each of them held the worst of the worst. Those men and women who had committed the most violent atrocities against their fellow man were kept there. Those who had done the unspeakable would endure the harshest of punishments, and it was all deserved. She needed to know, so she could keep her sentiment in check.

It was also a place where the archdemons, the highest echelons of evil, made their homes. The "big nasties," as I called them, had grown that way by feeding on the pain and suffering of those whom they violated there. The Necropolis was composed of three rings, each one for the severity of the punishment the souls would endure there. I had been here only once, and it was to personally deliver an Austrian man who had killed millions in his attempt to create what he believed was a master race.

The cylindrical structure came into view as we walked down the embankment away from the vile gas of the Underbog.

"That does not look like a place you want to go," Vera said as we walked further, getting closer to the middle of the crater where the structure stood.

"It's not, especially with who's waiting for us there."

"It would be nice to know what I'm getting myself into this time," she said.

"You really wouldn't," I replied, hoping she wouldn't push the subject, but she did.

"My ass is on the line here, too," she said. "Who or what exactly is going to be waiting for us?"

"It won't matter, if you follow the plan. Stay here" I said. But she just looked at me, and I caved and explained.

"And these demons, who are they?" she asked.

"Azazel you already know—he's the Avatar of Envy—if he's brave enough to show up. Vargaz is the Avatar of Fury—quick temper, quicker sword hand. Hexas is the Avatar of Fear—uuuugly fucker, but not a bad fighter. Ashtaroth is the Avatar of Violence—he's very slow, but very, very strong. And Serran is the Avatar of Deception—she's the one we really have to worry about. If push comes to shove, I can handle the others in a brawl, but we won't see Serran coming. So again, follow the plan and we will be okay, got it?"

"Got it," Vera replied. "So these guys, they don't like you, do they?"

"Not so much."

"Why?"

"Let's just say I never like playing by their rules."

"They have rules?"

"No, and that's exactly the point. I do."

We arrived at the outer wall and I cocked back my fist and drove it into the massive stone doors that kept the fortress sealed. They opened with a groan, announcing our visit. The outermost ring of the Necropolis was known as The Blade. The souls stuck there were herded like cattle to be butchered and reconstructed only to have it all happen again later. The screams penetrated the stone like it was hollow, and echoed through the halls. We stopped only a few times before walking deeper into the structure.

The middle ring was known as The Gorge. Here, the souls were given that which they desired, in extreme excess. Gluttons were forced to eat until their insides erupted from fullness. Those who lusted for the flesh were pleasured so much that their genitals were destroyed and reconstructed to be done again, and so on through the lists. Less physically painful than the first ring, it destroyed the idea of comfort, poisoning the minds of those in it against their vices. The apathy which those here showed toward all things enjoyable sucked the light right out of the world, and it was overtaken by a drab grayness that even to me was unsettling. I couldn't imagine how Vera felt. We stopped again only a few times before continuing.

The inner ring was known as The Shame. This ring's worst pain was reserved for nonphysical suffering. Those condemned to this place were forced to tear down that which they valued most in themselves. Those who were vain were cursed with insatiable itch, and so they ripped at their own flesh, destroying the image they held so dear. At its center was The Seat, where the throne for the archdemon Gorgoroth once sat. Next to this was a curled horn from which the demon once used to summon his court. He had long since vacated, but the chamber remained. It was here that Lawrence Kennedy was being held, and where the real danger awaited us.

The black stairs that descended to The Seat were steep and difficult to walk on, built that way so anyone walking up or down would fall and be deposited back into the circle below. I told Vera to stay here and to be aware of her surroundings. The demon lords were around. I moved carefully down the slick steps and into the arena where the throne was. At the base of it, wrapped in spiked chains, was the soul of Lawrence Kennedy. Beside him I saw only one of the demons I expected.

The thick armor plating that covered Ashtaroth's slimy flesh was sheen, like a polished piece of obsidian. He had blades mounted to his forearms, running from his elbows out past his fists. He towered at least thirty feet high, and, like most demons, fancied himself a more powerful force than anything the size of a human. His ignorance of my capabilities was to my advantage.

"Release the soul!" I belted at the enormous demon.

"If you want him, then you best try and take him," Ashtaroth thundered.

"This is your final warning," I said, knowing full well that my foe would not simply give up and let me have him. But then came something I did not expect.

"Why is he so important to you?" the demon asked. I thought for a moment. These were not the words of a demon (at least not *this* one). There was a puppet master pulling the strings.

"Does it really matter?" I asked. "I am the reaper, and he is a lost soul. He belongs to me."

"And the other one, is she a lost soul?"

"You would do best to keep your distance from her," I replied. "She has a bite."

"Does she now?" came a voice from outside of the pit. I turned toward it, knowing what I would see. Vera was herself wrapped in chains and being carried down into the flat by Vargaz. All according to plan.

"And where's your puppet master?" I asked as he set Vera down. Fire erupted from his nostrils as his blind rage overtook him, and he rushed toward me. I felt my hand move and become like steel. It reshaped itself into a blade as I had learned it would when I needed it to. As the demon charged, I moved like lightning, driving my fist into his chest, stopping his momentum as I touched the tip of my blade-hand ever so slightly on the soft flesh between the chin and throat of the demon. He froze as he realized he was outmatched.

"Back the fuck up," I said calmly to the demon who was now torn between his rage and imminent dismemberment. His desire to remain intact won out, and he stepped back to where he had left Vera.

"We still have them," Vargaz hissed as he placed each of his hands on Vera and Larry.

"The souls themselves do not matter to me—just some information. I get the information I want, you get what you want—them. Sound fair?" Vargaz didn't speak, which told me he wasn't in charge. A glint in his eyes refocused him and he finally spoke.

"Who says we want the souls?" he asked.

"If not them, then what do you want?" I asked.

"You!" I heard bellowed out from behind me as Hexas burst from the shadows and swung his ax at me. Everything was exactly as I imagined it would be. It was like child's play. I twisted myself to the side and the ax moved past me harmlessly. My arm moved quickly and the sharpness of my forearm moved through the tentacles hanging from Hexas's face, as if they were not even there, and into his neck. His arms went limp and his grotesque body fell lifelessly to the floor, while his head spun to the side and landed behind me. I turned and drove my boot into the demon's severed head. The sound of the crunching bones echoed through the pit. He would be back, like they always were, but at least for this fight, Hexas was one less problem to deal with.

A ghastly roar followed the crunching bones, and with it the behemoth that was Ashtaroth charged once again. He lowered his shoulders and head. The armored plating of his exoskeleton interlocked, effectively turning him into a massive battering ram. I turned and ran directly at the charging beast, letting out my own war cry. He picked up steam as he got closer and his spiked armor erupted out toward me in an attempt to impale me. As he did, I released. My body fell flat and I slid beneath his attack. My arms went up together and into his underbelly. Much like they had done to Hexas, they split the massive demon's gut wide open with ease, spilling his entrails on the dirt of the pit. He fell to his side, writhing in pain.

I vaulted myself upright and leaped onto the armored pauldron of the beast. I drew back and struck, digging my arms into the soft, unarmored backside of his neck. I pressed again, sinking deeper until I felt the bone, and brought my hands together. I felt his skull dislodge from his spine, and I pulled, casting his head to the ground below and jumping down after it to give it the same treatment I had given Hexas. When the echo of smashed skull faded, I turned to Vargaz who, once again, had done exactly what I had thought he would. He held Vera, still tied up, in front of him, his sword to her neck.

"Back!" he yelled, once more caught between his overpowering anger and his will to not be destroyed.

"You should have listened to me," I said to the flustered demon. He looked back at me, trying to figure a way out.

"What?" I said. "The puppet master not coming to save you? Well?" He was lost in his situation. Killing the girl would mean his own destruction, and letting her go was not a guarantee I would not do the same to him. And so the agreement I had planned finally came to fruition.

"Okay, okay, okay," Vargaz said. "Here's the deal: I let you all go, and you let me go. Deal?"

"Deal," I said without hesitation. "I will let you go. Now untie the girl." The sword moved from Vera's neck and went behind her to undo the chains. The bindings fell to the ground, and, as they did, Vera turned toward the demon. Vargaz's scream shook the entire structure as she drove the platinum crucifix we had gotten from Vince into his forehead. He stumbled backward, trying to pry it out from where it had melted into his face. Eventually he reached the edge of the pit and ran into the wall. His screaming continued until it was silenced by my boot being delivered to where the cross was stuck. His skull fell to pieces as I pulled my leg back, and his body fell limp next to it.

Vera picked up the cross and put it around her neck. "He told you I bite, motherfucker," she said as she kicked the crumpled corpse.

One more to go, I thought as I turned back around to where Larry had been lying. A cloud of insects and smoke appeared above him, and from it emerged Serran. She did not look happy as she stood over the man that was the key to fixing this whole situation.

"You killed my pets," she said, jamming her heel into Larry's ribs, causing him to release a weak groan.

"You know the drill, Serran. They'll be back; it just takes time. But then again, I didn't think you gave a shit about whether they come back or not. I figured you as more of the selfish, manipulate-the-universe-to-get-what-I-want kind of bitch. Not that there's anything wrong with caring for a fellow demon. I just didn't think it was your style. To the point, I am not someone that you should play this game with. Give me the soul and walk away. If you harm him, I will hunt you down—I don't care how long it takes—and I will end you. It will be slow, and I will make sure you know that it was the worst decision you ever made. Am I clear?"

"Crystal," Serran said, completely unfazed by my threat.

"You legitimately think you can handle me, don't you?" I asked. "I carved right through your trap, and you still think you can win."

"I know I can handle you, darling; and, honestly, it's amusing that you think I can't. I can say a word and kill you both."

"Leverage," I replied. "It's always good to have it. But I'm sorry, Serran. In this case, you just don't."

"I wouldn't be so sure, Grimm. You're in my world now. I have the leverage here, and in yours."

"Oh, right. You mean your assassin up on earth, who, as of this moment, is supposed to have Vince at gunpoint; who, at your word, is ready to close the crucible and sever the connection? Is that what you're talking about?" I asked.

The smugness melted off her face, as if she had just stepped into hell and the flames were peeling it from her face.

"As soon as your name was mentioned I had a feeling that you might think a little outside the box. I took another trip on the chair and gave my guy a little heads-up when we went back for this," I said, reaching over and lifting Vince's platinum cross that hung around Vera's neck. "And in case you didn't know, he has a small army at his disposal up there. So I think you're overplaying your perceived leverage, don't you?"

Her confidence was gone, and she knew it. I gave it a moment to sink in before speaking. "My turn now, bitch. Vera."

Vera walked over to the battle horn next to the old throne of the Demon Lord that once resided there, and gave it a hearty

110

blow. The sound filled the Necropolis and it began to shake. Tortured souls that had been kept within the Necropolis began to appear from the entrances around the inner circle. They were the same souls that I had released as we made our way to the inner ring. The skeletal faces of the masses stood silent, their gazes like fire, fixated on Serran.

"Now, I'm willing to let you walk away, go on about your pitiful existence, provided I get the soul unharmed. As for *them*," I said, glancing around the balcony overlooking the seat, "I wouldn't count on them being so forgiving. Now, I told them to give us three minutes, and then you're all theirs. If I were you, this is where I would start running."

Serran stepped away from Larry, gave me the same look of hatred that I swear Vera sometimes did, and made a break for the narrow black stairs. I rushed forward and tore the chains off Larry before helping him to his feet. He was weak, but mostly unharmed. We made our way to the edge of the pit and worked our way out, turning back only once to see the mob carrying Serran back into the pit for her punishment.

We exited the Necropolis the same way we'd entered. But now it was silent—the screams of those being tortured were gone. There was only one scream left, and I had a feeling that no one cared about it. I looked at Vera who had her arm wrapped around Larry. She smiled at me and we stepped back into the bog to find our way back out.

As we made footfall on the barren wastes where we had entered the blast of hellfire hitting our faces was intense, even more so then when we had first arrived. The wave of heat tearing at their flesh, coupled with their exhaustion, caused Vera and Larry to collapse. I helped them both up and began the long walk back to the where Vince still held the crucible open for us. As we moved, the journey became harder. Larry couldn't take it; he fell time after time. It was becoming clear that his spirit was in much worse shape than he outwardly appeared. And so he went over my shoulder while I helped Vera trudge through the unrelenting inferno.

The charred outline of the pentagram where we'd first arrived appeared in the distance, and a small glimpse of hope spread over Vera's face, knowing that her suffering was nearly over.

"We're almost there," I said, and an almost instant vigor jumped into Vera's steps. But what felt so close suddenly became so far. Like fields of wildflowers emerging from the snow, the ground cracked and a horde of lesser demons sprang from the earth between us and the exit. The legion before us hissed in contention at our passing, and I felt the hope stolen as Vera's weight sank down on my arm.

A cloud of fire and smoke emerged in the center. The conflagration passed, and from it stood Azazel. In that moment I only wished that I had crushed his head beneath my boot while I had the chance.

"I can't let you leave," the demon said, confident in his position on the board. I let Vera go and she slunk to her knees.

"Be ready to move with everything you have," I said as I placed Larry beside her, and she helped him up. I moved away from them toward my adversary. I could hear her shoes on the dirt behind me start to follow, and my hand went back to signal her to stay where she was. I stepped forward a few yards and spoke.

"So you've come to play, then, Azazel?" I asked, a grin of

defiance on my face. Anger crawled over the demon's face. My mockery had done what I wanted it to.

"I will make you all suffer!" the demon screamed.

So I prodded more.

"Sure you will," I said. "Just like the others did. I mean, look at me—they destroyed me, brought me to my knees. But you're different, right? You're fierce. That's why you were invited to join them in their little plot. Ferocity, right? Oh, my mistake—you weren't. Because you don't have what it takes. That's why you stay relegated to the tower. Because you're not good enough to hang with the big kids."

The cascade of emotional responses from my insults took their toll, and Azazel reacted. He released his war cry and the myriad of smaller demons charged. I felt myself snap into focus, and my hands became blades once more. I pressed against the ground and rushed forward to the clash. It was like a wave hitting a rock. I carved through the group with ease, casting the ruined corpses of the lesser demons to the side as I went, clearing a path. I was only a few yards from Azazel when I made my leap. Both arms came down like executioner axes, and as they did the demon's eyes widened. They passed harmlessly through the puff of flame and smoke, and as they did I emptied my lungs at Vera.

"NOW!" I bellowed. Vera lifted Larry as best she could and made a break for the charred pentagram. It was a clear shot between them and it.

I rushed back toward them to keep the path clear. The swaths of lesser demons, felled by the wide arcs of my arms, landed and began to pile quickly as Vera and Larry did their best to be quick. The sound of disappointment left Vera's lips as her foot caught one of the severed limbs that landed in her path. She hit the ground hard, and were she really breathing she would have knocked her air out. I grabbed her arm, and in one quick jerk she was back on her feet and in motion again. I scooped up Larry and then I made a mad dash for the exit.

The burning sky opened and a pillar of light descended over the now-glowing pentagram. I could see Vince's hand and forearm protruding from inside it. Vera jumped, and I saw her wrap her fingers around Vince's wrist. In a flash of light she was gone and safely back in the physical realm. I heaved and moved Larry's weight to make him easier to carry, and went for it. Thirty feet, twenty, ten—it was the longest three steps I had ever taken. I reached my hand up, and the same pillar of light that had just taken Vera took my hand as well.

I could feel myself rising out of the barren waste when I felt the tug. I turned around and saw Azazel's hook lodged into Larry's back, who until that moment had been unconscious.

Larry released a piercing yell and sprung awake, as if he had been fine the whole time. I felt myself leaving. The pull of the physical world was too strong; there was nothing I could do. I pulled back against Vince's grip to try to buy myself time to free Larry from Azazel's grasp, but I couldn't. I looked down at him. His eyes were wide and he was scared. The time to get a real answer would never come. I needed to get what I could and hope that it was enough.

"Who was it that killed you?" I yelled, struggling with all my might to keep from being pulled out of hell. The fear in Larry's eyes was overwhelming. He did his best to fight the pain and give an answer. He opened his mouth and as he did a second hook rose up and pierced his neck from behind, silencing any words he was about to speak. He cringed at the hooks in his neck and back pulled him toward the swarm of demons around Azazel. But in that instant of intense pain and total horror he found his center and grabbed my forearm. I felt his fingernails sink in as he clawed at me. He looked back at me and then made sure I saw the mark he had left. I didn't have a chance to understand before he peeled my fingers open to let him go. And just like that, the hooks pulled him from my shoulder and into the crowd of demons. I saw him move away from me, and then, a moment later, there was a flash.

I was standing back in the basement of The Velvet Orchid, arm in arm with Vince. I heard the sigh and felt the rise and fall of his chest pressed against mine. He took a step back and smacked me on the shoulder. I stood, speechless, the image of Lawrence Kennedy falling away from me replaying in my head over and over. I could hear something in the background, but it was muffled. It didn't matter—I was lost in Larry's sacrifice.

"Cyrus, Cyrus!" I finally heard, and snapped back. Both Vera and Vince were practically screaming it at me. I blinked a few times and responded.

"Yeah?" I said.

"You okay, buddy?" Vince asked.

"Yeah, I'm fine."

"Where's the soul?" he asked.

"Gone."

"Gone? What do you mean gone? You mean all that work was for nothing?"

I shook my head.

"Then what do you mean?" Vince continued.

I turned over my left forearm where Larry had scratched me to see what he had left. Two very distinct images were carved into it. One was that of an ankh with a line through it, and the other was a triangle. I reached down to touch them, but before I could they were gone.

"What does it mean?" Vince asked. "What the hell does that tell us?" I thought for a moment, but nothing came to mind. The three of us stood silently around the crucible, feeling broken and defeated. We had a clue, but it was vague at best. No one said anything for what felt like an eternity. Then Vera spoke.

"I know what it is," she said.

"Okay, then," Vince said. "Who killed him?"

"It's not a who; it's a where."

"What does that mean? 'Where' killed him?"

"No," she said. "He's saying that who killed him doesn't matter. He's telling us where we need to go to find more."

"More what?" Vince asked.

"I don't know, just more."

"Okay," I said. "So I guess this means we're going on a little trip?"

"Yep."

"To where exactly?" I asked, half-excited and half-scared.

"To where it all started," she said. "Egypt."

6

A Shadow Amidst the Darkness

I awoke to the sound of squealing rubber and a mild shake as the wheels met the hot tarmac of Cairo International Airport. I clenched my eyes shut and blinked repeatedly in an attempt to wash away the haze that filled them. I had never slept before, and waking up was simultaneously a wonderful and terrible experience. My entire body felt tight and sore, like I had once more stepped into the flames of the underworld. I was overcome by an overwhelming urge to extend my limbs, and so I did. The tightness of my first night of sleep drained out my fingertips as I realized that a simple stretch was all that was needed to release the tension. I felt foolish for not having already known how that worked.

I looked over at Vera, who was awake and opening her mouth wide as if she was trying to stretch as I just had, but with her face. I could see the fine lines of musculature in her cheeks as she did, and for the first time began to understand how humanity found some features attractive. Her jaw was solid and straight, more masculine than feminine, but, if anything, it enhanced her beauty. Or at least I, with my limited understanding, thought it did. My observation was shattered as she placed her hand over her nose and blew, her cheeks expanding over her strong jaw like a puffer fish. When she was done she stuck her pinkies in each respective ear like she was cleaning something out of them.

I must have had a look on my face as I watched her because she caught me and asked what I was looking at. I had no answer and knew from experience that divulging the train of thought that had led me to look at her would not have been a good idea. So instead I decided to just ask her why she had done that.

"Why did you hold your nose and blow?" I asked.

"What do you mean, why?" she asked. I didn't know what to say. So I simply and stupidly asked it again.

"Like, why would you do it?"

I heard a male voice speak.

"It's because of the pressure change," Vince said from the seat next to me. "When you fly, the air pressure changes with the elevation and it cause your ears to hurt. Sometimes it helps to do that to equalize the pressure."

I turned to him and nodded. "Good to know." I felt like a little kid, learning about the world from those who lived in it. I had been here millions of lifetimes over. But trying to live in it, as one of them, was showing me how little I really knew about human life. So much knowledge, so little understanding. Such was my current existence.

We disembarked and made our way through customs before getting into our cabs and heading to the hotel where we would be staying. When we got there I helped Joe, along with Terry and Frank, two other men that Vince had chosen to join us, take the bags from the trunks of the cabs. We began rolling into the hotel, and I watched as everyone crooked their heads to look out over the city. They were all taken aback by the location.

There was much more green in Cairo than any of the others had realized. I had been here many times over the millennia and already knew that to be the case. I find it interesting that no matter what the situation, humans will always take the time to take in the sights and smells of a new place, even if they don't have that time to spend. I wondered for a moment if it was because they were aware of their mortal existence, or perhaps it was from that childish sense of wonder that never quite fades. I then realized I was doing exactly what they were doing, only my scenery consisted of the people themselves, and I smiled a little.

Once everyone was inside and settled, the group converged on the room where Vera and I were staying. She had completely rearranged the room and moved every flat surface to the open space at the foot of the bed, and had begun unloading a bag she had dedicated to her research on The Answer.

Papers and books were strewn everywhere, and I felt like I was back in the basement of the church. I felt a slight pull and my mind rushed back to my time with Adrian. A feeling of what I assumed was sadness rose up in me and I pushed it back down as best I could. I was a bit lost in the moment, and it took a while before I realized I was being yelled at.

"Cyrus!" I finally heard Vince yell, and snapped out of my trance.

"Yeah?" I replied without thinking.

"You okay, man?" he asked.

"Yeah, I'm fine," I replied halfheartedly. "Just feeling—remembering—someone." Vince gave me a suspicious look and decided to let it go. We all turned our attention to whatever plan Vera had in store for us.

In the middle of the large pile of documents was an old hand-drawn map. On it were three distinct circles, added more recently, either made by Vera herself or someone else. Joe spoke up first, his impatience showing through.

"So, why did we fly out to the Middle East?"

"We're not in the Middle East, Joe," Vince said. "We're in Africa." Vince's piercing stare told Joe to sit down and shut up, even though his lips never moved. Joe did exactly that.

Vera gave a quick rundown of everything that had transpired up to this point.

"I don't understand," Vince said. "I mean, I get the link, but why did we have to come to Egypt? Because I just spent, like, twenty grand to fly our asses out here on a whim with no explanation. I think it's time we have one."

We all looked at Vera for the answer. Vera pulled the map out and showed it to us more closely.

"We're here to find this," she said, pulling out the dagger and placing it on the table. Its glow was fainter than ever. "More specifically, its origin."

"You're fucking kidding, right?" Vince was clearly not happy with her answer.

"Well, before we were so rudely interrupted by the men with the magic guns, we discovered that the link between all of these ancient religions was their connection with death—more specifically, their view of Death as a deity. This item is imbued with something that is capable of piercing the Veil between the physical and spiritual worlds, allowing damage to be done to beings on the outside of our realm. I believe that whatever birthed this item originates here, in Egypt." She grabbed the map and held it up.

"If my thinking is right, what we're looking for will be somewhere in one of these cities." She moved her finger to each of the circled areas on the map. "Each one of these markers is one of ancient Egypt's most prominent cities: Memphis, Thebes, and Amarna. In their own time each one served as capital of the Egyptian empire. I believe we will find what we're looking for in one of them."

"Okay, but why exactly do you think here?" I asked. "What about Egyptian mythology makes it so special? It can just as easily be any of the other religions."

"Okay, well, the symbols the fucking security guard scratched into Cyrus's arm I totally get point us here," Vince said. "But, like I said, I just blew twenty grand flying us here and you're fucking saying you think you narrowed it down to just a few places? Off a fucking scratch? How the fuck did you do that?"

"Calm down, man," Joe said. "I'm sure the lady knows what she's doing."

Vince took a deep breath and finished his thought.

"An ankh and a triangle could maybe represent a pyramid or a tomb, but there are thousands of tombs in this country. Hell, I bet a bunch of them are buried and haven't even been discovered yet."

"Bear with me," Vera said. Her confidence wasn't shaken in the least by his outburst. "On the surface, the symbols can seem like they don't give us much. But really, they tell us everything."

"And how's that?" Vince asked, starting to get impatient. "The ankh is the symbol for life. The triangle is a pyramid.

Life and pyramid. How does that give us everything?"

Vera waited a moment for Vince's impatience to pass before continuing.

"Yes, Vince," she said. "The ankh is life, but that's not what Larry clawed into Cyrus's arm. He clawed an ankh with a line through it. He crossed it out. Which means it didn't mean life. It meant no life. And what is the opposite of life?"

"Me," I replied.

"Right," she continued. "And to the Egyptians, you are?"

"Anubis, the god of death."

"Okay, so death. Death and pyramid—same fucking thing as life and pyramid!" Vince's agitation surfaced again.

"We're not looking for a pyramid, Vince. That's not what it means," I said as pieces started to fall into place in my head. "We're looking for a shrine." I looked at Vera for confirmation.

"Exactly!" she said.

"That narrows it down, I guess," Vince said, realizing that there was indeed a bigger picture to the discussion.

"Yes, it does," Vera continued. "Specifically, to those three cities. Those three cities, in their own time, were the capital of the Egyptian empire. And because of that, they will have a large shrine dedicated to the god of death, which is why I think we should start there. But I also think there's more to the symbology—really, the more important part."

"The triangle!" Joe said, far too excited for his own good.

"Right . . ." It almost sounded like it was out of pity, to not hurt his feelings. "When I was doing research on these religions, long before this mess ever started, I learned a lot about all of them. It's important to understand that, yes, the triangle is a representation of the pyramids, but not because it represents death, but quite the opposite. The Egyptians made

122

their tombs in its likeness because to them triangle is sacred. They believe that the pyramid's point was a gateway, and that it will send the soul to heaven."

"I'm lost again," Vince said.

"Okay," Vera said, plumbing her knowledge for more lore to fill in the blank. "The Egyptians didn't view heaven like we as Christians do. They had many gods, the mightiest of which was Ra, the sun god. In early Egypt, he was the creator and ruler of, well, everything. The pyramid didn't send you to some floating paradise—it sent you to the sun, to be with Ra, God."

"Okay, well, I guess that makes sense," Vince said.

"None of that's really important."

"Then what the fuck?"

"This part is. The Egyptians also worshipped math. It's how they built all the wondrous things they did. It was more than just the point of the pyramid that was sacred to them. The geometry of the shape itself was special as well—the right angle in particular—the line from the point of the pyramid, through its center to the base. In fact, of all the geometric shapes they worked with, the right-angle triangle was the most sacred to them."

"Okay, so the math is part important, how?" Joe asked, seeing that Vince was lost and trying to not be upset.

"Well, the hypotenuse of the right triangle is likened to another one of the Egyptian gods," she said.

I felt the last pieces of the puzzle fall into place, and the revelation hit me. I was excited at the information, and it came out of my mouth almost instinctually, as the missing connection was now staring me in the face.

"Horus!" I yelled, and immediately realized my reaction was

a bit too much.

"Who is likened to?"

"Jesus Christ," Vince said. His anger vanished and his eyes widened as the connection was finally made whole.

I, too, was impressed. She found something so enlightening all from some simple scratches on my arm. But in my gut it didn't feel right. It still felt incomplete. Something was missing. All it meant was that Larry had pointed us in this direction. It didn't tell us that we would find the source of the Answer here.

"We're missing something. How do you know the Answer is here?" I asked, hoping Vera had what I was missing.

She did.

"That's where the science comes in," she said. "You see, the radiation that the dagger gives off is photonic."

"It's pictures?" Joe asked.

"Photonic means it uses light, dumb-ass," Vince said.

"Horus was the god of the sky," I said. "Ra's power flowed through him and down to the people of Egypt. So because Horus channels the sun's power, you're saying that the blade was forged to be wielded by him? To kill a god?"

"Yes," Vera said.

"But I never interfered in the affairs of these people. Anubis is almost never present in any of the Egyptian myths. I intentionally never intervened," I said, feeling the very human need to defend myself.

"I know," Vera said, keeping to the point. "How did Horus become god of the sky?"

"His father, Osiris, was killed," I replied.

"By whom?"

"By Set, the brother of Horus." What I had been missing

came to me, and I said it for everyone else.

"Set was the god of chaos," I said. "The Answer wasn't forged to kill me; it was forged to kill him."

"Right," she said. "And Jesus Christ is Horus. Several millennia and lord knows how many translations down the road. Jesus, like Horus, battles chaos. The devil. And like so many things lost in translation, a god of death and a god of chaos become blurred. Eventually, in a little passage at the end of a religious text, it is death that leads the charge. How did you put it? 'And hell followed with him. And power was given unto them over the fourth part of the Earth, to kill with the sword, and with hunger, and with death, and all the beasts of the Earth.'"

The room fell silent and it was as if all the heat and life had been sucked from it.

"Cyrus," Vera said, "to these men you are not just death, you are chaos. You are the end of all mankind. And in their twisted version of reality you are Set, rival of Horus—Jesus—whatever. You are their Satan. And they have a weapon, built to destroy what they think is you. Built from a religion that had died long before the writings they are following. These men are trying to save the world, and have no idea that if they succeed they will destroy it."

"So what does finding the dagger's point of origin do for us?" Vince asked.

"If we can find how they made it, we can unmake it," Vera said. "All energy has an opposite. If I can understand how the radiation is created, I can formulate a way to neutralize it. If I learn enough, I might even be able to make Cyrus whole again. And if I can do that, I can also create a way to do the same to any weapons that these fanatics are using. Then the magic bullets are just bullets again. They will pass right through him. Death would be immortal again. We win."

"Well, ain't that some shit?" Vince said. "A weapon literally forged in light. So we're going to use the power of darkness to save the world."

"Yeah, I wouldn't quite say it that way. And now we're at the really hard part," Vera said.

"How so?" I asked.

"Well, when it comes to information on this stuff, the Internet will only take you so far. And I'm out of ammo. So now we need a real expert—someone who knows not only the history of these three cities, but also the mythology that goes into it. Someone who believes the insane truth of our situation and is willing to help us."

We all sat silently for a moment. It was a tall order.

"So where do we start?" I asked.

"The only profession where belief in mythical items goes a long way," she said. "Treasure hunting."

The sound of bone on wood echoed through the narrow alley and disappeared amidst the bustle of Cairo. We all stood silent for a moment before the door opened and a short Egyptian man of medium build pressed the wood away from the stone enough so he could stare at us with suspicion.

"Min anto?" the man asked in Arabic. We all just stood for a moment, unsure of how to respond.

"Who are you?" he asked again, this time in English.

"We're looking for a Dr. Ahmrin Muhdjasa," I asked as politely as I could.

The man's eyes squinted and ran side to side before he

replied. "And what do you want with him?"

I looked back over my shoulder to Vera, who handed me the dagger. We had wrapped it in a black cloth. I opened the cloth and revealed the glowing stone of the dagger. The man's eyes widened, so much so that I thought they were going to fall out of his head. He slammed the door closed and we could hear the man unlatch the chain inside. The door flew open and he quickly beckoned us inside. The door slammed and the man began furiously locking it again. When he was done he turned to me. He was breathing like he had just run a marathon.

He turned back to us and, as he did, I saw a small glint. He drew the pistol from his waistband and raised it toward me. Joe and the other two men reacted, leaping toward him, knocking him to the ground, but it was too late. The echo of the shot snapped within the small enclosure, and everyone inside went deaf for a moment. I stood still, unsure of what to do. Then I felt it—hot, uncomfortably so. I moved my hand toward my neck and then I heard the drip. I looked down and saw the droplets of red careening toward the dirty concrete of the floor. I pressed my hand on the hotness and felt the bleeding. I felt my head become light and then Vince's arms caught me as my vision turned to black.

I awoke to darkness and the uncomfortable beep of a heart monitor. The room smelled like disinfectant and vomit. Vince was next to my bed, asleep. I looked at the clock on the wall.

2:41 a.m.

How long had I been out? I tried to talk, but my throat was tight, and the words didn't come out. I reached up and felt the wad of gauze and tape on my neck. I shifted myself in the

127

bed and poked Vince in the arm. He vaulted awake.

"Hey, man, you doing okay?" he asked reassuringly. I feigned a smile and nodded. I thought of how different it was being the one in the bed and not the one watching as people gave false reassurances to their dying loved ones. My mouth felt coarse and tasted like some ungodly foulness I had never experienced. I made a gesture for water and Vince promptly delivered. The moisture hitting my mouth and throat freed them up and I was able to speak.

"What the hell happened?" I asked before taking another drink.

"We found the guy," Vince replied.

"That's good, right?"

"Yeah, it is."

"Did he say why?"

"You can ask him yourself, tomorrow. He's agreed to help us. He and Vera are at the hotel now ironing out the details and game plan. Right now, you need to get some rest. The doctors said you got lucky. Quarter of an inch and it would have killed you."

"When can I get out of here?" I asked.

"Tomorrow morning. Now, chill out. I'll be here all night."

I closed my eyes and tried to relax. We had what we needed, someone to help us find answers. I sank back into the darkness like I had done so many times before. Little did I know that this time would be very different.

I felt my body erupt into a seated position. I was breathing heavily, and my skin was sticky from the sweat. I had had a nightmare. I knew that because I had seen people react in this way before. I tried to focus my thoughts on what I had seen that made me so afraid, but it was gone. I could see nothing but the shadow of a figure vanishing.

I looked around the room; it was empty. The clock read 8:41 a.m.

As it struck 8:42, Vince walked in with breakfast. His brows scrunched and he placed the food down.

"You okay, man?"

"Yeah, I'm fine. Had my first nightmare." I looked at him, unsure if I was supposed to be proud or not.

"Brutal," he said. "What was it about?"

"Not sure, just a shadow, or maybe, shadows."

"Meh. Don't sweat it. That shit happens all the time. Hungry?"

I nodded and he brought over some terribly overcooked eggs and sausage. I was mid-chew when the doctors came in to check on me. I did as they asked and went through their battery of questions, feeling more mortal than I ever had before. The physician nodded and shook my hand before signing my discharge papers. I got dressed and headed for the door. I couldn't wait to be out of that place—ironic, considering how much time I had spent in hospitals from the other side.

I stepped out into the brisk morning air. Terry was waiting outside the hospital with a car. He got out and opened the door for us before getting in and driving us back to the hotel.

When we arrived, Joe and Vera were loading up an SUV with equipment. Joe waved us up, and Vince and I got out while Terry parked the car.

"So, where to?" I asked. Before I could get an answer I felt Vera thrust herself on me and wrap her arms around my neck.

129

The pressure on my wound was uncomfortable, and I pulled away a bit. She looked up and it was plain to see she was holding back tears. I didn't know how to react, but I felt an emotion in my sternum—boiling. I froze for a moment, not knowing what to do, and so I repeated my initial question. "So where to?"

The emotion in Vera's eyes dissipated and was replaced with anger, I wasn't sure why. She walked away and continued loading before answering the question.

"Memphis," she said. "We think that's where it is."

"Where what is?" I asked.

"Doc, get out here. This is your deal," Vera yelled into the cab. Dr. Ahmrin Muhdjasa got out of the vehicle. Had his skin been lighter it would have lit up with embarrassment.

"I am so sorry," he said. It sounded genuine. I wanted to ask him why he pulled the trigger, but I let it go. There would be time; we had a long drive ahead of us. I nodded toward him to accept his apology and remained silent so he could keep talking. He paused for a moment, forgetting where he was. "Right!" he said. "We are looking for the Urn of Ra."

"Which is?" Vince asked.

"It is what made this," Muhdjasa said as he pulled a shard of broken stone from his waistband. It had the same glow as the dagger. "This, this right here, that which was built to kill a god. The fire of heaven. This is but one shard, one of many born from the urn. I have been searching for it for decades. No one believed it was real, until you knocked on my door."

Vera chimed in from her packing inside the car. "The doctor was a bit taken aback by my team's research. Before we acquired the dagger, there was only one known stone imbued with the waters of the urn. It was purchased in the 1920s by a private collector. No one has heard anything about it in almost a century. The doc says he's seen it, and that's where he got the small shard he carries with him."

"When was this?" I asked.

"Paris 1972. There was an anonymous philanthropist who displayed this shard. The team was given twenty-four hours to examine and give our best guess. None of us had any idea what it was. I don't know what it is, but something about the shard called to me. I became obsessed. I stole it. I sacrificed my entire academic career for a glowing piece of stone, on a whim. The man who had the stone looked for me for almost a decade. It took me seven years before I made it back home to Egypt. This stone cost me everything. I have to know what it is."

Vera looked at Vince and me. I wondered if she had told Muhdjasa our theory. It didn't matter; he was using us and we were using him. As long as we got what we needed and were able to find a remedy for it, who cared.

"So, why Memphis?" I asked.

Muhdjasa produced a very old document. The papyrus was not in very good condition, and it was plain to see that Muhdjasa didn't really care about its historical value. He pointed at the hieroglyphics on it like we knew how to read it.

"Here, it says right here, 'Let those who would bathe in the fire of heaven relinquish themselves in the jewel of the old kingdom,'" he said.

I thought back to the early years of Egypt, and the pharaoh Sekhemkhet. Not sure why—history would scant remember him—but for some reason in this moment I did. He ruled for only half a dozen years, and left little behind—only one pyramid that he was buried inside. I thought about when I came for him. He was not afraid. But he said something that at the time had no meaning, but at this exact moment it did. "In the fires of heaven everything be banished—god, demon, and even death." I tapped him on the shoulder and he smiled at me. After that I did what I had always done: my job.

"I know where it is," I said. "The urn is in the pyramid of Saqqara."

"How do you know?" Vince asked.

"Something I heard a long time ago. It's there, I'm sure of it."

No one questioned what I said, and we began to finish loading the vehicles. It wasn't ten minutes before we were on the road toward our destination.

The crunch of limestone beneath the tires of the two SUVs silenced as the vehicles stopped. We got out and began to unload. The field of sepulchers was huge. There were many tombs within its borders they couldn't all be seen at once. It was early afternoon, and the groups of tourists taking pictures would provide fantastic cover to sneak inside. We hid our gear in the packs we were carrying and joined one of the tour groups, doing our best to blend in. Joe, dressed in full camo, was not doing a good job of looking like one of the crowd. Vera and I smiled as we heard Vince calling him a dumb-ass for what seemed like the millionth time.

It took almost two hours for us to make it to the pyramid. Joe gave us the signal to stay back and look occupied while he, Terry, and Frank made a scene to get us inside. We heard a rustle and turned back to see Terry and Frank in a knockdown, drag-out fight. Joe feigned trying to break them apart as the tour guide rushed to help.

That was our chance. We ducked into the entrance and Vince picked the lock on the gate that protected the tomb from unauthorized guests. I don't know how long it took, but it was quick, and we were soon inside, away from prying eyes. We continued in, using the walls as guidance through the pitch black, until we were sure turning on the flashlights we brought would not give our presence away.

The tomb itself was unfinished, but somewhere amid the winding corridors we would find the urn, I was sure of it. Muhdjasa knew the layout somewhat and did his best to direct us through the dimly lit passages. It took two wrong turns and twenty minutes to find the burial chamber. A few lamps left by archeologists were placed very deliberately in the corners of the room, but had clearly not been turned on in months, if not years. Vera, Vince, Muhdjasa, and I decided that this was the best place to start. We lit the lamps and began to unpack.

I felt a strain in my neck where the bullet had grazed me, like something was trying to push its way out from the wound. It was uncomfortable, but given the fact that I had been shot, I didn't think much of it. When we were done, we let the doc do his thing. The walls were covered in writings and pictures. After another hour Vera got bored and went to ask Muhdjasa if she could be of any assistance. As she walked away, Vince spoke:

"You know she likes you, right?"

"Sure I do," I replied. "That's what friends do, like each other."

"That's not what I mean," he said. "She's into you."

I knew what he was talking about, but I had never understood that part of human emotion. Instinct was something I had never needed. The idea of procreation was completely foreign to me. I understood the reason for it, but all the things that went into it were just beyond me. It wasn't that I didn't want to know. I had tried, several times, to understand it, but it had never clicked.

"It's too complicated," I said to Vince. "I wouldn't know where to begin, and besides, we have more important matters to attend to."

"I'm just saying, you're a man—at least for now—and she's a woman," Vince said.

"I'm not exactly a man," I replied.

"Yeah, well, being the immortal personification of death is probably why she's into you in the first place. I mean, how often do you get to have a crush on someone or something like you?"

"Not helpful."

"Just saying."

"Fine," I said. "Teach me, then. It's not like we're doing anything else, anyway."

The next few hours flew, and I didn't understand a damn thing that Vince told me. Everything was counterintuitive, which he said was the point. It wasn't supposed to make sense; it was supposed to be about something you feel, not rationalize.

We looked up to see Joe, Terry, and Frank walk in. They had really gone for it. Cuts, bruises, and scrapes adorned both men. Really, they shouldn't have even been standing, they were so beaten down.

"Glad you boys finally made it," said Vince. "What took

you?"

"Had to sneak back in after dark," said Joe.

I nodded at Vince who looked at his watch and then turned his wrist toward me. 8:37—the day had disappeared. They came in and sat down with us. No sooner had they done so, we then heard Vera snapping her fingers for us to come and look.

The five of us stood up and made our way through the flickering light to where the two doctors were standing. Vera's hand grasped at my sleeve and pulled me to the front of the group.

"This is important. Go ahead, Doc," she said.

Muhdjasa redirected the light to a hole in the wall, above which were the hieroglyphs in question. He moved his hand to them and read the illuminated symbols.

"'He who seeks the light of the gods must first stand beside them.'"

"Which means?" Joe asked.

"It means you have to die," I replied. Everyone looked at me. I continued. "In most cultures, passing on from the physical meant that you have the opportunity to gain entrance into some sort of afterlife. Whatever is hidden here is calling for someone to die."

Everyone was silent. I thought about it for a moment, and something else came to me.

"Maybe it's not death," I said. "Does anyone have something long that can fit into that hole?" Joe reached into one of the bags. He pulled out a retractable baton and flung it so it would extend.

"Will this work?" he asked.

"Should do fine," I said, and he handed it to me. I slowly

135

extended the metal into the hole. A sharp snap sent a vibration through the baton and into my hand, causing me to let it go in surprise. I grabbed the handle and pulled it out. A narrow groove had been made about a half inch deep into the steel, a little over a foot into it where it had been struck. The mark was precise and clean, clearly made by a blade that had been triggered when the baton went in.

"Yeah, so I'm not putting my hand in there," Vince said. I smiled; no one else did.

"Agreed, and we just saw what I thought we would," I said.

"Which is what exactly?" Vera asked.

"Self-sacrifice," Muhdjasa said. He grabbed the light and started tracing it around the room, speaking as he did. "The person comes into the room and does the series of prayers. See?" he said, tracing the six ritual prayer areas around the room. "Eventually they end up here, at the last one. They place their arm into the hole and slice. Then I'm presuming they bleed to death."

"Death is the side effect," I said. "We don't need the death—we need the blood." I pointed to the ground. The stone in the ground had very fine channels carved into it—deep enough for liquid to run inside, but not enough for us to notice under our shoes. I motioned for the light, which Muhdjasa handed me. I shined it at an angle across the floor.

"Is there a grade to this?" I asked.

Vera and Vince immediately dropped down and took a closer look at the stone floor. Vince snapped his fingers and a moment later Joe handed him a bottle of water. He poured some on the floor and we all watched as it rolled slowly away from the wall we were gathered by. I followed it with the light until it hit a circle in the middle of the room where it stopped.

Everyone moved to the center of the room. I leaned down. There was a breeze, incredibly faint, coming from where the water went into the crack.

"How much water do we have?" I asked.

"Three more bottles," Joe said. He'd grabbed them from the bag and was bringing them over. I looked at Vera.

"How many ounces of blood are in the human body?" I asked.

She shrugged. "I don't know—wrong kind of doctor."

"Four-point-five to five-point-five liters," Muhdjasa said. Vera, Vince, and Joe looked at him, surprised. "What? The Egyptians drain the blood when they mummify someone."

"And we have how much?" I asked.

"We have four bottles total," Vince said. "So, eighty ounces."

"That's about half," Muhdjasa said.

"Looks like some of us are donating," Vince said, pulling out his knife. Joe grabbed it from his hand and replaced it with a bottle of water. Joe slid the steel across his palm, clenched his fist, and squeezed. As he did, he cleaned the knife and handed it to Terry and Frank. They did the same. Muhdjasa motioned for the knife.

"It's okay, sir," Joe said. "We got it."

"I've been searching my whole life for this," said the doctor with conviction. "Don't think for one moment that I'm not going to be part of this ritual." He took the knife and cut his palm like the others. The blood ran from the four men's hands and into the crevice at the center of the room. I watched as it hit the clear water from the bottles Vince was emptying. It swirled like crimson and silver under the lights before vanishing into the circular drain.

After a few minutes a loud pop rang through the room. A

137

subtle vibration rumbled underfoot and began to grow in intensity. A blinding light began to pierce the ground around the drain and then it sunk. The floor opened and almost like dominoes falling, the stones of the floor descended into a spiral staircase. The area near the hole slid open as well, forming a ramp where the body of the sacrifice would have slid down.

We looked down into the area below. The room beneath was alight. It shimmered as if starlight was captured inside, trying to escape. None of us had ever seen anything like it.

Muhdjasa went first, his excitement hurling him forward like a kid in a candy store. I looked at everyone else; only Vera wanted to go. I gestured to Vince to make his way down, but he would have none of it.

"That's all you, man. You know I've seen my fair share of religious insanity. Don't plan on adding another culture's shit on top of the pile I've already accumulated."

"Suit yourself," Vera said, her tone very subtly calling him a sissy. She grabbed my hand and pulled to follow the giddy doctor.

At the bottom of the staircase was a landing. The room was rectangular, about fifty feet long and twenty feet wide. The majority of the room was a large pool filled with liquid that gave off the same glow of the dagger. A mosslike plant covered the ceiling and walls. Tiny particles of the plant fluttered in the light and caught the glow before settling on the liquid. A narrow bridge extended lengthwise across the center to another landing. Muhdjasa was already on the other side, along with what looked to be exactly what he had been looking for. A pedestal with a bowl made of solid gold in the center.

Vera and I began to move across the bridge. I looked into the pools: dozens, if not hundreds, of handless skeletons rested at the bottoms of the glowing pools, those who had undergone the ritual. It was strange that the water was so clear in spite of it being filled with corpses and likely thousands of years of dust. I let it go when we made it to the other side where the doctor was.

"Anything interesting?" Vera asked.

"Yes!" Muhdjasa said, the adrenaline in his veins still clearly reflecting on his personality. "Look here," he said, pointing into the bowl. The gold beneath the glowing liquid was engraved with hieroglyphs.

"What does it say?" I asked.

"'Like fire to the field, the light of the gods burns the creatures of the shadow,'" the doctor translated. He paused for a moment. "What does that mean?" he asked.

"No idea," I replied. "Keep going."

"'Just as day turns to night, so does life turn to death. The souls of the unworthy rise again to feed on the just. Argul Andrugathane, the shadow amid the darkness. Like a plague, they must be cleansed. Burned with the waters of holy light.'"

"This is it," Vera said. "This is what I needed. The water is the source. Doc, the dagger—dip it in the water."

Muhdjasa produced the stone knife and dipped it into the pearlescent pool. He yelled and withdrew his hand.

"Ouch! What the hell was that?" Vera and I looked over. There was motion in the water. They were small and almost see-through.

"What is it?" the doctor asked, clutching the red bands on his hand.

"Jellyfish," Vera said. "Tiny jellyfish." She had one of the empty water bottles and dipped it into the pool, collecting some of the water and jellyfish.

"How is this possible?" Muhdjasa asked. "Everything should be dead after this long."

"It's a mini-ecosystem," Vera said, holding up the now-glowing bottle. "The jellyfish are bioluminescent; they eat the plant particles that fall from the moss, and give off light."

"Where's the dagger?" I asked. Muhdjasa picked it up from the floor where he had dropped it from the jellyfish sting. It was glowing brighter than ever before. This was definitely the stuff we wanted. We walked back to the golden bowl, and the doctor continued the inscription.

"'Be warned: the light is fed by the black moss. Just as the water brings death to the dead, so the moss brings death to the living. Only those of sound body may leave here. All others must be consumed by the fire.'"

"That doesn't sound good," Vera said. She reached over and looked at the cut on Muhdjasa's hand. It had begun to look discolored. The blood vessels were black, and flesh had begun to flay. "We need to go now," she said, and tried to pull him toward the stairs.

"Not without the pool!" he argued.

"It's not worth your life," I said, and attempted to help Vera grab him. He struggled and pulled away. As he did I heard a yell from upstairs. It was Vince.

"You guys need to get up here! Something not good is happening!"

Vera and I looked at each other; the doc had made his choice. We dashed across the bridge and back up the spiral staircase to the main room. Joe and the other two men were on the ground and gasping for breath. We turned over their hands—black and flayed just like Muhdjasa's. He should have been sick like

140

them. But I knew men's bodies; his adrenaline was keeping him going. Vera poked her head back down the staircase and yelled to him one last time. As she did, the room fell silent. Everyone was looking at me. I could see the panic on their faces. Vera yanked my head to the side and looked at the bandage on my neck. I could see on her face that the same black pestilence was on the wound.

The heat drained from the room and I felt what I had felt millions of times before—ghosts. I reached over to Vera's hand and took the glowing water from it, holding it up. The light bounced off the walls, and I felt my heart jump as I saw the walls move. It was like spiders crawling across them, running from the light. I watched as a million empty eyes stared into me. Then, just as they had fled from the light, they moved toward us. Like a swarm of locusts, the Hexen buzzed, ready to descend upon us.

I turned toward Vera to tell her it was time to go. The slight shift in my body was all that was needed. A cascade of black rushed into me. I felt like I had been hit in the chest with a wrecking ball. I landed on my back and slid a few feet. I looked up to see Terry and Frank disappear into a wave of Hexen. Vince had Joe in a fireman's carry and was making a break for the door. The wave of shadows flooded toward them and I did the only thing I could think of, throw the bottle. I called out to Vince as it left my fingers. It hit the wall and lit up. The light pushed back the Hexen and Vince scooped up the bottle midstride before disappearing into the tunnel that led back to the pyramid entrance.

As he did, half the wave pursued, and half turned to me. I rolled toward the spiral staircase and slid down it on my back into the light of the chamber below. Vera was inside trying to revive Muhdjasa, who had finally succumbed to the poison, but it was over. I ran over and grabbed the dagger and her hand. I peeled off my shirt and dipped it in the water before draping it around her.

"We have to make a break for it," I said. "Stay low and go straight for the door. One of the lamps is still on, but it's not lighting much. Get there as fast as you can."

"What about you?" she asked. I raised the dagger and gave it a little shake.

The room above sounded like a hurricane. Shadow amid the dark my ass—it was a storm.

"On the count of three," I said, and began my countdown. "One, two . . ." Vera turned to me and her lips met mine.

"Three!" she yelled, and darted toward the tunnel.

I rushed up behind her and clashed head-on with the torrent. I felt myself become the reaper and let it unleash. Everything slowed. My hand and the dagger cast down the shadows one by one as the sound of Vera's boots grew more distant. I turned to the side and saw the glow of my shirt moving into the tunnel. I spun and swung, cutting as large a swath as I could into the ocean of shadow before I made a break for it.

Nothing but the darkness surrounded me as I cleaved through the Hexen toward the tiniest glimmer of light left behind by Vera's exit. I slammed into the stone by the tunnel and gave one last swipe with the dagger before rushing up the ramp. I darted down the tunnels following the glow of my shirt and praying that Vera did not take a wrong turn toward the surface.

The flash of moonlight nearly blinded me as I broke into the open air. I could feel my heart racing as I sprinted across the crushed stone of the courtyard. Vera was only about twenty feet in front of me, and just behind was an army of Hexen. I could see the SUV we had arrived in. Vince had it running and was waiting only on us. I saw the tires start rolling as Vera made it alongside. The door was open and I could see her yelling at me. I didn't hear anything except the sounds of my own heart pounding and hard gasps of my own breath.

Just a few more steps, I thought. I reached out and grabbed Vera's hand, but my grip wasn't good enough and it slipped. I turned my head to look behind me, and shouldn't have. They were as close to me as I was to the SUV. I had only one more chance before my frail, mortal body was out of gas. I jumped and caught Vera's hand. She pulled me as hard as she could, but she wasn't strong enough. Then I felt it. It was like a skyhook had grabbed me by the pants. White as a ghost, but strong as ever, Joe hoisted me up enough for me to get my leg into the car.

I patted him on the shoulder and he did the same to me.

"You okay?" I asked. He didn't answer. I watched as his eyes rolled back as the last bit of color drained from his face before he fell onto the seat. Everything went silent after that. I remember yelling and watching as Vera desperately tried to revive him. I remember Vince's hands shaking and Vera's makeup running down her cheeks. I remember thinking, *We have what we came for, but was it worth it?* I have seen and felt so much death, but nothing ever like that.

I was frozen in the moment. And in that infinite second, I understood why people mourned. Why, misguided as it was, people wanted me dead. They never wanted to go through losing someone they cared about. And in their minds I didn't just threaten someone—I threatened everyone.

I had never experienced misery before, and given the

143

opportunity, would never like to again. It hurt, deeply and relentlessly. And I couldn't help but think it was all my fault. I understood the logic behind why it wasn't, but still, it didn't make me feel better.

It then that I realized the weakness that was coming over me. I was mortal, but I was not like these men. Or maybe I was. For the first time ever I understood what I was like to be dying. The sickness was spreading into my system. Two parts of the same coin, the dying and those who mourned the dead. I was at that moment both of these things.

Thinking back on it now, I don't think any degree of physical pain could ever equal what I had felt. In the end, we had what we needed, and because of that I keep telling myself that his sacrifice was worth something. It had to be.

The next few days were spent in the hospital. The wonders of modern medicine had long since found remedies for the black moss. And through the physical pain was minimal the entire experience was terrible. Being weak and unable to even help yourself it torturous. Feeling like a burden to others is so much worse than I could have imagined. Yet, this was something that nearly everyone has to go through. It's part of life, and it is an unspeakable tragedy.

None of us talked much on the way home. I wasn't sure if it was the emotional overload, or if we all wanted to give each other a chance to grieve in our own way. Vera stared out the window of the plane for the entire duration. Vince put on his headphones and slept. I could do neither of those things. I just sat and ran the events over and over in my head. I touched the bandage on my neck and knew that it and the ointment beneath were all that kept me away from the same toxin that brought me to thinking about it in the first place.

It was pointless, but I just kept wondering if there was anything I could have done differently. I felt so guilty for letting any harm come to anyone. For so many millennia I was callous to people's passing; it was just part of the natural order of things. Now, however, it was something that directly affected me, and it had given me new perspective on the concept of death.

Vince buried Joe the day after we got back. It was very difficult for me to watch. Not the funeral, but Vince, in so much anguish. I had seen so many funeral precessions but had never once been party one. The pain of loss is real, and lasting. I had never understood the logic of grief. I had always said to myself that I understood the biological responses that brought it about. But there is so much more to it, and I now understood why.

Before that funeral, I had never thought of any place as "home" before. I was everywhere, all the time. If anything, I may have viewed the nether as home. I was there as much as I was on Earth. But for some reason, I didn't. These people had brought me into their lives. They made me feel at peace, more so than I had ever been. And because of that, I decided that wherever they were would be home. Home, it was a comforting concept. I had been missing it my entire existence, but no more.

Vince went back to the club. He told me he wasn't sure how much he wanted to be involved anymore, though he knew the stakes. I said I understood, and for the first time I did. If it were me, I would want to follow through. Maybe because Joe died for the cause and leaving it incomplete would make his passing meaningless; but I'm not Vince, and I can't say what he felt or why. He held his pain, and it showed.

Vera didn't get much of a chance to show emotion. We returned to the murder investigation and theft we had hurried away from. Out of the frying pan, into the fire. I offered to don my detective's getup and assist with getting Detectives Aaron and Marx out of her hair, but she declined. She said the fewer people that saw me, the better.

I was to stay in a hotel until things had calmed down on the ARC campus. I sat alone for days until she finally came to see me. Eventually, the investigation hit a dead end, and she was not a suspect. After that, she checked me in as a visitor to the ARC on-site living quarters. She said she had an on-site residence that she didn't use much and that I should stay there to be safe. She handed me off to Prescott, who walked me down to the residence. It was small but cozy.

Another whole day passed, and I waited for her the same as I had at the hotel. Things continued like this for almost a week, and, aside from the small checkups, we had not spoken. I hoped we would this time. I stood up as I heard the door open and shut. I thought about it and wanted to ask how it had gone with the investigation. As I saw her, the look on her face said that I just needed to shut my mouth. She looked like she had been hit by a truck, exhausted.

She stumbled into my arms and her emotions erupted. She had kept strong all week and it was finally time to let it be over. I could feel her tears soaking through my shirt. I don't know how long she cried before finally pulling back and giving me a kiss. I didn't react. I didn't know how to. She began pulling my shirt off, and I just froze. She started pushing me toward the bedroom, but I stopped her. I knew what she wanted, but I was not ready for anything like that. She felt my discomfort and stopped. I picked her up and carried her to the bed anyway. I placed her once-again weeping frame onto the bed and gave her a kiss on the forehead before tucking her in.

I don't know how long I stayed up; time didn't exist. The sunlight peeked into the window, and I felt my tired eyes begin to water. As the star rose into the morning sky I heard a stir from the bedroom. I was lost, staring at nothing, when Vera walked into the room. She was ready for work. I was so out of it I didn't even realize she had showered. I was exhausted, too, and yet I could not sleep. So many things raced in my mind. For the first time I understood what people meant when they said, "I feel like shit." I guess it was part of being human. I had been chewed up, digested, and run through the ringer until there was nothing left except the putrid waste. Metaphorical, and yet eerily true.

"You look like shit," Vera said, echoing my thoughts.

"You know I was just thinking that. I mean me, not you. Not that you could ever look like shit. I mean . . ."

"I get it," she said, a small grin spreading over her face at my ineptitude. Honestly, it made me feel good. First smile I had seen on her face in a while. She walked over to the couch and sat next to me. She took my hands in hers and, without saying a word, nodded in appreciation. I knew what she meant. She would have done anything to feel better the night before. My refusal of her was a good thing. She would have regretted it. I don't remember the rest of the conversation; I'm not sure I even participated. I only remember her handing me a few pills and kissing me on the forehead before heading out the front door.

I took the pills and slept. It was horrible. I relived every terrible moment in that tomb. I watched over and over as the spark in Joe's eyes faded into nothing. I felt so helpless—not because I couldn't save him, but because I should have been there for him as he crossed over. It was killing me that I couldn't be there. He was lost, he and so many hundred thousand others stuck to wander the dark until I could be restored. It played in my head over and over until I heard the door close and rose to the world soaked in sweat. I sat up on the couch and rubbed my eyes before standing.

"Aaron and Marx came by today to give a progress report on the murder investigation," Vera said. "They have been working closely with Ramsey and Prescott on the situation. The good news is, it's being treated as one case. They said they will do what they can and come back in a few days and let us know what they have found. Honestly, I think they're just fishing. Oh, also, they asked for you. I said that I didn't know where you were. That you we're doing your own investigations. I hope that's okay."

I nodded, half answering and half trying to shake off my nightmare.

Vera walked over. She could see I wasn't in good shape. We sat for a moment without speaking.

"I have some other good news," she said.

"What's that?"

"I think I'm close to figuring it out."

"Figuring what out?" I asked, fuzzy brained from being still half asleep.

"The Answer, the properties that make it what it is. And from there, how to fix you. Well, make you, *you*, again."

All the shit melted away as I heard those words. But at the

same time, I felt my heart sink. I was learning so much trying to live as a human, along with all the pains and tragedies that they go through. And how because of that, when something good happens, it's that much better. Ultimately, however, I had a job to do, and that was more important than anything I could learn from living. It was selfish of me to even assume that anything I could possibly learn was more important than my job. I decided that I should give the reaction expected and did. She talked about the science of it. I zoned her out and just stared into her eyes, nodding along in agreement as she spoke.

All I could think about was that I was going to be myself again. And maybe I didn't want to be. I would be safe. I could clean up the mess that had certainly been created in my absence. And then I could do what I wanted to, hunt down the sons of bitches who presumed they could fuck with life and death. I had made it a policy, millions of years ago, to create as little impact on the world as I could. But these people were messing with something way beyond their control, and they would pay for it.

"Come on," Vera said, done with her explanation. She took my hand and led me to the bedroom, tucking me in the same way I had done for her the night before. She changed and got into bed with me. She leaned over and gave me a kiss on the lips before rolling over and turning off the lights. I felt myself finally relax as the light faded and began to fall into an actual restful state. I felt myself descend into it as Vera's words washed over me like the night.

"Sleep well, Mr. Grimm. We have a long day ahead of us."

7

The Hard Choice

The anxiety that had been building over the past few weeks all came together at once and felt like a ball of fire in my chest as I stepped through the glass doors and into Vera's lab. I had tried hard to put the feelings that had been stewing inside me to rest since we'd returned from Egypt, but they just wouldn't die. I wasn't the only one. I had heard that Vince had gone back to The Velvet Orchid and tried to drown his sorrows in what I'm sure was high-end Scotch.

At the beginning, I believed Vera's decision to keep me hidden in the ARC guest quarters was a good one. But by this time, it had begun to feel more like a prison cell. All the while, the knowledge that whoever had set this tidal wave of events in motion was still out there, working toward their goals. They had the mainframe, and with it at least part of the information contained within. My only solace was in knowing that they still lacked two of the passkeys, which now resided on-site beneath a now vastly superior security system.

It had been almost a month since we'd returned. The worst part had been the silence. Up until the point that Vera started staying with me in her on-site residence, I was all alone. Everything felt so disconnected. All I could think of as the bright lights of the overhead halogens beat down on me was that it would soon be over. I would be myself again. I would be everywhere once more. And I could finally end this madness and go back to a boring, uncomplicated existence.

I heard the glass doors seal behind me. Then there was only the echo of my boots on the hard tile of the laboratory. Ahead of me was another set of glass doors leading into another round, glass room. At the center of that was a tall cylindrical pod tilted at a slight angle about eight feet high. It, too, was white except for a glass plate on the front just the right size for whoever was inside it to look out of. I knew as I looked at the device that that was what Vera and her team had built to try to restore me back to my original state.

I thought about the story Vera had told me to remember that morning in case I was asked. She said that I was to tell them that I was a volunteer for studying the effects of photonic radiation on human brainwave activity. I only kind of knew what that meant, but I trusted her to know, and that was good enough.

As long as it worked.

I heard steps from my right side and looked to see a man leaving what looked like a control room. As he walked down the three steps toward me I could see past him and spotted Vera working on something inside. He extended his hand as he got closer and a wide grin spread across his bearded face.

"Mr. Jones," he said, looking at his hand and waiting for me to reciprocate. I assumed that the name was a fake one Vera had given him to keep me anonymous. I smiled and reached out to take his hand, giving it a hearty shake. I felt the human side of me think that that might very well be my last handshake. "It's a pleasure to meet you," the man continued. "My name is Dr. Harold Gardener, and I appreciate what you're doing here."

"Thank you," I replied, not quite sure what he was talking about. I was curious, and so I asked, "What exactly am I doing here, Doc?"

"Well, what did Dr. Essalte tell you?"

I repeated the story she had given me, glad I had thought about it a moment earlier.

"Well, that's technically correct, but do you understand what is going to happen to you?"

I shook my head, doing my best to act confused. I figured that I would appear more human that way.

"Well," continued Gardener, "this application process is confidential, so I'm not surprised you weren't given more information. How can I put this?" He paused. I could see the little gears in his head turning and trying to take the complicated scientific terms and convert them into something understandable and not scary. When he had it, he continued.

"Basically, you're here to help us test an experimental procedure that may very well prove the existence of the human soul," he said.

Well, at least I knew the lie that Vera had sold to the rest of her scientific colleagues. I'm not sure why, but it made me think that that was the reason she had left me so alone. Doing real science and weaving a web of lies for everyone else to follow. I could only think that what she had achieved was amazing. I felt something warm in my upper chest when I thought about it. She knew so many things, among them the truth. And she took that knowledge, and her knowledge of people, and did this for me.

I nodded at Dr. Gardener and let him direct me through the process. I had no idea what he was talking about, but he was clearly very excited and enthusiastic, which boded well, I supposed. I smiled and nodded as he gave me a tour of the lab and produced a long-winded speech with mountains of scientific mumbo jumbo that I couldn't follow. After a moment I zoned him out entirely and instead played the explanation that Vera had given me in my head.

Everything is energy, Cyrus. Even matter, at its base level, is energy. Protons, neutrons, electrons, all of it. All energy vibrates and resonates with its own very distinct frequency. Because of this, we can identify an energy by its vibration. Even souls. This is very good, but also very bad. Because all energy is distinct, it means it's static. If you change it, it ceases to be what it was; it becomes something else. Just as positive and negative charges cancel each other out. Everything has an opposite. That's why the Answer was made. It was built with the very specific purpose of canceling the vibration of a soul. A positive side, and a negative side—that's how we're going to fix you. We know how the Answer works, and we've made its opposite. With that, hopefully we can repair the damage that was done to you.

It flashed in my head as if it were replacing whatever was coming out of Dr. Gardener's mouth. I nodded when he asked if I understood. I didn't want to be rude, after all. We finished our tour and wound up right where we started, at the second set of sliding glass doors which opened. I walked with him over to the device and he pulled it open. The hiss of air rose out as he broke the seal and slid it open. I stepped up and got inside, lying back against the padded part. It was comfortable—not something I expected. Honestly, I figured comfort would have been an afterthought. I smiled to myself as he asked if I was comfortable. As I nodded, the glass doors slid open for Vera. She walked in, eyes buried in her iPad. She handed it to her assistant in a bright-yellow shirt and pointed out something on it before the person nodded and ran off to do whatever she had instructed.

"Thanks, Harold," she said to Gardener. He nodded and walked away.

"You like it?" she asked, leaning in close and grinning from ear to ear. "I took a tanning bed and reworked it."

"You know, I knew it looked familiar," I replied, smiling myself for some reason. She leaned in close and spoke low enough so that only I could hear.

"I've had a few tests. I injected some mice with a solution composed of saline infused with the bioluminescent properties of the jellyfish. In larger doses it killed them—sorry, I know, more work for you when you're back to being you. Anyway, in smaller doses they became weak—physically fine, but it was like they were extremely tired. Gave me something good to work off of. I did the inverse-radiance treatment that this machine does on them, and good as new. So there's nothing to worry about; I know what I'm doing."

As she said those words to me the ball of fire in my chest vanished and I felt at peace. I had trusted her from the start, but the confidence of her saying it made it all the better.

She took my wrists and ankles and gently wrapped them in the harnesses to keep me from moving. She leaned in close and gave me a kiss on the cheek. As she stepped away I saw her push back some tears. She mouthed *good luck* and walked away. She made her way back to the control room where Dr. Gardener and her assistant were waiting. After a moment

154

some protective barriers moved into place around them. She gave one last look at me and held up her hand, fingers crossed.

The lights around the pod I was strapped in dimmed and I heard Vera's voice come over the intercom. "Inverse-radiance test number one hundred and forty-seven, human trial number zero-zero-one. Time: 9:33 a.m. August fourteenth. Beginning phase one." As she spoke the top of the tanning bed began to move and closed over the top of me. The panel of glass on the front aligned perfectly so I could see out—or they could see in, not sure which was more important. I heard it lock with a loud metallic click before the intercom came on again.

"Beginning phase two," Vera said. "Charging radiance coils." The coils around me began to glow. The light was a vibrant blue; it reminded me of lights I had seen on the undercarriage of a car while watching a show called *Cops*. The glow of the lights made me feel strange, both lighter and heavier at the same time. Vera's voice sounded over the intercom again. "Inverse-radiance bombardment in T-minus seven minutes." I looked through the glass at a black digital clock with red numbers that turned on and began counting down.

The assistant in the booth with Vera and Gardener scurried out and ran to the glass doors where Saundra the receptionist was waiting. I could see the confused gestures of the assistant. She was anxious and didn't know what to do. She ran back over to the booth and talked to the two doctors who were fixated on me. Vera gave her young assistant some direction and the young lady ran back out to where Saundra was waiting.

"You doing okay in there?" Vera asked over the intercom. I nodded, unsure if she could see me.

"Ms. Essalte," the assistant said, breathing heavily as she ran into the booth again, "Saundra said this person could not wait."

"She's going to have to, Janice. Tell Saundra to make something up. I don't care what it is, but we are in the middle of an experiment that we can't just stop halfway through."

Janice ran off one more time, and Vera turned to me, realizing she was still pressing the intercom button. "Sorry about that," she said. "You can talk, by the way. We can hear you."

"I just hope everything is okay," I lied. Quite frankly, I didn't give a shit. I just wanted to be back to being me.

I watched Janice scamper back to the booth once more and tell Vera something that made her face turn pale. Vera stepped back toward the terminal. She was shaking and looked lost in a daze before composing herself and hitting the intercom again.

"Cyrus, this is important, and you need to hear this." There was panic in her voice. Whatever was happening was not good. I felt the anxiety begin to flutter once again in my sternum. Apparently, I needed to start giving a shit. I dreaded asking, but I had to.

"What's going on?" I asked.

"The person who is here to meet me says she's Ana Harmond."

The words registered, and as they did the ball of flame erupted from the embers and made my chest feel like it was going to burst.

"Make sure she doesn't leave," I said. Vera nodded and turned back to Janice.

"Tell Saundra that I'll meet with her and tell her to call

Detectives Aaron and Marx and tell them to get down here ASAP. No one else is to know, and make sure that Saundra contacts the police discreetly. Am I clear?" Janice nodded.

"What the hell is going on here?" Gardener asked.

"She's a person of interest in a murder investigation," I said. "I'm actually a former detective who is consulting with the local authorities. The specifics of the case are confidential. If you breathe a word of this to anyone, I will charge you with obstruction of justice. Are we clear, Dr. Gardener?"

The doc froze and then replied with a simple, "Yes, sir."

Janice ran back into the booth. "Ms. Harmond is on her way here, and the detectives are also en route. No one else knows."

"Good job, Janice," Vera said.

I watched from my suntan bed as Ana Harmond stepped up to the sliding glass that led into the outer ring of the lab. She was dressed in a black pantsuit and scarlet heels that matched her lipstick. One thing was abundantly clear: this was not the same woman I had seen dragged away in terror while her husband lay bleeding out in their bed. She was calm, collected, and beamed with confidence. She was not someone who appeared to be here under duress.

I thought back to that night and how, in retrospect, that look on her face was the only reason I was here. Until she looked at me I had every reason to not care. All I had to do was wait for that little twinge on the back of my neck to hit and pick up her soul as the nefarious characters dumped her body into a river. One look, that's all it had taken. It had all led to this

Even now I still didn't know why Ana could see me. Vera's exposure to the radiation of the Answer had given her the gift. But to my knowledge Ana had had no such contact. All my damn curiosity had done was cause pain. And because of it, I was sitting in a tanning booth about the get zapped with who knew how many lumens of artificial light designed to heal a broken soul. *What the hell is really going on?* was all I could think.

Watching Ana stand there, appearing in perfect physical condition, made me feel like nothing that had happened up to this point mattered. It had been a waste of time. Pointless pain all because that girl had given me one look. And now she stood before me, as far away from danger as she could possibly be. And why? Her eyes told the tale. The confidence of an impending victory burned in them.

I have seen entire civilizations crumble because of that look. So why was I surprised? I shouldn't have been. None of what had happened was her fault; it was mine. I understood at that moment that it wasn't because she had looked at me. It was because I wanted to be seen. Endless eons spent cleaning up messes, treated with nothing but disdain for so long. I just wanted to be important, but no one cared. And why should they? I had created this imaginary scenario where I could be more than just the garbage man, and it had caused me to lose sight of the importance of what I was meant to do. I had played right into her hands.

The realization played over and over in my mind as Janice walked from the booth to the glass doors. Though I couldn't hear them, I imagined them making their whoosh sound as they separated. I felt my eyes blink and I jerked against my straps as I felt a vibration startle me. The splatter of red stuck to the glass, along with bits of bone and gray matter that were expelled as the bullet exited Janice's skull. Her body collapsed. The vibrant yellow of her shirt turned black as it began to soak up the blood pooling around her.

I jerked and twisted in my restraints as Ana advanced on the control booth with her pistol drawn. Gardener took two to the chest and fell back into the booth as he tried to close the impact-resistant safety glass and seal them safely inside. Vera grabbed the door handle and yanked it as hard as she could, but the fallen doctor's legs were in the way and it wouldn't close. She grabbed him and pulled as hard as she could to clear the obstruction. Vera made one last lunge for the handle to get it closed, but it was too late—Ana had got her leg in. The door closed hard on it and I saw the pain on Ana's face as the heavy glass careened into it, throwing her off balance and halting her advance.

Vera composed herself and steadied her position, pulling as hard as she could. She knew she couldn't get it closed, not as it was in that moment. But it was keeping her assailant at bay, so she had to keep trying. She had to hope that one of two things would happen: Ana would retract her leg and the door would safely seal her inside, or she would hold Ana at bay long enough for either ARC security or the detectives to arrive and save her.

I could hear groans and screams of the two women as they struggled. As they did I began to feel the warmth of blood dripping from my fingers as the restraints began to tear into my skin from struggling.

I've said it before, but there is nothing worse than being forced to watch someone you care about being hurt, and not be able to change it. I could hear myself yelling amid the

159

backdrop of the life-and-death struggle I had a front-row seat to. There was movement out of the corner of my eye. I saw Aaron, Marx, and Prescott in a full sprint toward the sliding doors. *Just a little longer*, I thought.

The deafening sound of gunfire struck my ears through the intercom. I looked back at the booth where the muzzle flashes lit up. Ana had put the gun through the opening and was firing. The confined space amplified the sound, and as round after round echoed in the tiny room I knew that it would be too much to stand. I watched as Vera's hands instinctively moved from the door handle to her ears, and, as they did, the door opened and in went Ana. She pressed the magazine release on her sidearm and pulled another from inside her coat.

The sounds of the glass doors moving and clink of the slide chambering another round in Ana's gun happened simultaneously. Aaron and Marx moved into the corridor toward the office where Ana held Vera at gunpoint. Prescott remained outside with his radio in one hand and pistol in the other.

I could hear the two detectives in the background yelling for Ana's to "freeze" and "drop it," but they had no effect. She knew that if she turned toward them to fire they would drop her before she made it all the way around. So, she stayed trained on her target.

"Tell the bozos to drop it, Grimm, or your girlfriend goes bye-bye," Ana said, diverting her gaze just enough to make sure I had heard her.

"You fucking bitch. When I get out of here I'm going to fucking rip you apart!" I yelled back.

"Now, now, don't be like that. Let's keep this civilized and everyone gets to go home safely. Now, tell the cops to lower their weapons."

"Not gonna happen," Aaron yelled from the back.

"If you don't want to get hurt, little man, put the gun down," Ana yelled back.

"You'll eat eight rounds, four from each of us, before you can even turn around," Aaron replied. "There's nowhere left to go. Drop the shit!"

"Last chance, Grimm. Tell him to drop it, or he's just more collateral damage."

"You have no moves, Ana. Give it up and you don't leave here in a body bag."

"You see, that's the problem with you 'Eternals.' You think you're so much better than us. Your arrogance lets you think that I'm in a position that I don't want to be in. You think that I came in here without a game plan, without knowing exactly what I was getting myself into. But you're wrong. I'm in control. I say what happens. Who lives and who dies is up to me right now. I'm giving you the opportunity to save lives. You don't fucking tell me I'm going to leave here in a body bag, because you have no idea who you are fucking with. I decide who wins today, and trust me, it's not you."

I tried to think what she had. I surveyed the room and saw nothing. She didn't have anything; she couldn't. It was all glass, and there was nothing there she could use. But I had learned that humans were not like demons—they were unpredictable. Because of that, I decided to err on the side of caution and try to learn more. If nothing else, it would buy time for more help to arrive.

"Okay then, Mrs. Harmond," I said. "I'll play your game. What do you want?"

"Tell them to lower their weapons."

Ana peered out of the corner of her eye. I was never good at reading people, but even if I was, she was stone. It was my move and I needed this chess match to continue. "Marx, holster," I said. I watched the anger spread on his face as he looked at Aaron. Aaron nodded and Marx slid his steel back into its leather.

"Your turn," I said.

"Both of them," she said.

"Not a chance. Now spill: What do you want?"

"You already know," she said.

"You're not getting the other two passkeys," Vera said.

A smile spread over Ana's face. "You know, I had forgotten about that. Those would actually be a bonus. I think I'll have those, too. Give me the keys."

"Go to hell, bitch!"

"Temper, temper," Ana said. "You're a pawn playing a game of kings. Give."

"You haven't answered the question," I said, not letting her get away with the redirect.

"Very right, Mr. Grimm. Actually, I'm here for you."

"Come get me, then," I replied.

"Not dead. Dear me, no. I just need your signature."

"My signature? What do you mean?"

I felt my anger rise up as Ana rolled her eyes at my question. "You guys really are that stupid; you still haven't figured it out. Well, I had to give you the benefit of the doubt."

"I am not one of the four horsemen. I am not here to bring about the end of days. You have this situation entirely wrong."

"No!" she yelled back. "*You* have this situation entirely wrong. You still think this is about you. Pawns playing a game of kings. Okay then, let's see if, once I give you a broader look at the board, you can move out of check. After all, there's no fun in playing the game if your adversary doesn't see the mate coming. Tell me what you know."

"It's a trap, Cyrus. Don't do this," Vera said.

Ana moved forward and pointed the gun at Vera's face to silence her.

"Let me tell you a story. It's a story that will portray for you just how little control you really have. Imagine if you will, an organization. The leaders of this organization realize that the state of the world is such that to save it, drastic and immediate steps must be taken. Call it divine providence if you will. They need something very specific: information on how a very old, very lonely spiritual entity exists. He is very powerful and very difficult to track down. He is everywhere, but nowhere. This organization learns, through thousands of hours of research, that the reason for this is because he can make copies of himself and go anywhere in the world that he needs to—part of the job, after all. Knowing this, the organization comes up with a plan: to feed on his curiosity and, in turn, force a meeting with someone he won't be able to resist. A scientist with a unique gift: the ability to see across the boundaries of reality, a gift granted to her very deliberately by this organization. Their hope is that this entity will take the bait, and, if he does, they will funnel him, guide his movement until they can get what they need: a fragment of his soul. The organization lays the foundations for the ruse and drives it on its way. Granted, there were some hiccups along the way. Your friend, the exorcist? We didn't see that coming. But nonetheless, here we are. With exactly what we need: a digital blueprint of you, stored right here, not ten feet away from me. So, tell me, if everything has led to this point, do you really think your cop friends are going to stop me?"

I did not know what to think. I could only ask her, "Why?"

"Nuh-uh, me first. It's my move, remember?"

I thought for a moment, but it was only a moment. "Vera, give her one of the cards."

"No way. Fuck this bitch. She's messing with our heads."

"Vera, I need you to listen to me. Think about it. She's not here for these—what can she really get with it?"

"Access to another quarter of the mainframe's data, that's what!" Vera replied.

"I mean, what's there that's going to help them?" Vera thought for a moment and leaned over, pulling the blade from the console and removing one of the data cards.

Ana pulled out a portable card reader and held it out for Vera to swipe, which she did.

Ana placed the device into her pocket and placed her hand to her ear. "Did you get the scan?" she said. "Good. Now, where were we? Oh, that's right, your turn."

"Why do you need a piece of my soul?"

"Such a foolish question that doesn't improve your place on the board in the slightest. But you get your answer, anyway. You said earlier that you were not here to start the apocalypse. Fine, I believe you. That doesn't matter—it doesn't mean the apocalypse isn't coming, anyway. And it damn sure doesn't mean you're not going to be part of it. I'm going to use your soul to save as many as I can. Do what you will no longer be able to."

"How will you do that?"

Ana gave me a smug look and the edges of her lips turned up. It wasn't my turn.

"Give her the other card," I said.

164

The anger fuming on Vera's face as I asked her to turn over the last piece of her research to this woman made me think that I had to think of better leverage. This was about to turn into a war. And at the moment, we were losing.

"No," Vera said. I'm not good with tones, but this one I knew. She would die before she would hand it over.

"Vera don't do this," I said, doing my best to de-escalate the situation from my constrained position. She pulled her badge from the blade and held it between her hands, slightly bent.

"Do it, and I pull the trigger," Ana said.

"Pull it, and I put my entire clip between your shoulder blades," Aaron yelled from the hall. "Then you get nothing, bitch—not the card and certainly not the print from the system."

It felt like time moved at a snail's pace as the edges of Ana's lips curled upward. Then she laughed. The sound of it echoed through the lab. I felt a chill run down my spine, and I'm sure I wasn't the only one who felt it.

"You think I don't already have what I need? I've had the scan of the 'Eternal' for the better part of a week, Detective. You haven't heard a single thing I've told you. I'm here because I choose to be, not because I have to be."

"It's not possible," Vera said. "The security measures we have put in place guarantee that no one gets in that we don't want."

"And that has stopped me, how?" Ana asked.

"Enough of this bullshit, Detectives. Shoot her."

The echo of Aaron's boot hitting the tile as he took a step made the world sound hollow. I wanted to say some-thing—anything—but I had no words. My anger at the situation was pressing on me and I wanted to yell at them

165

to fire, be damned if she was holding the cards she said she was. I felt the words on my lips, but she spoke first.

"No. Take another step, Detective, and it will be the last thing you do."

"Fuck you!" Aaron yelled.

"Fine," she said. "I told you not to press it, and everyone walks away. But it seems you don't believe me." Ana turned and looked at me. "Just remember, Grimm, it was you who did this." She paused for a moment, her smug grin curling up again before she spoke.

"Take them," she said.

It took only a split second. Out of the corner of my eye I saw the movement of the sliding glass and then heard the muted thud of the rounds reverberating in the outer hall as Prescott moved into the outer lab and began firing into the backs of Aaron and Marx. I watched in horror as the two men fell forward and lay motionless, pools of red forming around them. I jumped, twisted, and yelled, fighting against the restraints as it happened, but I could only watch.

My hands were shaking, and I was breathing heavily as I looked back toward the booth where Ana Harmond was looking at me, the same snide look on her face. She turned her attention back to Vera.

"Now, give me the key," Ana said.

Vera was crouched over, tears were running down her face. I could see her hands shaking in fear at what might happen. "Snap out of it, Doc," Ana said, but Vera just trembled on the floor. "Hey!" Ana yelled, finally bringing Vera back to the moment. Vera rose slowly, the black of her makeup running down her face.

"So, clearly your Mr. Prescott is really *my* Mr. Prescott,"

Ana said.

"Fuck you," Prescott said from the hall. "You have what you came for, now get out of here."

"I have what I need, but not what I want. Doctor, the key," Ana said.

"No."

"You don't really have a choice. You can give me the card and I walk away, or I kill you and take it anyway."

"No," Vera said again. She was absolutely calm.

"You have no more leverage." Ana's voice began to show her irritation.

"But I do," Vera replied. "I have him."

She looked at me, and I felt the fire in my chest begin to swirl. I didn't understand. Vera continued.

"You see, without this card we slow you down. We don't stop you, but it hinders your progress. Am I right?"

Ana didn't respond.

"And ultimately, he's more powerful than anyone you have on your side. He might not know the whole story, but he has a starting point. And that's all he will need."

"So? He's just a man, now. Most of his best tricks are gone," Ana said.

"Are they?" Vera replied. "Cyrus, what does the clock say?" I turned my attention to the red numbers as they ticked down: four, three, two, one, zero.

"It's done," I said.

"You made a mistake coming here, Ana," Vera said. "Before this moment, we were trying to find you, help you if we could. But all that changed when you came here. Because he's won't be trying to save you anymore. Now you're the prey." A look of confusion and anger spread on Ana's face.

"Cyrus?" Vera said in a voice shaking with fear.

"Yeah?"

"When she reloaded her gun, what color were the bullets?"

I thought back and answered, "Gray."

She looked at me with tears in her eyes. "When this is over, come find me." With those words, the bent card in her hands overextended and snapped. The two broken halves fell through the air in slow motion as she lunged for the initiation button on the console.

There was a flash of gunfire, a spray of blood, and a feeling of anguish as I watched her fall to the ground. Then, nothing but the blinding light.

8

Breaking All the Rules

The coils on the inner walls of the chamber burst to life, and, like the fire from a thousand suns, the light consumed me. There was no sound. My lungs emptied as I yelled, but it, too, was swallowed by the light. The tears fought their way from my eyes but evaporated into the fire along with my sight. I could feel the blood running down my hands, but there was no pain. The only sense left to me was smell, and it was that of burning flesh. I was trapped in the hopelessness of the moment as I burned.

My movement slowed, and it became harder to struggle against the restraints. The running blood had stopped, and I could no longer move my fingers. I gave a desperate pull against my restraint and felt a break. It was like a dead weight had been lifted. As the charred flesh and dried bone crumbled, I raised the stump where my hand used to be, while the rest fell to the floor. I felt my ankles start to go next, and then my knees. I tried to stay upright but knew that I wouldn't be able to for long. I pulled the other stump free and tried to push against the chamber. But there was almost no muscle left; it was over.

This was to be my end. Burned in the chamber that was built to heal me. I was not afraid, though I suppose I should have been. More than anything, I regretted that I would not come for her. She died to save me. But it was all for nothing—I was not saved. I wondered for a moment if I would be like them. But I guessed not. Unlike man, I was not a soul in a vessel. It was all me. Off to oblivion, just the particles of a ruined spirit. Who knew? And, really, who cared?

The ankles gave, and I began to fall. What was left of me stayed propped up against the chamber, unable to move. There was not much, but I was still here, trapped as a frail husk. The whine of the coils died, returning me to the silence. Then that was interrupted by the sound of the seal breaking, and the chamber began to open. My charred frame tumbled onto the floor. Strangely, I could breathe fine. I did my best to pull myself across the ground, but I could not see and did not know where to go. As I pulled, I felt my arm begin to change. It was becoming easier to move. A few moments later, I felt my eyelids crack, and I could see.

A flood of power washed over me, and I rolled onto my back. I turned my head. The black of burned flesh began to fall off, and I watched the muscles rebuild right before my eyes—arm, wrist, palm, fingers. I turned myself over and looked out the glass toward the control room. The panic on Ana Harmond's face as she saw me changing right in front of her was satisfying. I began to stand, and she started to move toward the sliding doors. I was still stiff, but that would be over soon, and she was right to be afraid.

I felt my power return to me, and with it the whole world changed. The last bits of charred flesh fell to the ground,

170

turned to dust. As they did, I felt myself shift planes. I once again stood between the worlds of the living and the dead. I walked toward the lab entrance, half-corporeal and half-astral. My quarry bolted from the outer lab and into the hallway. I reached the exit and passed through the glass like it wasn't even there.

The anger pulsing through my now-translucent veins was intoxicating. It felt good, and it shouldn't have. I heard Saundra attempt to scream as she was gunned down at the entrance of the lab. As she passed on, her spirit cried out, and the anguish of the world collapsed in on me. All those dead whom I had not been there for were crying out. I could feel myself drawn to them. I was whole again, and it was my job. I needed to do it. My time as a human had made me understand what the feeling was—hunger. I craved to grant them their respite, but for now they would have to wait. First, Ana Harmond and Nathan Prescott would join them.

I knew the trail of bloody footprints would lead me to my prey. It was only a matter of time until they were mine. I was no longer bound by the constraints of the mortal realm, and that meant no matter how fast they were, I was faster. The sound of a closing door alerted me, and I moved toward it. I phased and passed through the door to find more tracks. The echo of footfalls in the narrow corridor told me that they were in a full sprint. The corners of my lips curled as I gave chase. I was enjoying my hunt. I wanted to take my revenge. The thud of another door slamming directed me, and I passed through it as well. Three doors later, I was right on their heels.

The duo made a sharp turn and went down a flight of stairs.

I could hear Prescott telling her that it would lead them to the service elevator and out to the hazardous material disposal exit. The elevator doors closed, and the box began to descend. I moved through the safety doors and into the shaft. I felt my hand turn to an edge. I thought of cutting the cables on the lift, so they would plummet to their doom. I decided against it. That was too good for them. They had made this personal, and I was going to make damn sure they knew it.

I stepped off the landing and into the shaft. The rush of air I felt as I fell was exhilarating, but I needed to focus. I passed through the roof of the elevator and unphased. The force of my weight landing on the elevator floor made the entire box shake. There was nothing but panic in their eyes as they found themselves trapped. I could have very easily made it their tomb. The firearms came out and their muzzles flashed, but each round moved through me like I wasn't even there.

The bell dinged as we reached the bottom floor, and, as it did, I grabbed each of them and drove them through the steel. I could hear the air being knocked out of them as they landed and slid across the ground, along with the broken elevator doors. Their momentum was stopped as they hit the cinder-block wall in the back of the room and cried out in pain.

"Help!" Prescott yelled, and two ARC security guards came running from down the hall. They drew their sidearms and fired. I moved toward them like lightning and brought my hands down across the barrels of their guns. The severed steel fell to the ground, and with another quick move I slammed each of them to the ground, rendering them unconscious.

I turned back to my prey. Prescott sat up against the wall and was trying to fight through the pain to stand. Ana, on the other hand, was crawling toward her gun, like it was going to

172

help her. I decided that I would let her reach it and fire away in vain so that she would know that she was powerless to save herself. She scooped it up and did exactly that—one, two, five, nine rounds that did nothing.

"I win, bitch," I said as I started walking toward her. "And when I'm done here, I'm going to find your little organization and tear them apart, just like you."

"Fuck you," she said, pushing the magazine eject. "They'll be ready for you, anyway." She began to crawl away from me as she slammed her last clip into the sidearm.

I move quickly to overtake her and reached down. I grabbed her by the back of neck and pulled her to her feet. I lifted her entirely off the ground and pulled back before slamming her against the wall. I could feel her shoulder blades splinter as she hit the reinforced blocks. Her entire body seized in pain and she yelled. It felt good to hear her suffering.

"I'll make a deal with you," I said. "Tell me where they are, and I'll end this quickly. Only those who are in charge will die. Enough innocent blood has been spilled by your little crusade."

"We're saving the world," she choked out as I held her suspended by her neck against the wall. "Do you really think that I would betray that cause because I was offered a quick death? Do you think God would forgive me if I did?"

I felt anger again. So, I pulled back and slammed her against the wall once again. "There is no God!" I yelled. "He is a figment, created by people to help their fragile little minds come to terms with one simple truth!"

"Which is?" she asked.

"You are a shadow—energy coalesced into a singular mind and bound into a physical body by the universe. When you

173

die, I collect what's left and you get recycled, over and over and over again."

"Then that's how God made it."

I felt my fist penetrate the reinforced bricks as I reacted to her response. "THERE IS NO GOD!" I screamed, my face a fraction of an inch from hers.

"Just because you don't believe doesn't make him not real," she said.

"I've been here for hundreds of millions of years. I've seen this planet die and be reborn a dozen times, and you care to lecture me on what I believe. If God were real, I would have seen him. I've seen everything else that there is to see."

"Everything until a girl got dragged out of her room and turned to look at you."

"Enough bullshit," I said. "Where are they?"

"Fuck . . . you . . ."

"Fine, we do this the hard way." I felt the power surge into my hand as it turned black and hard as diamond. It was sharp—sharper than it had ever been. It took but a flick of my wrist to do what I wanted. I took her leg at the knee, and she cried out. There was no one to hear her, save for the man who would follow her shortly.

"Shall I repeat the question?" I asked.

"Go to hell!"

"Been there," I replied. "And when we're done, I'll hand-deliver you." I paused to give her a moment to try to move past the pain.

"Where?" I yelled.

She tried to spit in my face, but it passed right through. I flicked my wrist again and took the other leg. I felt her writhing in my fingers, and I liked it. I wanted her to suffer, even though it felt horribly wrong. I needed to do this. More was at stake here than revenge. But as I held her in my hand—shaking, scared, and in pain—my hatred was turning into pity. I needed to try a different approach. I was beginning to feel that I was going to run out of body parts, or that she would run out of blood before she cracked.

"I understand what you're trying to do, Ana," I said. "You believe that what you are doing is for the betterment of mankind. But I'm going to tell you something. Your organization is but a small perspective in a much larger reality. I have been watching humanity since its birth, and I'm going to tell you the brutal and horrible truth. Mankind, as a whole, must save itself. You can't; I can't; even God can't. As a species you must decide what is and is not the best thing for you. And that will either lead you to true salvation, or it will lead you to destruction."

"Our work is that of God," she said, her weakness evident in her voice.

"Let's say for a moment that it is, and you succeed. What then? God takes a very small percentage of the human race to live with him in heaven and the rest are left to suffer as hell consumes the earth? Would it not be better to help those who are not worthy become the best of you? Make them what it is God desires so that when your rapture comes, everyone gets to rise with him. Is that not a nobler endeavor?"

"You don't understand."

"What don't I understand?"

"You are he who brings about the end. You can't know any more than your part. Even if I tell you, you won't understand."

"Try."

"It won't matter," she said.

175

"This is your chance to prove me wrong. Your chance to possibly make me your ally, if what you tell me makes more sense than what I already know. And yet you refuse to take that chance. Why?"

"Because if you unite the four then we might not have enough time to save those people we can."

"What do you mean?" I asked.

"Again, it doesn't matter. This is just one more move in our chess game."

"It does matter!" I said.

"Why?" Ana asked.

I had to think for a moment. She asked again, "Why?"

I didn't answer.

"WHY!?" she screamed.

"Because it was important to her, and I can't let her down!"

"So, I took one of your royals off the board, and now you don't want to play the game anymore?" She smiled weakly and gave the same maniacal laugh she had before. "The best thing about my demise is that I will still have the girl."

I felt my anger rise and I flicked my wrist once more, sending her left forearm to the ground. She cried out and then began laughing again.

"What?" I asked through gritted teeth.

"Come find me, Cyrus. Come find me. Such great words—poetic, really—so full of hope. Better get started; you have a lot of searching to do. Several million souls you'll have to sift through. And while you sift through the wreckage left behind in your absence, I will find her, and I will bury her in the darkest pits of sorrow where you can never reach her. Even if that means I go there with her."

"Fuck you!" I yelled, giving her another slam against the

wall.

She spit blood and smiled once again.

"You say you'll save the world from us," Ana said. "Because we're wrong. Well, let's see how committed you are. You claim to play on the side of good. Here's your chance to prove it. Do you waste your time chasing the girl, or do you try to stop my team? She made the hard choice, Grimm. Can you? The pieces are moving. Check."

I thought about what she was saying. It took me away from the moment. She saw it, raised her hand, and pressed the pistol to her temple. The sound was muffled by the skin, producing only a thud. The bullet emerged from the other side of her head, and the contents of her skull went with it, leaving a streak of red across the cinder block. I froze for a moment and then dropped what was left of her.

I felt panicked. I couldn't let her get away. I closed my eyes and connected to the life stream. I let myself sink back into my job. I could feel them everywhere—millions of souls that had been left abandoned by my absence. So much sorrow, worry, and sadness, all at once.

My eyelids opened, and I looked around the room for Ana. She was gone. I tried to focus and pinpoint her, but there was too much interference, too many souls crying out at once. I had to start processing them before I would be able to see clearly. I let myself go—a hundred thousand impressions, going to the strongest cries first. I moved as fast as I could, but I was running thin. Too little butter over far too much bread. I don't know how long I was there, but by the time I was finished, the pool of blood on the floor was dry.

Millions of souls that had been left behind had all been addressed. I felt better and worse at the same time, for none of them were Ana or Vera. She had gotten away; to where, I did not know. I came back to my senses and put myself back in autopilot with my job, but there was still more to do. She had asked me what was more important, and the answer was simple: stopping her order. But how I was to do that was a question not easily answered. Then I heard a cough from the shadows. I had forgotten about him. I moved toward the sound, and it spoke.

"Cyrus, I'm so sorry. I didn't know what to do. They have my daughter," Prescott said.

"And you didn't think to tell me?" I said, my anger beginning to swell again.

"They said they would kill her. I didn't know what else to do."

I was pissed, but that wasn't going to help me. I needed to let it go. Nathan Prescott didn't know the stakes of what he was involved in. Hell, he might even have been having a breakdown with what he had just seen. He was clearly afraid of me, but other than that he seemed okay. I needed to just walk away, as there were more important matters to tend to. I decided to leave him to the authorities and move on. He was but another pawn used and discarded by Ana and those she was aligned with.

"Wait," Prescott said as I headed for the exit. I didn't want to stop, but it was like he had grabbed me with his words.

"What?" I asked.

"I was just doing what I had to, to save my daughter."

"That doesn't make it right."

He didn't answer. I turned my head and looked back at him to give him one last chance before I left.

"Then let me help," he said.

178

"And how exactly are you going to do that?"

"I don't know. I'll do anything. Just help me save my little girl."

The pain in the man's eyes was piercing. I believed as I looked into them that he might actually be willing to do anything.

"Fine," I said. "Did you kill Ramsey?"

"No, he has no idea what I've done."

"Then get him, convince him to help, and meet me at The Velvet Orchid."

"That's not exactly in the good part of town."

"You said anything."

"You're right, I did. What do you need me to do?" he asked.

"Dress light."

The home of Nathan Prescott looked like what you would expect for a man who was the security chief for a multibillion-dollar tech corporation. There were a few kids walking down the street, but otherwise it was quiet. There was no sign that anyone was inside the house, but I could feel them there. For some reason, I could only feel them. It was strange, almost like something was clouding my senses. I remember thinking that I was simply still adjusting to being whole again and shrugged off the uneasiness.

My heart was pounding as I approached the home. I moved closer to the window I'd decided was the best point of entry. Before my time as a mortal I would have never imagined being anxious about a situation. There had never been a need. But so much had happened. Now I was so much . . . *more* than I had been before. I was scared, and excited, and focused.

Before I even realized it, the window was open, and I was in. I landed on the tile of the kitchen floor and realized I could have just walked through the wall.

I took a deep breath and pushed the anxiety away, moving back into the strength of my being. My senses heightened, and I instantly had a better sense of the home. I could hear the men talking upstairs. The girl was close to them, but I needed a better indication of where. If I was going to achieve what I wanted, then I would need Prescott. And to get him, I needed to get his daughter out of the house safely.

I made my way to the steps and began to move up them as quietly as I could. The men were in the upstairs loft and had the television on. I was nearing the top when I heard it—the wood creaking beneath my feet.

The men's conversation stopped and the sound of at least one of them getting up and grabbing his firearm was clear. I had to make a decision: Did I risk it and go for the girl, or did I play it safe and hope he assumed it was just the house settling? I chose the latter and darted down the stairs.

The man moved down the staircase slowly, and for some stupid reason decided to speak.

"Is anyone there?" he asked. I didn't reply, of course. "Come out or I'll shoot. Then we kill the girl."

Had I not gone through what I had over the previous weeks, I would have stepped out. Dead people were always so honest. There was no need for them to lie, so why would he? But I knew better now. Then the guard made his last mistake: he fired. The bullets whizzed by me and embedded themselves into the wall opposite where I was hiding. The other guy upstairs vocalized his displeasure at the harsh sounds, but I didn't care. All I cared about was that the holes where the bullets were lodged into the wall were missing something, a glow. I knew then that their firearms would be useless to them. I just needed to make it to the girl before they did.

That's when I made my move.

The man on the stairs had turned his head to yell back toward his partner. This was it. I moved out from behind the corner and bolted. The soaked-in power I had scarcely known for some time made me fast—faster than I remembered. I don't even think he could have stopped me if he was looking right at me. I felt my arms turn to blades, and time was slowed. He caught the motion out of the corner of his eye and began to turn, but I was already on him. I gave one swipe with each hand—one at the neck, and the other at the waist.

I was already at the top of the stairs by the time the three pieces of the guard had fallen to the ground. The other man saw it and broke out in a full sprint toward the bedroom where little lady Prescott was being held. He turned and looked back at me, panic in his eyes, and fired his weapon. The bullets passed through me as if I wasn't even there as I closed the gap between us.

The splinters of the door frame went flying as he kicked the door open to the child's room. He started to raise his arm, pointing his gun at her. There were a few loud pops and then a scream. I could feel my teeth gritted and my eyes were closed. They shouldn't have been. I hate to admit it, but I was scared to see what had happened. I looked at my hand and saw red dripping from my fingertips.

The man was in front of me, but he was standing still. I tilted my head and looked around him from the side. I had hit my mark. The angle was just such that I had taken his hands and the gun out, creating the first pop. I moved around him and into the room between the child and him. Then I looked at the results of my second strike. It, too, had landed. The line of red ran from his bottom rib to his hip on the other side. He was still breathing. His legs and torso had fallen against the door frame, making him appear as if he were still intact.

Had he not fallen in just that way, he would have bled out in a few seconds. I had killed him, but he was still alive (at least for *now*). His eyes followed my movement. His shallow and quick breaths were the only sound in the room. I felt bad for a moment as I watched him suffer. Part of me wanted to think he deserved it. He was supporting an organization that was trying to bring about the end of the world, wittingly or not. But there was also that part that knew it was wrong. I moved closer to him and made another quick swipe. Then he was gone.

I felt the anxiety swell up in my chest again, and I turned around. One round had made it out of the firearm, creating the second pop. It was in the wall beside the trembling little girl. He had missed by an inch. She was safe. Thinking back, I probably should have said something, but I didn't know what. I took a step back from the terrified child and walked out of the room, being sure to knock the still-propped guard out of the doorway so he could not be seen. I saw her jump out of the corner of my eye as the body hit the floor with a thud.

I walked to the bathroom and grabbed a towel before returning to the little girl's bedroom. I walked slowly to the corner where she was. She was covered in blood. Blood I had inadvertently sent her way when I dispatched her would-be assassin. I took a knee next to the child; she was weeping, like you would expect any child to in that situation. I reached out my hand, and she flinched. I wasn't surprised but knowing that she was afraid of me still stung a little.

"It's okay, Emily," I said as softly as I could. "I'm a friend of your daddy's. He sent me here to save you." Her eyes turned up at me. She was still scared, but at least she wasn't shut down. I sat and used the towel to wipe some of the blood off her hand. "It's going to be okay," I said. "We're going to take you to your daddy real soon, I promise." I inched closer as the cloth soaked up the still-warm liquid. Before I knew it, the little girl lunged and threw her arms around my neck. She pulled me in close and held on tight. I didn't know what to do for a moment, but it was almost like I was her father, and I instinctively wrapped my arms around her and held her close. She stopped crying, and I felt her grasp loosen.

"Let's get you cleaned up," I said. "Then we will go see your daddy, okay?"

She nodded and reached out her hands for me to start wiping them down. I thought in that moment that I would have been excited that I had found my leverage, but that isn't what I felt. Even now, I can't explain it. All I know is that it was pleasant.

The embrace between young Emily Prescott and her father made me feel warm, like I had when she'd wrapped her arms around me and I'd hugged her back. When they stopped it was the elder Prescott that was crying. I would guess that whatever I had felt when she hugged me was the same as he felt, only more intensely. It elicited such an emotional response from the man that I couldn't help but be fascinated. But I was also disappointed. Disappointed in myself. I could feel it, just as he could, but all I could do was analyze it. I couldn't envelope myself in it to understand more. I saw the redness around his eyes and I thought of how I had learned so much, but still knew so little.

Vince motioned to one of the nearby bouncers, and he came and took the little girl by the hand and led her away. "Take good care of her," he said as they left the room, and received an acknowledging nod from his goon.

"You look like shit," he said to me, a smile on his face. "Then again, you also look to be you again. How does it feel?"

"Good," I said. "Nice to be back."

"Glad to hear it. Where's Vera? Did you ever embrace your human side and make a move? C'mon, man, I want details."

His smile evaporated when I didn't smile back. I didn't have to say a word; he knew it wasn't good.

"What happened, Cyrus? Where is she?"

"She's gone. That's why we're here," I said.

"Was it them? They found her?"

"Yeah, they found her, us. It happened while she was putting me back together. She saved me, Vince."

He was silent for a moment, but the emotion had to go somewhere. The tidal wave of profanity that spilled out of Vince's mouth, as he stomped around the room throwing objects in his grief and anger, was nothing short of jarring. When it was over he was in his chair with his head in his hands, taking deep, measured breaths.

"When I find the son of a bitch that did it, I'm going to wring that motherfucker's neck," Vince said, making the gesture with his hands. I looked at Prescott, who had started to stand up, clearly to take the blame. I lifted my fingers but a few inches to wave him off, and he sat back down.

"So, what's the plan, boss?" Vince asked.

"Well, it turns out that the person who did this is already dead," I said.

"You got the son of a bitch?"

"Not exactly." I explained the entire situation. "I need you to open the portal again, so we can go in and find them," I said.

"But can't you *feel* souls?" Ramsey asked. I had forgotten that Prescott had brought Ramsey as I had asked. His question let me know that Vince had brought him up to speed on events.

"Yes, I can feel every soul on earth, which is the problem. There are two that are missing, and if they aren't here then there's only one other place they can be."

"So just go in and get them," Vince said. "You can move into that realm freely now. You don't need me to open a portal for that."

"Yes, I can move freely, but it's not just me going. I've been there, and I've taken a look. They're not in any of the easy-to-find places. And unfortunately, we're on a time crunch. Whatever the organization has planned, they're going to do it soon, and I have nowhere to start. I'm going to need some help finding them in any reasonable amount of time, and that means I need someone alive."

I looked at Prescott, who took a deep breath as he realized he was going to take a trip into the fire, just as he had promised he would.

"So, what's my job, then?" Ramsey asked I was surprised he had wrapped his head around the situation with such ease.

"When I find them, I'm going to . . . apply some pressure to Mrs. Harmond," I said. "As soon as I have what I need, I'm going to get you the information. It's your job to take that information and turn it into something we can work with in finding these assholes, so we can stop them."

"Sounds easy enough," Ramsey said. "One problem with the plan—you said that to find the girls in any timely manner would require help. If hell—limbo—whatever—is so large that you need help to find them, how does only one extra set of eyes help you in any significant way?"

"He's not there to be an extra set of eyes. I know exactly where I can find someone who can find the girls quickly," I replied.

"So, if I'm not going with you to look, what is my role?"

"Well, this is the part where I remind you that you said you would do anything if I saved your daughter," I replied. "Do you still hold fast to that promise?"

Prescott nodded reluctantly. But I had done what he had asked, and he wanted to make good on his promise.

"Good," I said. "This 'person' who can help us is someone I have unfortunately had the displeasure of working with from time to time. In his realm he is simply called the Duke. But humanity has many names for him: Satan, Lucifer, the Beast, Apollyon. The list goes on."

"We should really not be doing this," Vince said.

"You're right; we shouldn't," I replied. "You see, there are rules that I follow—things that I'm to never do, because it can cause a whole lot of problems. I don't interfere with human affairs, I don't kill, I don't save, and I don't pull souls from the fire. The list is not short. But at this point, I'm throwing the list out."

"Thank you," Prescott said, realizing that what I did for his daughter was something on my list.

"I didn't do it for you," I said. "But I did it. That's what's important."

"I understand," Prescott said, this time with conviction in his words.

"I don't think you do. You see, we're going to do something beyond anything you can imagine."

"And that is . . .?"

"One of the things I've learned in my dealings with the Duke is that he, like so many others, has a weak point. He can't resist a bet. So, to answer the question of your role, Mr. Prescott, it's simple: I'm going to do something I really shouldn't, I'm going to make a deal with the devil, and you—or more specifically, your soul—is what we're going to wager."

9

The Cradle of Fire

The sound of rushing wind was cut sharply by the cries of pain coming from Nathan Prescott. I watched as the scorched tempest (that would be hell) flayed him. I wanted to feel bad for his suffering, but in my mind, he deserved far worse. Vera had gone through this same thing without a single complaint. It was only fitting that he would endure the same torment to try to save her from this place. I gave him a moment to grow accustomed to the environment before waving him forward.

Prescott did not move very quickly, despite my urges. It would have been easier to just kill him and ferry his soul where we needed to be. But the thought of leaving the little girl I had saved only a few hours earlier without a parent for the sake of expedience would be crossing the line. I had weighed it in my mind over and over, every time we had to stop to take a break. Logically, killing him and moving quickly was the right thing to do. The fate of potentially billions of people was on the line, but I couldn't bring myself to do it. One child's life should not have been more important than the task at hand, and it wasn't, but I still refused to do the smart thing, all the same.

It was only a few hours before we reached the Cliffs of Judgment. The look on Prescott's face as he stared out into the infinite black of the chasm put a smile on my face. It made me think of my short time as a mortal, and how humans took the simple things in life for granted. The very idea left me in wonder. I imagined what it was like to see something wondrous, through his eyes, that I took for granted. We walked along the edge of the red stone until we found one of the many carved staircases that led down into the void.

We descended into the blackness for nearly five hours before the silence of our long walk was broken. One of a thousand kinds of lesser demons skittered across the walls now towering above us, and the sight of it drove Nathan to say something so he could take his mind off the reality of the situation.

"So," was all he said at first.

"So," I replied.

It was silent for a moment. He was uncomfortable. Good—he should have been. He was about to enter into the parts of hell that mankind writes about in its religious texts.

"I didn't realize this place would be so . . . big," he said.

I thought for a moment how best to respond to his comment and decided the truth would probably be the best.

"Yes, it is. It's actually the same size as Earth. Because, you see, we're still there. This place is just the world behind the world."

"Interesting. So, when you brought me here, technically everyone remained just a few feet away from us, just in another dimension?"

"Yes and no," I said. "We don't move into another dimension;

we just change phase."

"Okay . . . so what does it mean to change phase?" he asked.

"Everything in the universe is composed of energy. When you break it down to a base level, it's energy. Protons, neutrons, electrons, they make up matter, but they themselves are energy. All energy has a wavelength, it vibrates. That vibration is like a fingerprint. Take emotional energy, for example. Anger vibrates in a certain way—that vibration is the same thing for everyone. Anger is anger. It is the same everywhere, same vibration. Make sense?"

"Kind of. So, you're saying that when we moved here, we didn't really *move*; we just changed vibration?"

"Exactly," I said.

"That's really cool."

"It would be cooler if we didn't have to be here in the first place right now," I said. I needed to let it go. I needed to keep a clear head, and holding a grudge, justified or not, was not going to help me—us.

"Sorry," I said.

"You're right," he said. "I got her killed; this is my fault. I just want to make it right."

I felt the nagging anger I had been clinging to slip away from me. It made me feel immensely better almost immediately.

"We will," I said. "You will."

I looked down over the edge of the steps. The walls converged on a small spark of red light at the bottom of the hole. I looked up; the walls did the same at a small spark of white in that direction. "We're halfway there," I said. Prescott nodded.

There were another few minutes of silence before Prescott began to ask more questions.

"When we came here, we stood on that marking, Vince did his thing, and we were just here. I'm wondering how that actually works. I mean, isn't this weird? I shouldn't really be here, should I?"

I thought for a moment on how best to explain. "No, you shouldn't really be here. Humans are unique. Rocks, trees, animals. They can't change phase. They are stuck on that side of the fence. Technically, everything has life energy in it. When things die, that life energy returns to what I call the Source. It gets recycled and infused into new creatures. Humanity calls this the law of conservation of energy."

"So that's what happens to everything else," Prescott said. "How are we—humans, I mean—different?"

I didn't speak immediately. I didn't actually know. I had never really thought about it. It was as though at the same moment he asked me, the answer became clear. The little part of me that had experienced being human knew the answer, and I smiled a little to myself as it spilled from my lips. "Honestly," I said, "you make yourselves that way.

"Humans acknowledge their own existence. To you, you are more than just the body you live in. It's a shell, and the thing that makes you, *you* is just trapped inside of it. Because of this, you are two separate pieces, bound together. Spirit energy exists natively on one side of the fence, and physical energy on the other. Understanding that your soul and your body are separate creates a dichotomy that is unique to humanity. A man dies and comes back to life because his body pulls his spirit back across the wall. You stand on a portal and phase into this place, and your spirit pulls your physical form over. Not all of it, but enough to give you form."

"That's insane," Prescott said with a look of bewilderment

on his face.

"I completely agree, but it's the best explanation I have."

I looked back over the steps; the landing at the bottom was in sight. "I can see the bottom. You have enough time for one more series of questions, so make them good."

"You said that I stood on a portal to get here. Does that mean that we can only phase in certain locations?"

"Yes," I said. "It's like there's a piece of cloth draped over the world, separating the two. The Veil. The portals are small spots where the cloth has worn a bit thin."

"And you kind of slide through?"

"Yep," I replied.

"And just how many of these places are there?" Prescott asked.

"The cloth has been around a long time," I said. "So, quite a few."

There was a moment of silence. I tried to ignore it, but that small amount of humanity I had experienced made me feel uncomfortable. I stopped and turned back toward him.

"What?" I asked.

There looked to be almost pain in his eyes. "Cloth doesn't wear that way. There has to be bigger holes out there, right?"

It was my fault that I had told him to ask good questions. I paused for a moment. The truth wasn't exactly something I wanted to get to deep into at that moment. What we were doing was important, and I didn't want to say something that might make him lose it.

"I'm guessing the silence means yes?" he said, knowing the answer.

It was too late. I was committed. "Yes," I said.

"How many?" he replied almost instantly.

"Seven. But they are nothing to worry about; they're just a bit easier to slip through."

"How much easier?"

"A bit," I said again, sharply. I was relieved when we were finally at the bottom of the stairs. "Time to go."

I began to walk quickly toward the stone doorway at the end. I felt the pressure of Nathan grabbing my arm. A small pulse of anger moved into my chest. I turned and pushed him away.

"Cyrus, how bad is it?"

"It's not. They have been there a very long time. Forget about it," I said.

"This is important; I need to know."

We did not have time for this. The situation was about to get dire, and I needed him focused. "No, you don't!" I snapped. "This—this conversation has nothing to do with what we're about to deal with. Shit is about to get very real, and I need your head right, got it?"

"Yeah, but—"

"No buts. The seven sites are sealed—they don't open, and they pose no threat to you or your little girl. Continuing to talk about it has nothing to do with what we are about to do. End of discussion."

Prescott looked at me with what looked like sheer terror in his eyes. "I think it might," he said.

As he said it, it was like every part of me fell backward. I stood, but I was falling. "What do you mean?"

"She spoke of it," he said. "Over the phone."

"Who?" I asked.

"Ana."

"And who was she talking to?"

"I don't know," he said.

My mind was going crazy with what it could be. All I could think of was that if Ana Harmond knew about the seven seals, the organization's plans were significantly bigger than I thought. He was right—it *was* important—and it potentially did affect him and his daughter. Hell, it affected everyone on that side of the Veil. But right now, it didn't matter. I needed it to not matter. Even if it did—even if it could matter right then—the same answer was at the end of the path. The path that started here, at the bottom of this chasm.

There were countless cracks with bits of orange light struggling to climb out of them. The stone was hot as we walked across it. The little spurts of hellfire were like hands grabbing at our feet as we walked across the searing basalt. It moved ever so slightly as it floated atop the molten stone beneath. Across from the landing point of the stairs was a door, carved directly into the stone. Flaming runes were inscribed on it. *Ves Muul err Hagaat*—The Cradle of Fire. I put my hand behind me to signal Prescott to stop, and he did. As I approached the towering stone a shrill voice seeped through it.

"Who is it that seeks an audience with our Lord?"

"You know who it is. Open the door," I said.

"I'm sorry, I didn't get that. Who is it?"

"Do not try my patience, imp. Open the door or I will open it for you," I replied, making sure he could hear the impatience in my tone.

"I'm sorry, my lord, but no one enters the cradle without due cause."

I looked at Prescott, and he stepped back. My hand grew black and began to burn hotter than the fire we were now standing over. I slashed with my hand—once, then again, over and over. The cuts were clean, right through the stone. I pulled back and hit the now-fragile door and sent the pieces careening out into the realm of fire. I stepped through the door and saw the imp half crushed beneath some of the rubble I had just cast out over him. I walked over to him and bent down.

"I told you to open the door," I said.

The imp struggled to move the stone, but it was futile.

"My master will not be pleased about this intrusion, nor the treatment of his disciples."

My hand moved out to his neck. My fingers wrapped around his scrawny frame, and I gripped him tightly. "You listen here. He doesn't give a shit about you, or that fucking door. I could rip you apart right now and no one would care. Now, where is he?"

The boney finger of the imp pointed out toward a cliff. In the distance I could see a pillar of flame climbing into eternity. It looked like the boss was at home. Good.

I yelled for Prescott, who ran up behind me, as we approached the cliff. From the top we could see what were called the Pits. Squirming within them were the countless souls of those doomed to suffer until they had paid their karmic balance. From here they were just flecks of motion, but I knew what went on there. I pointed to the pillar of flame in the far distance and informed my companion that was where we were going. He reluctantly nodded.

The cliff, much like the chasm we had just come down, had a sheer face, save a disfigured staircase that led down. The fire subsided as we moved toward the landing that would lead us through the Pits and then across the Fields of Anguish. It had been a very long time since I had been here. Now, even more so than any time before, I really didn't want to be there. As we descended, Prescott asked what the motion was; I prepared to give him the short version.

"Is that where I'm going to end up?" he asked.

"Unlikely," I said. "Those in the Pits are there because they failed to honor their debts. Good people, bad people—everyone is held to the same standards. The conventional idea of hell isn't real. It's not fire; it's not brimstone—not always, at least. Mostly it's reliving your greatest failures. Everyone comes here at some point in their existence. Depends on how many lives you've lived and whether you could keep your promises."

"So, I best not chicken out of our agreement, then."

"Wouldn't recommend it."

"Why debts, though? Aren't there worse things than not keeping a promise?"

"Yes, there are worse things, and there are places for those things. This place is the land of fraud. This is where the liars come, but not just any liars—those who betrayed the trust of someone who needed them. It's what he likes. His currency is deception, and what better a prison for him to have than for those who made deals and didn't follow through."

As we got closer to the Pits, the fire subsided and the heat went along with it. It grew darker and darker until we reached the bottom. The ground was obsidian and had a distinct sheen to it; we could see our reflections. There were relatively few screams of pain as we walked across the risings above the Pits; only tears of sadness coming from men and women who had wronged others by their own actions or inactions. I hated being there. I had taken every one of them by the hand and

196

comforted them before returning them to the Source, and this is where it had sent them to serve their sentence before being given another chance. I wondered, many times, if these punishments were just. But it was not my choice to make. I was just the garbage man, cleaning up the souls for the big machine of existence.

The voice of Nathan Prescott cut through the cries of sadness. "I can't believe God lets this happen."

"God doesn't," I said.

"What do you mean?"

"There is no God."

"So, *you* bring them here?"

"No . . ." I said. "I take them to the Source, and it decides where they go from there."

"Hate to break it to you, but this 'Source' thing you take people to—that's God."

"No . . . it's not."

"And how do you know?"

"Because like you said, God wouldn't let this happen."

"Then what is it?" he asked.

"The best way that you will understand it is that it's like a big coin sorting machine. And like that machine it doesn't play favorites, it only sorts. Souls with different states go to different places. Some are taken here; some are immediately sent back to earth to live again; some stay as spirits; and a bunch of other options. Not God."

"Then, where is he?" Prescott asked.

"Nowhere," I said, starting to get irritated.

"How do you know?" he asked, not sensing that I was losing patience.

"I don't, but I just do, you know?"

197

"No."

"Look, none of this shit matters! Let's just do what we came here to do and move on!"

I came down out of my anger and could see that he was crying. I rolled my eyes and thought to myself how weak he was as a person. Then I realized that he wasn't talking to annoy me or challenge me. He couldn't handle where he was and that was how he was handling it, by talking. Prescott fell to his knees and his face went into his hands.

"I'm sorry," he whimpered. "I don't know why I'm acting this way."

I kneeled down next to him. My anger turned to compassion, but I didn't know what to do. I had pushed him over the edge and I needed to fix it but didn't know how. *What would Vera do?* I asked myself. I leaned in close to him and pulled him into my chest.

"I'll get you through this. Just a little bit further, okay?"

Prescott nodded into my chest and sucked all his emotion back in before standing up.

We needed to be quick, so I picked up the pace and tried to keep him talking.

"So what else do you want to know?"

I could hear him wiping the tears away from his face as he readied his question.

"So those seven bigger holes you talked about earlier . . ."

"Yeah, what about them?" I asked, unsure of where this was going.

"You said they were easier to come through, but nothing did. You said they were sealed. Well, seals wear out."

"Not these seals."

Prescott ignored me. "What happens if one of them opens

up?"

"Nothing," I said, hoping he would leave it there.

He didn't.

"That doesn't make sense. Why doesn't anything happen?"

This was not something I wanted to answer, but I couldn't risk him breaking down again; he might not snap out of it. So, I answered. "I said they're easier to slip through. That doesn't mean there aren't any stipulations to go along with that."

"So, what makes them different?"

We we're getting into the stuff that mortals aren't supposed to know and aren't supposed to know for a reason. But I didn't have a choice. We weren't going to make it away from the pits before I would have to answer.

"Remember how Ana talked about 'Eternals'?" I asked.

"Yeah, I didn't understand."

"You're about to," I said. "You never tell anyone this, got it?" I was hoping he would say that he wasn't so sure he wanted to know any more. I gave him time to say it, but it never came.

"Okay . . ." he said.

I gritted my teeth and spilled. "In the beginning there wasn't just me; there were six others. Unbound by time, like me, they governed a piece of existence. They were Karma, Truth, Justice, Wisdom, Grace, Will, and Order. Each of the Eternals is bound to one of the seven seals. Nothing goes through one of the 'big' holes unless the Eternals say it does. That's how the realms remain separate."

"You said six plus you. I didn't hear Death on that list," Prescott said.

"That's because it's not. Technically, I am Order," I said.

"So, when the book of Revelations depicts death riding upon a pale horse, that wouldn't be you?"

199

"It's a book written by men who think they know God but have no idea what the truth is."

"But don't they talk about the seven seals in the book?"

"Yes, but the seals don't just break. They have to be broken by Eternals themselves. And that's not going to happen."

"Why not?"

"Because there's no reason for them to be. Each of the Eternals is like me—powerful. And each seal would have to be broken willingly."

"And Ana and her followers want to kill you to prevent the end of the world, and it's all bullshit?"

"Yes. There are a lot of things I know, and even more I don't, Nathan. But one of the things I'm sure of is that humanity will go to extraordinary lengths to defend the things they care about, and that includes ideas."

"Which is why I'm here," he said with sadness in his voice.

I nodded solemnly. When I raised my eyes, I could see the end of the line. The barrier between the Pits and the lands of the Duke were separated by what I can only liken to a transparent wall of glass. It rippled and warped just a little as it held back the flames of the Fields of Anguish.

I pointed out over the fields to the towering inferno in the distance.

"Brace yourself!" I said. "This is going to hurt."

"That looks really. . .really far away," he said.

"It is," I replied. "Probably a few weeks."

"A few weeks? In that? I thought you said we were short on time."

"We are, but time runs slower here, and this deep in hell, time practically stands still. A week in the fields is but a moment on the surface."

I lowered my shoulder and rushed forward. The barrier broke and fell like shards of glass from a window. From that point the pits ended, and the Fields of Anguish began.

A blast of hellfire tore into me and tried to push me back. I turned around to see Prescott hit by the same wall of flame. He stumbled and fell as the fire gouged chunks of flesh from him. He cried out in pain but gathered himself and rose to his feet. He struggled to speak, but slowly was able to force the words out.

"This . . . this is . . . mu . . . much . . . better," he said as he forced a smile that was quickly wiped off by a blast of flame. He was making jokes; it was a good sign.

"You sure you're okay?" I asked.

"It's better than listening to all those people suffer," he said. He was toughening up. I liked it. He would be fine, at least for the trek through the fields.

We fought against the flaming tempest for several as long as he could before resting. The hours turned to days, the days to weeks. Through it, Prescott held his own, a far cry from the image of the man in my mind. I had pictured him as weak and easily influenced. But that wasn't the case anymore. He had a different kind of strength, one that I couldn't quite peg, but it was there all the same.

As we drew closer to our destination, the heat became more intense, making progress slower. But it was easy to see the pillar of flame that rose from the heart of Blackhold, the Duke's palace now. And the closer we got, the more strength it seemed to give Prescott. Its immense size stood out even against the fiery storm that swirled around us. We were almost there.

I felt almost weightless as I stepped out of the torrent of

flames and onto the more polished obsidian at the base of Blackhold. Prescott came in right behind me and took a nosedive onto the hard surface. I could see the steam rising from him as he lifted himself to his feet. He was out of breath, but his resolve was unshaken. He had done well. But the hardship was far from over. I could hear the laughing of imps and other demons coming from inside the keep.

The building itself was ornate and well made, built to withstand the tempest of hellfire for all time. It would have stood for millennia had it been composed of corporeal matter. Adorning the outside were rows of various types of carved demons. They stood watch on each side of the long, wide steps the led to the antechamber. The stairs themselves were steep, much more so than would have been acceptable across on the other side of the Veil. At the top was a massive black gate with a carved obsidian dragon adorning the frame. Its eyes glowed with an ominous burning orange, as if the fires of hell were dancing inside of them.

We moved up the steps and between the black wings of the dragon into the antechamber. Before us was a long, cavernous hallway that would lead into the throne room where I was sure the Duke would be waiting for us. There were four pillars on either side that ran the length of the room. They, like the floor, were comprised of black volcanic glass and were accented with what I can only describe as red gold. The dancing light on the blood metal made the room itself feel alive. There was nothing but the feeling of dread as we walked the sheen path through the center of the room.

The echo of impish laughs reverberated as we neared the end. The way the distant light from the fire in the throne room danced across the mirrored stone and crimson gold reinforced the thought that the fortress itself was breathing. I thought back to the previous times I had been here and did not remember it being this way. When we reached the end, I was glad to be done with it, until the discomfort rose back up as the cackling of the imps came to an abrupt halt.

The power held within the words as they were spoken hit me like a hammer to the chest.

"Come in," they said.

Had the construction been anything less than it was the entire building would have shaken. I looked over at Prescott, who was still like iron. The echo of the voice faded, and we took the first steps up another small flight of black stairs—ones that would lead us to the Demon Lord's throne.

The smooth decor turned to sand and ash as we stood at the top of the stairs. In the distance we could see the pillar of flame rising up from behind the black throne. As we got closer we could see the fires rising into the infinite void through what looked like a tear in the world. It spewed from the scorched and jagged earth as if it was an artery pumping the very lifeblood of hell into the sky. What started as a crackle of flames became a roar, and the world around us drained of color.

When we were close enough to see, I noticed that there was no one sitting on the obsidian throne. Instead, standing motionless at the bottom of the stairs that led up to the empty chair was a figure draped in a black shawl over long robes and a hood. I motioned to Prescott to stay back, and he did.

I approached the figure. Its hand rose when it felt I was close enough. Its fingers were protruding from beneath the black cloth. They were long and boney, a sign of a harsh tenure here. I attempted to yell over the roar of the flames, but I knew my words would be drowned out. The figure didn't respond; it just stood there with its hand out for me to stop. As if it was trying to reach out and touch me, feel me. I tried a few more times to yell but got no response. So, I did what I should have done from the start: I focused. In an instant a shard of me broke off and appeared next to the cloaked figure.

It was but a part of me, but it was real enough. I grabbed the cloak from behind and pulled the figure in close to me before placing my hand to its throat.

"Where is he?" I asked as threateningly as I could. There was no answer. There wasn't even a reaction. Just a black shadow hiding the face of the creature beneath the cloak. "Where is he?!" I belted into the face of the figure. I could feel my rage building and my patience growing thin. All of it fell away as a sound emerged that cut right through the howl of the flames.

A great laugh emerged from the heart of the fire, and from out of the flames strode a man in a stark-white suit. His eyes, like his hair, were of the deepest black, empty and cold. He was clapping as he walked toward me, clearly amused. I, however, was not. In a puff of black smoke and bright orange, he vanished. A moment later there was another puff of orange and black. The man appeared again, legs crossed, sitting on the black throne.

It was the Duke.

The Duke snapped his fingers, and there was a burst of wind. The pillar of flame withdrew into the world, and, as it did, it sucked everything toward it. I watched as the force of the wind pulled Prescott off his feet and hurled him toward us. The shard of me cast the figure I was holding to the ground and leaped in front of Prescott, catching him before he was sucked into the swirling flames as they fled back into the depths. It was only a few moments, but I'm sure from the look on Nathan's face as I sat him down, it felt like forever. I walked to where Prescott was sitting and absorbed the shard of myself.

"Great show," the Duke said. "The look on his face was priceless." He flailed his arms and imitated how Prescott had looked as he was being hurled through the air.

"Yeah, great show," I said sarcastically.

"Oh, c'mon, Grimm. You have to liven up a little. Get it—'liven up'?"

I gave no response.

"Tough crowd," he said. "Then again, it is you. I shouldn't expect anything more than the morose stare of the man who would be Death. So, what can I do for you?"

I thought about whether I should be up front or spin a tail, then I remembered it was indeed "me" and, different or not, sometimes you have to play to expectations. "I need your help," I said.

"Interesting," the Duke said. "With . . .?"

"Finding someone—well, *two* someones."

"And what do I get out of this?"

"Potentially, a soul," I said.

"Whose?"

"Mine," Prescott said as he raised himself to his feet before dusting off the ash and sand.

"I can bring you a soul anytime," I said. "But it's something different when they come willingly, wouldn't you say?"

"I would very much agree with that," the Duke replied.

"So, shall we speak terms?" I asked.

"You have my attention."

"The two people I'm looking for, I know that you know how

205

to find them. The deal is, you tell me where they are, or—even better—bring them to me. In return, Mr. Prescott will submit himself to the *Orros Uhlgat*. If he fails, he's yours. Deal?"

I wished for a moment that the black emptiness of the Duke's eyes was not exactly that, so I could read him. The silence was hard to bear. From the corner of my eye I saw Prescott beckoning me over. I slid slowly back toward where he was sitting.

"What the hell is an Orro, or whatever the hell you said?"

"It's a test," I whispered back.

"Of what?"

"Your goodness of heart," I said, and then moved back toward the throne.

"Well?" I asked. The Duke didn't answer. It was then that I realized that his focus had changed. He wasn't thinking about the deal; he was staring at—no, *into*—me. I saw it and felt the power in me flash to the surface, as if I would have to defend myself at any moment. I stymied it and asked again, with more authority, "Well?!"

The Duke shifted in his black throne before speaking. "You know, something is different. About you, I mean. Can't quite put my finger on it, but I think something has gotten into you."

I looked back at him, my gaze like stone. He fidgeted for a moment before vaulting off his chair and giving a short clap. I can only describe it as giddy, like a child getting a new toy. He moved unnaturally quickly toward me, stopping at arm's reach. The lids around his atramentous eyes squinted as his lips twisted and curled before finally settling into a smile. His lips parted and revealed a set of vibrantly white teeth. Those split as well, revealing a black-and-blue tongue. He ran it along the front of his chomps before settling it once again inside his mouth. I could smell the fire and brimstone on his breath. It made me want to put my fist into his mouth to block the stench.

When he was done staring I asked one last time, "Well?" I put no false weight on it, but my anger was present with every letter.

"You know, there are times when you think you know someone, or something. Times when every minuscule detail is within your scope of understanding. And then there are times when it isn't. I often find that it is in these times that you get smacked in the face by something you never would have expected. This is one of those moments, Mr. Grimm."

"The first or the second?"

"The second. And, mm-mmm, I like the way it tastes."

"You are trying my patience," I replied. "What are you getting at?"

"You," he said. "More specifically, your emotional growth, or at least that's what I think it is. I can't tell, and that makes it exciting. You are exceptionally intelligent, and unparalleled in your knowledge of this world. But the one thing that you could never understand, that eluded you, even though you thought it didn't, was human emotion. So nuanced, it is impossible to intellectualize. And yet, somehow, you figured it out; which leads me to conclude that—"

I didn't let him finish. My fingers grasped his black tie and I pulled him toward me. My other hand clinched, and I swung. My knuckles dug into his cheek and neck. The force lifted him off his feet and sent him tumbling. He would have landed flat on his back had it not been for another puff of fire and shadow that deposited him almost exactly where he began.

He winced in pain at the strike and began to move his jaw around. Then that pain turned to a laugh. It grew louder, which only made me angrier.

I moved like lightning and grabbed him by the neck. Then I squeezed. The cries of pain once more turned into laughter. I had had enough. I struck him again. But the laughing continued. I slid my hands to his head like I was holding a melon. There would be no more laughing. I felt the bones turn to dust between my fingers as I squeezed. As his head disintegrated in my hands, so did the rest of him. His body vanished in flash of ash and smoke. The empty white suit hit the sand and burst into flames, and then it, too, was gone.

I waited a moment, knowing what would happen next. I felt the ground tremble, and a moment later the land heaved and the massive pillar of flame erupted once again from behind the black throne. Just as before, the Duke emerged, clad in white and clapping.

"Ohhhhh, I am very amused," he said as he vanished and appeared again on the obsidian chair in a flash of smoke. "I never thought you would lay a hand on me. Then again, I was giving a monologue right before it happened. So, I guess I had it coming."

"Shut up," I said, as politely as I could.

"Now, now, don't be rude, Cyrus. You are a guest in my house, remember that," the Duke said, his tone descending into the solemn kind.

"And if I don't?" I asked, responding to his veiled threat.

There was another flash of black, after which I felt pressure on my neck. I came out of the daze to see the smoke dissipate from where the Duke had been sitting. He was behind me, and had his hand around my throat, pulling me toward him. I crooked my head and looked behind me. In his other hand he held a black sword. He had shoved it through my back. I looked forward again and I could see it jutting out of my sternum.

"I will treat you in kind," he whispered in my ear. I thought that I would have been furious, but I wasn't. Instead I thought back to every interaction I had ever had with the Demon Lord. No one would go so far as to calling him a friend, but he wasn't an enemy, either. He was a negative force in the universe, to be sure, but not my enemy, especially not now. Everything came into perspective in that moment as I watched his sword protruding from me. I needed him to understand it as well.

I reached down and grabbed the black blade and twisted. The metal splintered and gave. I pulled the broken steel and cast it to the side. With my other hand I took hold of his, the one on my neck. I grasped firmly and twisted as well, though more slowly. As I did, I turned around. The sound of the broken hilt falling away from my back into the sand coincided with the painful lurch of the Duke as he fell to his knees under his gnarled arm. I turned around and spoke to him like the old acquaintances we were.

"It is important that you understand this," I said. "I am not who I once was. There are things in motion that mean a great deal to me, and, as such, I am a little touchy right now."

"Clearly," he replied through his gritted, sparkling teeth.

"Now, I'm going to let you up in a moment, and when I do, we're going to have a nice, civil conversation. At the end of it, you're going to realize it's a good deal, accept it, and we both get what we want. Okay?"

The Duke nodded, and I let him up. He stood, and I extended my hand. He grabbed it and gave one firm shake. He rubbed his shoulder, which I found odd, given the decidedly less pleasant treatment his skull and pride had just endured. He snapped his fingers back into place and walked away from me. There was a slight tremble, and then a large stone table rose between us from the sand. The chairs slid out by themselves, and we took our seats across from each other. I gave the same proposition I had before.

"You know, Cyrus, I appreciate that you are growing; it takes a lot to change, and I respect that."

"And I appreciate that, but it has nothing to do with my offer," I said.

"Ah, but you see, that's where you're wrong, my friend—very wrong. It has *everything* to do with your offer."

I felt a bit of worry shiver up my spine. The hairs on the back of my neck were at attention. He continued.

"Knowing what I know now, that thing I discovered earlier was exactly what this deal needed," he said.

"And what is that?" I asked.

"You see, emotions make things real; they put things in perspective. Give consequence. Strong reactions make for understanding. Just as I'm sure the hairs on your neck are a little bit, shall we say, aware. They tell you to be afraid. You shouldn't be, and yet you are. Your instincts tell you that you should be. You can tell a lot about a person not from their actions, but their reactions. Wouldn't you agree?"

"This means what exactly?"

"It means I decline your offer," the Duke said. There was a small pause before he spoke again. "Come see why."

I had almost forgotten about the cloaked figure I had cast to the side when we had first arrived. It walked to the table and stood beside the Duke.

"Now," he said, "just because I have declined your deal doesn't mean I don't want to give you what you want." He nodded to the figure. The bony fingers moved out and up toward the hood and pulled it back.

My heart sank into my stomach as I saw the skeletal face of Vera emerge from beneath it. I vaulted from my chair toward her. She vanished in a puff of smoke as I landed in the sand on the other side of the table.

"Where is she!?" I demanded.

"Reactions, my friend. Reactions speak volumes."

I stood up and grabbed him again, preparing to take his head off a second time. I expected him to resist, but he didn't. I could feel the stench of sulfur on his breath and the pearly sheen on his teeth staring back at me. I had overplayed my hand. I shoved him back into his chair and walked around the table to my seat. The Duke straightened his alabaster coat and sat smugly, head cocked slightly to the side. He spoke as I sat back down.

"I have the other one, too," he said.

"How?" I asked. "How did you even know?"

"Know what? Where to find them? Or that you love her?"

"Where to find them. Wait, what do you mean *love*?"

The Duke cackled madly. "You don't even understand it yet. Oh, that's good. It's going to make the pain so much sweeter."

I sprung from my seat and pointed my finger in his face. "Listen here, you motherfucker. You hurt her, and you're going to wish it was possible for you to die!"

"You know, Cyrus, I love these moments—so tasty. This one right here is easily the best thing I've had in the past few millennia." He paused for a moment, waiting for me to react. I didn't.

211

"Still oblivious?" he asked. "Okay, I'll spill. I wasn't talking about her pain. You see, that pain doesn't matter. She's endured plenty of that in the centuries she's been here with me."

I thought about it and remembered how time works in this place. She had been gone for so little time to those on earth. But for her, it had been much longer. She must have thought I'd forgotten about her. The Duke's words brought me back to the present.

"It doesn't matter—we will get to that part later," he said. "For now, let's get back to business. Sit."

I didn't.

"Sit the fuck down!" he said. I wanted to punch in the prick's glistening white teeth before I sat. But it wasn't going to help me. So, I did as he commanded.

"So, I have what you want. Now let's talk about how you get it," he said.

"What do you want?" I asked.

"Just a favor, or two."

"What kind of favor?"

"The best kind: the kind I save for later—or maybe not. I haven't decided. It's more fun that way," he said, "So, what do you say, Mr. Grimm? Would you care to roll the dice?"

"Do I have an alternative?" I asked.

"Not really."

I thought about it for a moment. I knew who I was dealing with, and he wouldn't have been pressing me for this deal if another way was available to him. That meant what he asked for would be big. But, my balls were in the vise, and this son of a bitch knew it.

"Fine," I said as I stood up.

The Duke followed suit, checking the buttons on his white coat. He was making me wait. After what felt like an hour, he stretched his hand across the table. I looked at it for a moment, then at him. His pearly whites were beaming back at me.

"So, just to reiterate," I said, "you get a favor, and I get the girls, right?"

He closed his lips and momentarily grew less smug before giving a small nod and reasserting his hand.

I stretched mine across the table and took his. His lips separated, and he looked at my hand once more before giving it single hearty shake. As the deal was completed, a rune of red and gold emblazoned itself on the back of my hand. As it did I squeezed his hand and felt the bones in it collapse beneath the pressure. As this occurred I pulled him closer—close enough to whisper in his ear.

"Oh, and just so we're clear," I said. "You try to fuck me over on this, and I will make you wish that you were capable of dying. Got it?"

I released his hand, and he pulled its mangled form away from me before resetting the bones in a series of painful sounding pops. The sheen of his teeth was more apparent than ever as his lips curled up at me. The stink of his breath wafted across the table with the words that I knew would set our agreement in motion.

"Oh yes, my dear Mr. Grimm. I understand perfectly." He paused for a moment as a final pop rang out as he reset the last bone in his hand. "But I don't think you have to worry about that."

I waited patiently for him to hold up his end of the bargain, but he just stood there, his big fucking grin mocking me.

"Well?" I asked.

GRIMM

"Oh, right—you want the girls," he said.

"Yeah," I said. "That's the deal."

"Ohhh, I see. You assumed I would give them to you now," he said, his smile growing wider.

I felt my lips purse and my anger start seething into rage. My jaw clinched, and the grinding sound of my teeth cut through the wail of the scorching wind. I began to move toward him, my intent clear.

"Wait, wait, wait," the Duke said before clearing his throat. "I've decided that I will go ahead and cash in that favor right now. When it's done, you can have the girls, okay?"

"I'm listening," I said through my still-clinched teeth.

"I was planning on waiting, you know, for a more dramatic item. But I guess it really doesn't matter. This was on the agenda."

"What do you want?" I asked.

"Actually, I think you will rather enjoy this. 'Right up your alley' so to speak, What do you say, Mr. Grimm? Time to have a little fun?"

10

A Dangerous Game

I felt the warp of space around me as Nathan Prescott and I were drawn back over to the physical realm. He landed hard and took a deep breath as he felt himself return to the land of the living. The color bled back into his face, and he rolled over onto his back. There was silence in the room. Vince and Ramsey had expected me to come back with the girls, or at least Vera. I could see the disappointment on their faces when they realized she wasn't with me—and Nathan was instead. They stood up in anticipation of our news. I wanted to come right out and say it, but this was something that needed more than just a simple explanation. A change of scenery was first on the list. We walked up through the club and into Vince's office.

"So where are the girls?" Ramsey asked, his impatience driving the question. I thought of how best to answer, but Prescott blurted it out without thinking.

"He has them. He knew we were looking for them. And he's going to milk it for everything he can," he said.

"How could he have known?" Vince asked.

I gave Prescott a stern look, so he would keep his mouth shut. He caught my drift, but it was too late—the cat was out.

"I don't know," I said. "And what's worse, he knows how much they're worth."

"Fuck! What do we do now?" Vince asked.

"Plans change. I still made a deal with him," I said.

Vince and Ramsey stayed silent, each of them too scared at first to find out more. Eventually Vince spoke.

"And that means . . .?"

"He wanted a favor."

"I don't like the sound of that," Ramsey said.

"Here's where it gets weird," I said. "What he wants seems way too easy."

"What do you mean 'easy'?" Vince asked, his face brandished a look of concern.

"He just wants me to find and bring him a soul," I said.

"You already took him a soul," Ramsey said. "No offense, Nate."

"None taken," Prescott replied.

"A very particular soul," I said.

"And why can't he get this soul himself?" Vince asked. "He has the means to find just about anyone. What makes this one soul so special?"

I thought about what I was going to say. The next words that came out of my mouth would need to be chosen very carefully. But again, I didn't get the chance. Prescott filled in the blank before I could find a way to be delicate about the situation.

"He wants some guy named Gerald Flynn, whoever the fuck *that* is."

A look of horror washed over Vince's face as he heard the

words. He stood up, and the shock turned to anger just before he started pacing around the office.

"No," he said. "Gary Flynn? No! This—this is not how this is supposed to go. Of everyone it could be, it can't that motherfucker. Why him? Why!?"

Prescott was startled by Vince's reaction, and did his best to walk it back.

"He can't be that important, can he?" asked Prescott.

"You god damn right he is!" yelled Vince. "That mother-fucker took . . . he's the one that turned me into this. When he gets out of prison, he's mine—no one else's. Especially not some fucking demon. That son of a bitch has to answer for what he did."

I looked at Prescott, who was leaning forward, his hand over his mouth, knowing that he had really stepped in shit. He stood up and walked toward Vince, trying to calm him down. I heard the sound of the desk opening and the sharp metallic click of the pistol's slide. Ramsey leaped to his feet as well, and Prescott halted in his tracks, both of them with their hands raised.

"You don't fucking touch me!" Vince yelled, his head a whirlwind.

I kept my cool, never leaving my chair. "Calm down, Vince," I said as soothingly as I could.

"Shut up!" he yelled. "This is not right, not right."

"I never said it was. I'm just saying that's what I was asked to do."

"Bullshit!" he continued. "Why the fuck does he even want that piece of shit? There's no reason he could."

"Clearly there is," I said. "But that's something that we're going to have to figure out as a team."

Vince looked as if he were going to lose it—hell, for all I knew, he probably already had. I didn't expect him to take it well, but this was much worse than I had anticipated. His breathing sped up. It was happening—he was going to shoot someone. I had seen it in other people's eyes before. It was too late. It was damage control at this point. I needed to make sure when the trigger was pulled that the gun wasn't pointed at Prescott or Ramsey, or even himself. I needed his attention on me, and calm wasn't going to cut it anymore. I cast the chair aside as I stood up.

"Hey!" I yelled at Vince as I moved toward him. "Quit being stupid about this. We're not the enemy, and the Duke isn't the enemy—hell, fucking Gary Flynn isn't even the enemy. The enemy is out there, putting together and working on a plan to bring this world to an end."

"Stay away, Cy," Vince said, a look of pure anguish on his face. "This is not how it's going to be."

"Give me the gun, Vince."

"Stay back!"

"I said give me the gun!" I yelled as I stepped in front of him. A deafening pop rang out. I could see the smoke from the barrel of the gun. I moved my eyes up to Vince. His anger was replaced with terror.

"Oh my God," he said. "I am so sorry. No, no, no, no, no, no."

The gun fell limp in his hand. I grabbed it gently and placed it on the desk beside me. I approached him slowly, and he fell into my arms weeping.

"It's okay," I said. "Everything is going to be okay."

I could feel the emotional energy spilling out of him. As I held him, I remember thinking, that this would be the moment that would give him closure. He had already lost Joe and Vera soon afterwards. I honestly think that, for him, this was finally the chance for him to grieve. It wasn't Gary Flynn that set him off—it was everything else he had been through with me. The mention of Flynn was just the straw that broke the camel's back.

I don't know how long I held him, or how long he cried. But Prescott and Ramsey did the right thing and waited for him to finish. Vince lifted his head from my shoulder and gave me a look of thanks before glancing around the room through his bright-red eyes. It took only a few seconds for him to turn Italian again.

"This NEVER leaves this room," he threatened in jest (but not really).

Vince told the story of Flynn to Ramsey and Prescott. When it was over I brought the conversation back on track.

"So," I said, "the Duke wants Flynn."

"So, take him Flynn," Ramsey said.

"It's not that simple," Vince said.

"Why not?" Prescott asked. "You can just zap right in there, kill him, take his soul, and you're done."

"You're right, he can. But he also said it's too easy. The Duke wouldn't ask unless he actually got something out of it—something of real value. So, there's a reason he wants Flynn and it sure as hell isn't just to piss me off," Vince said.

"Okay, so what do we do, then?" Prescott asked.

"We find out why this is important to him," I said. "He made it very clear that whatever his favor would be was going to be painful, very painful. He may have been bluffing to get under my skin, but somehow I really doubt it."

"I can find out anything you need to know about Gary

Flynn," Ramsey said.

"Good. Do it," I said. "Nate, right now you're a fugitive, so you need to stay out of sight. And I know exactly where to hide you and still be useful."

"Sounds good," he said. "Where?"

"You get to find me the souls two cops you killed. I can help you get a bead on them, but you are going to have to go in and get them. Vince," I continued.

"Yeah?"

"It's possible Flynn is more valuable alive, as a bargaining chip to the Duke," I said. "Use whatever connections you have and give him an escape plan, in case I need to get him out."

"What are you gonna do?" Ramsey asked.

"I'm going to get us some help."

It had been a long time since I had seen any of the other Eternals. But in light of recent events, I believed it was time to change that. Oman is the aspect of Truth. The look of dread on his face as I walked toward him told me much about what he thought of my unplanned visit.

"What do you want, Cyrus?" he asked, his tone telling me *no* before I even asked the question.

"I need your help. Well, not just your help—everyone's," I said.

"Yeah, that's not going to happen. We don't interfere, you know that."

"No, we're not supposed to interfere, except in extreme circumstances. I think this meets our criteria."

"I don't think so," Oman said, his face still like stone. He turned and started to walk away.

"I was mortal," I said.

He stopped midstride for a moment.

"Walking around as a human does not make you mortal."

"I know the fucking difference, Oman." I paused for a moment to calm myself. "And I'm telling you, I was mortal."

He turned around and looked at me. His stone visage had become one of concern. I had his attention.

"That's not possible," he said, not quite sure he was right anymore.

"You are Truth," I said. "You know better."

"I—I don't believe this. How?"

"Long story. I just need to know you'll have my back when the time comes."

I waited for a response, but Oman just stood there staring at nothing. I realized he was looking at the truth. But I needed him here, at least for the moment.

"Oman? Oman!"

He snapped out of it.

"Yeah? Yeah, I understand," he said, taking a deep breath.

"Good. Tell the others and let me know when it's done."

"Be careful," he said.

"You know me," I replied.

"That's what I'm afraid of."

"Order Oman, not disorder. Always for the sake of balance."

"If you say so."

I could tell he would do as I asked. Then, in a flash of light, he was gone.

"What do we know?" I asked Ramsey. He waved his hand much like he had when I'd first seen him. I walked over. The

221

screen was just an avalanche of numbers and letters moving faster than I could pay attention. I started to talk, but Ramsey raised his hand and I fell silent.

"I'm almost in," he said.

"In where?"

"The good stuff. Prison medical records—specifically, the psych evaluations. I left the public records over there," Ramsey said, pointing to a stack of papers on Vince's desk. "Feel free."

I walked over to the desk and shuffled through the documents. None of it appeared to have any new information. I turned back to Ramsey, who let out an excited whoop as I did.

"Yes," he said. "I'm in!"

The information on the monitor was again scrolling very quickly, much faster than I could read it. Ramsey wasn't fazed at all; he just kept going as the information whizzed by. The document ended, and he leaned back in his chair with a look of confusion on his face.

"What is it?" I asked.

"Either these records are incomplete, or this guy is really, really messing with the heads of his doctors over there."

"Let's assume the records are right," I said. "What's going on?"

"Well, this guy is not—was not—an upstanding citizen before he was convicted of attempted murder. Nothing, and I mean nothing, I could find said that this was a good guy. Drugs, prostitution, theft, gambling, the works—you name it, this guy did it."

"Yeah, we knew that already. So?"

"So, since the first day he's been there, he's been quiet as a mouse. I mean a really, really upstanding guy. His interviews are super clean. This guy doesn't even swear anymore. No outbursts, no altercations, nothing. And people were after this guy in there. He just smiled and took their worst. It wasn't a slow process, either. He wasn't rehabilitated; he was just changed. Something snapped, and his psychiatrists know it. They have the same records we do. They know who this guy is, and they also know that the behavior he's exhibiting is very abnormal for someone with his history. He has daily interviews, and from what it reads this guy isn't even learning anything. Hell, he's probably teaching *them* stuff. I don't get it."

"It doesn't matter," I said.

"How can it not matter?" Ramsey asked.

"The point of this was to find out more about Flynn, to find out why the Duke wants him. Well, based on what you just told me, it's pretty obvious why."

"But it doesn't give us the underlying reason as to why he's acting that way," Ramsey argued.

"I agree, but we can't exactly get that information from out here, can we?"

Ramsey thought for a moment in spite of the obvious answer. "No," he said. "So, what are you going to do?"

"I need to talk to him."

"And you plan on doing that . . . how? Popping in, killing him, and popping out is one thing, but it's a maximum-security prison—you can't just appear out of nowhere and have a conversation with the guy. You also can't just walk through the front door, either."

"Actually, yes I can."

"As who exactly?"

"Detective John Graison," I said. "Okay, I need you to create a link between Flynn's attack on Vince and the murder of

Lawrence Kennedy. Hell, connect him to Detectives Aaron and Marx. I don't care. I just need the paper trail, and I can do the rest."

"Oh, that's good. And it just might be a challenge. Consider it done," Ramsey said.

I nodded and stepped away when the room lit up. The flash of light faded and from its origin point stood Oman.

"What the hell?" Ramsey said, shocked.

"I have news, Grimm."

"Go on."

"I contacted who I could."

"That's great," I said, relieved that I had support.

"No, it's not," Oman replied. I stayed silent. "I found Aiden and Wynn, but not the others."

"Why not? I don't understand," I said.

"They're not there. They're not anywhere. The three of us didn't just look, we scoured everything. Not on Earth, not in hell—nowhere. Which means they're either hiding, or . . ."

"They're not dead," I said. "They can't be."

"And how do you know?" Oman asked. "Humanity almost killed you. That's the reason all this is even happening, isn't it?"

"I know, but . . ."

"We will support you, but not at the risk of ourselves. Do you understand?"

I could feel a whirlwind of anger, frustration, sadness, and other things I can't even put into words churning inside me as I heard him. I wanted to lash out, call him a coward, but I understood why they had made that decision.

"Yes," I replied. "Keep looking; they're out there somewhere. Find them."

"We will do our best."

There was another flash of light, and then Oman was gone. I turned around and saw Ramsey sitting in his chair. His eyes were trying to swallow the room, and his chin would have fallen through the floor if it wasn't attached to the rest of his head.

"That was . . .?"

"Oman, the Aspect of Truth," I said. Ramsey blinked a few times, his mouth still open.

"And the other two he mentioned?"

"Aiden is the Aspect of Will, and Wynn is the Aspect of Wisdom."

"Wait, what? I don't get any of this."

"Yeah, well, I'll explain later. You have work, and I need to get going."

"Just quickly, who are the others?"

"Sai, Karma; Jaina, Grace; and Vaughn, Justice. Me, Order. List complete. Now get those documents set up."

A loud buzz rang out, and the grind of rusty wheels pulling open the chain-link fence quickly replaced it. It was only a few hundred feet to the front entrance, but it felt like a mile. I had walked on the Earth many times before this, and many times before had I walked into dwellings where the social outcasts of mankind were kept. But this was the first time that I had been anxious about it. There was no apparent difference this time versus any other time, but I couldn't help but wonder why this time felt so different.

I pushed the anxiety out of my chest and to the back of my mind. The sound of another buzz and unlocking of the doors drew my attention before the coldness of the steel handle against my skin washed it away all together. There were two guards sitting at a security station alongside a metal detector. I was directed to deposit all metallic objects into a plastic bowl for inspection before walking through the machine. They returned the personal effects I had been given by Prescott to blend in. I pocketed them and proceeded down the hall to another security station. This one was much more comprehensive and was clearly the line where it turned into a prison.

There sat a man inside of a booth with thick metal walls and glass. I heard the click of the speaker, and the man spoke.

"Go ahead," he said.

I placed my fake badge and visitation request into a drawer and closed it. The man opened it from the other side and scanned it into his system. After a few moments the light on his terminal turned green and he slid the documents back to me and motioned me in. A third buzz signaled the opening of the metal gate. I pushed it to enter. Another man walked me down another hall and opened a door. Inside were six booths. Each had a closed-circuit phone and small divider.

"What the fuck is this?" I asked. "I ain't no visitor; I'm a detective. This is not a courtesy call for this scumbag."

The guard's eyes widened, and he shuffled his feet, not knowing what to say.

"Yeah, this is for a case, guy. I need a more private setting."

I started walking toward the door, and he followed me.

"I need to get sign-off from my sergeant."

"What do you think this fucking paper is?" I said, waving the forged document around. "Here," I said, handing it to him.

He read it for a second and then handed it back when he

was satisfied.

"This way," he said.

The door to a large, empty concrete room opened, and there was nothing but a single steel chair and a camera in the corner of the room. The guard informed me that all imagery was recorded and to not attempt to hand the inmate anything. I acknowledged, and he closed the door behind me. I don't know how long I waited before the door on the other side of the room opened, but it seemed like quite a while. A guard escorted in Flynn, who was in gray jumpsuit and full shackles. The guard walked him to the chair and shoved him into it by his shoulder.

"He's all yours," he said before exiting the room via the same door he'd entered.

Gary Flynn looked at me for a moment, unsure of why he was there. But the look of confusion on his face fell away and was replaced with a small smile. I started to size him up in return, so I could decide how best to approach our conversation. I never got the chance.

"It's good to see you," Flynn said.

"My name is Detect—"

"Let's not do that; it's a waste of time," he said. "It's been a long time. You know, sometimes I forget how everyone looks, and I've missed that."

I didn't know what to say. It might have been bullshit, but I didn't know and it didn't really matter as long as I found out what I needed to. "Who do you think I am?" I asked.

There was a short pause. "Cyrus, it's me."

I looked at him, knowing I had never taken the time to get to know this man.

"You don't see me, do you?" he continued. "I suppose not;

this vessel is a bit misleading."

"Who are you?" I asked.

"It doesn't matter. The better question is, why are you here?"

"That's where you're wrong," I replied. "Why I'm here is the part that doesn't matter."

"Oh, but it does, my friend. As a matter of fact, the reason you're here is the only thing out of this exchange that really does matter."

He was right—the reason I was there was important. But he shouldn't have known that it was. Yet somehow, he did. So, I went along with it."

"Well, as it turns out, someone thinks you're important, and I'm here to find out why," I said.

"So, you were sent, then. Good. I'm glad you question the reason you were sent, because there's no way he would have told you."

"Told me what?"

"Why I'm important."

"So why are you important?" I asked.

"I'm not," Flynn replied, "but what I possess is, a key."

"What key?"

"You know, you were always so smart, and yet so unwilling to see what was right in front of you. Look at me. Really look at me," he said.

I stepped back and took a deep breath. I reached out to feel the soul that rested beneath the physical. There was nothing there—the man was dead—and yet there was something familiar beneath the flesh.

"You're not Gary Flynn," I said.

"No, I'm not."

"So, I ask again. Who are you?"

"I'm your best friend. At least I *was*, a very long time ago."

My mind felt like a blender being put on purée. My vision blurred, and I fell to one knee.

"What's happening to me?" I asked.

"You're waking up," he said. I lifted my head and the man sitting in the chair was no longer Gary Flynn.

"Vaughn?" I asked, not quite trusting what was before me.

"Yeah," Vaughn said. "And now you know why you can't find me."

"How did—how did you end up in here?"

"The same way you ended up in this cell with me: by choice."

"What does he want?"

"Me," Vaughn said. "And you as well, apparently. You see, I trapped myself in this body, so that he couldn't have me. But it appears he found a way to get me, anyway."

Everything fell into place in my head. "The key," I said.

"Yeah, the key," Vaughn said.

"He's going to use you to break a seal," I said. Vaughn nodded. "But it's just one. Breaking one seal gets him nothing. There are six more," I said.

"Are there?"

I remembered what Oman had told me, and that struck me, too. "No," I said, "he's already taken the others. With you he has three."

"And you make four," Vaughn said. "And four is all he needs to move across the Veil."

"He can't use me," I said. "I owe him one favor. And he just used it to have me bring you to him."

"Are you sure?"

I replayed the conversation in my head. I could feel his fingers wrapped around my hand and hear the words.

A favor or two.

I closed my eyes and gritted my teeth in frustration. I wanted to put my fist through the wall, and probably would have if it wouldn't have alerted the guards. "Fuck!" I yelled, and then again, over and over, before catching myself and taking a deep breath.

"Fuck is right," Vaughn said.

"So, what the fuck are we going to do now?" I asked, knowing that my plans were now shot to shit.

"You do your favor, and then you find a way out of the other one."

"I can't just deliver you to him," I said.

"And you can't refuse, either. You know what happens if you do. If that happens, he has you anyway."

"There has to be another way," I said.

"You know there isn't," Vaughn said. "Now do it."

"No," I said.

"Do it!"

"I won't."

"Then I'm sorry, my friend," he said. "It's not your choice anymore."

Vaughn stood up from the chair. He gave a smile that clearly meant good-bye and dashed for the wall. He rammed his head into it as hard as he could and split his forehead open, leaving behind a smear of blood. He cocked his head back and smashed it against the concrete again and again, a third time, a fourth. I felt like I was moving in slow motion as I heard the bone fracture and saw his skull begin to cave in. Five, six, seven, and he fell back, a bloody mess where his face used to be.

His body started to convulse as the guards rushed in through the doors. All sound stopped as the guards did their best until the medical personnel came into the room. But the body was still, just an empty shell now. My eyes darted around the room, and there was a small flash that only I could see. I felt his hand on my shoulder and I turned to see the face of my friend. I could smell the sulfur and see the white teeth in the shadows behind him. Then, like a cloud of smoke in the wind, they vanished.

I landed hard on the red earth, hard enough that I felt it crack from the impact. I made my way quickly back to Blackhold and climbed the obsidian steps. When I reached the summit, there was an army of demons between me and the throne. The Duke had prepared for my arrival. But there was power coursing through my veins. They would be little more than a warm-up. The smart ones knew it, and simply stood aside. After I ripped apart the first dozen or so, it became clear to the rest that I would carve through them as well, and they moved as well. An ocean of demons parted at my advance. They knew there was only one that I wanted.

The Duke sat at the same table at which we had made our agreement. There was an open chair across from him that I assume he had intended for me. As I came closer he stood and gestured toward it. I ignored him. I moved like a bolt of lightning and was immediately behind him. I drove my blade-hand through his shoulder and down into the stone of the table. I twisted, and he gave out a grunt of pain and then a laugh of contentment.

"I told you it would hurt," he said. "Now, let me up so we can talk."

"Is that your second favor?" I asked.

"Good, good," he said. "So, you did figure it out—at least that part. And no, it's not."

"Then you can talk from there," I replied, giving another twist of my hand. "So, what's the rest of the plan?"

"Oh, please. You really think I would tell?"

"No, but it doesn't hurt to ask nicely. Now, give me the girls."

"Sorry, but the deal is not complete. I still own you."

I slammed my free hand down next to his head, severing his ear. "Remember the part where I told you not to try and fuck me over on this deal? This is you fucking me over. Girls! Now!"

"No," he said, still trying to laugh through the hole in his chest.

I tried to calm myself and react rationally, intelligently. Killing him did nothing for me—he would be back, and I would have gained nothing. I twisted again and leaned down next to his good ear.

"I don't think you understand," I said calmly. "You give me what is owed, I let you up and you get to call in your other favor another day. If you don't—that's your call. But I won't respond in anger and give you what you want. I won't kill you. What I will do, however, is make it my personal mission to ruin your day, every day, until I do get what is owed to me. Got it?"

"Oh, yes, Mr. Grimm, I understand. But you forget I have time on my side. All I have to do is say no for however long it takes you to realize you can't win."

"Actually, I don't think you understand. You made a great observation last time we met: you told me I love her. As you are well aware, that is something that bodes very badly for you. You see, love is the enemy of reason. It makes people do things that defy understanding. It makes people do things that are not in their best interests. Now, I'm going to lean down next to you, and I want you to look into my eyes and tell me, does it look like I give a fuck about winning anymore?"

I put my boot into the door of Vince's office, vaulting it open. Vince and Prescott jumped up as it did. But as soon as they saw me their surprise was replaced with relief and they rushed toward me. Each of them took a girl out of my arms and brought them into the office. Though they were spirits, they held enough form that they could be held.

The ladies were in bad shape. Souls, for the most part, are forever; but, as I said at the beginning, that doesn't mean they can't be harmed. Damage had been done, and both Vera and Ana looked like decomposed corpses that I had just dug up out of a graveyard. They were intact, but they needed some rest.

"I don't understand," Ramsey said. I remembered at that moment he couldn't see them.

"I found them," I said.

"They're here?"

"Yeah," I said, pointing to what for him looked like an empty floor. "You've never crossed the Veil; you'll be able to see once you do. Vince."

Vince produced the dagger from inside a small safe beneath his desk. He handed it to Ramsey. I watched as his eyes opened and he saw the truth.

"Any questions?" I asked.

"Nothing from me. Might want to ask them, though," Ramsey said, gesturing toward Vince and Nathan.

"I'm guessing since you have them, everything went off without a hitch?" Vince asked.

"Not exactly," I said.

I walked over to where Vera lay on the floor beside him.

"Hey," she said weekly. She stretched out her hand and touched my face. "I knew you would come for me. Took your sweet time, though."

I remembered that for her it had felt like several lifetimes. It made me feel horrible that she had waited for so long.

"Of course, I came for you," I said. I leaned down and kissed her on the forehead. "You're gonna be okay. Get some rest."

I grabbed her hand from my cheek and placed it on her chest. She closed her eyes. Vince nodded at me, and I stood up to visit our other guest.

"You will get nothing from me," Ana said.

"I understand," I said. "I don't need you to talk; I need you to listen."

Her eyes widened in confusion. Her lips started to move, and so did my hand. I placed my index finger across her lips and said gently, "Shush."

"I think I understand why you did what you did," I said. "You're not afraid of me; you're afraid of what I become if my will is not my own. And you are right to be afraid. But it won't come to that, I promise. You see, I now understand what you claimed I never would. I've met the king on the side of the board across from you. We really are on the same side, and it's time you realized that. I don't need you to say anything; I just need you to think about that."

I turned to Vince and Prescott. "What did you find?"

They looked at each other. I could see that they did not want to disappoint me.

Vince shook his head. "Nothing," he said.

"They have to be somewhere. We need to find them."

"Well, I know this," Vince said. "Aaron and Marx sure as shit aren't down there."

He held up his platinum cross. "I used this to make a few nasties very unhappy. They spilled quite a bit. And they are not down there, I'm absolutely positive."

"Well, shit. Find out anything else?" I asked.

"There's a lot of movement of demons toward weak spots in the Veil. They're planning something."

"Yeah," I said, "and I have an idea about what."

"Care to share?" Ramsey asked.

"The Duke is going to try to tear a hole in the Veil and unleash an army of demons on the physical plane."

It felt like time had stopped after I said it. Too blunt, perhaps.

"So that's bad, right?" Ramsey said.

"Yeah, that's real fucking bad, asshole! Did you not fucking hear him?" Prescott yelled.

"Hey! Calm the fuck down!" Vince said. Prescott stopped and placed his head in his hands. "So, what's the plan, boss?"

"We need to find a new ally who's willing to put aside the differences and help us," I said, looking at the withered spirit of Ana Harmond.

It was dead silent. And then I heard her speak.

"Well, it looks like you figured it out. More impressive than I would have ever given you credit for."

I nodded at her backhanded compliment.

"I know where they are," she said weakly. I walked over to

her and took a knee.

"The cops?" I asked.

She nodded.

"Where?"

"We have them? The group has them," she said.

"Does that mean that you trust me?"

"It seems that we should have trusted you from the very beginning."

"Where can I find them?"

"I don't know where the church is precisely. It moves every few days. I can only tell you where it was."

I looked behind me. "Ramsey, if I give you a list of locations can you build some kind of math thing that will anticipate where the next location will be?"

"If the sample size is big enough I can write an algorithm that should be able to get us a pretty good estimate—so, yeah."

"Good," I said. "Start working on it." He put his head down and started typing.

I leaned closer to Ana. "Thank you," I said. "Thank you for believing in us."

"Just promise me that if it comes to it, you'll do the right thing," she said.

"I promise," I said.

Ana reached her hand out and grabbed mine. I gave it a squeeze. "I have another question," I said.

She nodded for me to continue.

"When we get there, I need to know who to look for. I need to know who's in charge, who to talk to."

"You already know who's in charge," Ana said. "My husband, Adrian."

11

What We Are

The last rays of the sun scattered as we approached the alleyway of the abandoned warehouse where we hoped to find the Church of Ordanis. Ana had explained to us that there was no actual saint they followed the teachings of—only a name. Ordanis: those ordained by God. They believed themselves the last line of defense between Lucifer and the Tribulation. We had figured out much of their fanaticism along the way, but it was different hearing their motivations from the inside. To an extent, I still believed them crazy, but it was controlled crazy; which is much more dangerous. For them, the survival of humanity was worth more to them than their own sanity. I couldn't help but appreciate their conviction.

It had taken us a few weeks to make our way here, and Vera and Ana had still not fully recovered. Outwardly, they looked fine. But their sluggish movements made me feel like we were vulnerable. Ramsey was having a hard time focusing. He was still adjusting to being able to see the dead. He couldn't help but stare at the girls. As we moved down the alley it became darker, until there was nothing but one flickering light over a chained door. I tried to reach out to see if I could feel anyone. It was like trying to see through a thick fog. I got nothing.

"You sure this is where we need to be?" Prescott asked.

"Math doesn't lie," Ramsey said. "It's here."

"Guess we should check," I said. I reached down and twisted the chain, severing it as quietly as I could. The door itself wasn't locked, but it stuck from years of nonuse. Only way we were getting inside was with some noise. I grabbed the handle and braced myself for a hard pull.

"Wait!" Vince said. He waved his hand and it passed through Ana's head. "How about we do a little bit of recon first?"

It was a good idea. "I'll go first and let you guys know," I said.

I stepped through the bricks and into the darkness of the warehouse. There were shredded pieces of plastic hanging from the ceiling. They were draped very strategically around the decrepit construction equipment left behind from when the renovators ran out of money. The room was massive and dark. Only a single faint blue light was illuminated at the farthest end.

I could hear people talking in the distance, from where the singular glow originated. I moved closer to the light, keeping to the shadows as best I could. There were dozens of men and women gathered around the blue glow. Half were dressed in tactical gear and carried automatic firearms; the others were in white lab coats. None of them was Adrian Harmond.

It didn't matter. We had the right place. It was time for Ana to play her part. I began backing up toward the door when I heard the lock of a slide behind my head.

"Don't move," the gunman said.

I jerked my head to the side, and he pulled the trigger.

The bullet sailed past my cheek. I spun around quickly and brought my now-bladed hand down across his wrist, sending his hand and armament to the concrete. I struck him in the shoulder with my other hand, open palm, spinning him around. I slid my hand up and grabbed him by the neck, pulling him close. He reached up and grabbed my forearm, but I had him firmly in front of me, ready to use him as a shield should I need to.

"Get in here!" I yelled. It took but a moment before the sound of rusted hinges rung out as Prescott put his boot through the door. Vince, Prescott, and Ramsey came in with firearms drawn and moved toward cover. I dragged the man back toward the group as the sound of more armed personnel could be heard entering near the blue light. The sound of boots and combat equipment subsided. Then, from the light came only one sound—clapping.

"Bravo, Mr. Grimm. Bravo indeed," Adrian said. "You know, I figured it would have taken you much longer to find us. Then again, it sounds like you had help." He waited for me to respond. I didn't. So, he continued. "You know, you can't win. You're numbered, outgunned, and outmatched. Give up and I'll end this quickly. Like how Vera went."

"Fuck you!"

"There it is: your sore spot. I like that you're learning emotion. Might allow you to understand why we're doing this. Then again, it doesn't really matter if you understand. It only matters that you're gone."

"You should be dead," I replied.

"Technically, I am dead, or don't you remember playing fake detective over my corpse? Which reminds me: the actual detectives are here. Come on out, gentlemen."

I could see the silhouettes of Aaron and Marx through the hanging plastic.

"In your defense, Grimm, if we didn't already know who you were, your detective work would have been very convincing," Aaron said.

"You see, Mr. Grimm, none of it was real. We played you to keep you out of the way," Adrian said.

"No shit," I said. "But why? I'm on your side. You could have just told me."

"On my side? Please. What would you have done if I said the plan was to kill you to save the world? The same thing you actually did, I suspect—fight back. So, I ran you in circles. Kept you looking until I could get what I needed from you."

"My lab data."

"The Quintessence, Cyrus. It is more than just a collection of measurements. It is what makes you, you."

"But why? To make your weapons more powerful?"

"So small-minded. I'm not stupid. I know that killing you under normal circumstances would make me just that. I know what it is you do. And I know exactly how important that job is to the continuance of this world. The souls of the fallen need guidance. It's part of the natural order. There must always be death. It just doesn't necessarily have to be you."

"You mean to replace me? I don't think you understand the scope of what it is I do," I said.

His worst fear was that I would be used to bring about Hell's reign on earth—a possibility that I stupidly walked right into the moment I shook hands with the Duke. I wondered for a moment if I should let him succeed. The Duke would no longer have me. And if he really did have a way to replace me, the world would not end. The cycle would be preserved.

This plan, which seemed fanatical only minutes ago, began to look like it had merit. Though I didn't understand the degree of technology at his disposal, if he could do it, the plan to kill me was not only logical, but completely reasonable. But I've heard it said that "no plan survives first contact with the enemy." This one would be no exception. I needed to know more before I would willingly sacrifice myself to his scheme.

"Who takes my place?" I asked.

"I do," Adrian said. "My burden for doing what must be done."

"And how do you know it will work?"

"I had to accept the possibility that I would fail to kill you in the church. So, before I ever put anything in motion there was a backup plan. If we succeeded, then the remnants of your soul would have been enough to complete my research. If not, I had another way of obtaining the information I needed. You see, I knew a very talented particle physicist with a good heart; someone who would do the right thing, no matter what. But I couldn't exactly just give her the research I already had—I would give myself away. So, I removed someone close to her and left behind something she could use."

"Dr. Crane and the dagger. You killed a man just to leave behind a clue?"

"The simple answer is yes. In the grand scheme of things, the life of Dr. Crane was completely irrelevant. But as you can see, the clue left behind was very important given that I failed to eliminate you in our first encounter."

"We just pointed you in the right direction," Aaron said.

"And I did the rest," Vera said.

"Oh, that's interesting. She is here," Adrian said. "It must have taken some effort to get her back from my wife, may she rest in peace."

Vince caught my gaze and I knew what he was thinking. He reached into his pocket and pulled the glowing dagger from it. I flicked my wrist, dispatched my captive, and discarded him to the side. The blade shimmered as it passed through the air, glinting in the blue light as it sailed toward me. I moved quickly, grabbing Ana's arm and pulling her close, like I had held the gunman a few moments before. I reached up, snatched the knife from the air, pulled it down, and leaned my head close to Ana's ear.

"You need to trust me," I whispered. "Tap my arm twice if you understand." She did it subtly, and then struggled just enough to make it look convincing.

"You mean this wife?" I asked. Adrian tried not to react, but he did. His small lurch forward and gritted teeth told me what I needed to know. The sound of the many firearms being raised to point at us echoed in the cavernous room. Adrian lifted his hand in protest.

"Yes, that wife," he said, trying his best to steady his anger.

"Good. Tell them to lower their guns."

"No. I think you have greatly misjudged your play here, Mr. Grimm. Like Crane, Vera, or even me, she is inconsequential." He said it with conviction. Had he not swallowed immediately after saying it, I might have believed him. My little pause spurred him forward.

"There are seven billion people on this world. A single soul makes no difference in comparison."

A true statement. But he had already given it away. His logic did little to sway what I already knew. She meant everything to him. He had already lost her once; and, just as I had made the mistake for Vera, he would do the same for Ana.

"I agree with you, Adrian, which means I will destroy her without hesitation if it means saving those seven billion." I pressed the tip of the blade even closer to Ana's neck.

"Wait!" Adrian said. "Lower your weapons," he continued, turning to his soldiers.

"On the floor," I said. "Slide them over."

"Do as he says."

The men placed their weaponry on the floor and kicked them toward us.

Vince, Prescott, and Ramsey moved forward when it was clear, and stood next to me. I lowered the dagger from Ana's neck. I could see Adrian's face as I let her go. He expected her to run to him, but she didn't. She, too, fell in line next to me.

A look of disbelief fell over Adrian's face as she looked up at him. He said her name, not sure what to expect.

"Ana?"

"He's on our side," Ana said.

His anger boiled over and he screamed back at her, "No!"

He turned his attention to me and continued his outburst. "You've poisoned her against me, what have you done?"

"Nothing," I said. Pausing for a moment to see if he had more to say. He didn't, so I advanced. I moved like a bolt of lightning between the draped plastic into the blue glow at the end of the room. My palm hit squarely on Adrian's Adam's apple and my fingers closed tightly on his jaw. The force was enough to lift him into the air, and I held him there.

"I want you to understand how angry I am with you," I said. I squeezed his face, and a muffled squeal came out. "Are we clear?" I asked.

"Mmm-hmm."

"Good," I said, lowering him and letting go. "I also want you to trust me."

I took a step toward one of his men. "Hold out your hand," I said.

He looked at Adrian, who nodded. I placed the glowing blade into the man's hand and stepped away from him. I turned back to Adrian, hoping my gesture had been well received.

"The ball is in your court, now, Mr. Harmond. Are you ready to talk?"

Adrian, Vera, Ana, and I talked long into the night, far past the point where the living would be able to continue. Much of the beginning was arguing, needing to express the emotional distress that all parties present felt. Trusting someone who has threatened your very existence is not something that is easy to do. But if we wanted to make headway and build something meaningful, it had to happen.

Vera in particular was having a hard time with it. She had been betrayed by her colleague, someone she worked with, albeit indirectly. Adrian hadn't trusted her with the research that she herself had pioneered. I fully expected Adrian to be defensive when she lashed out at him, but he wasn't. He had long since accepted what he had done, and it showed.

Adrian did not try to justify his choices; he just stood there, silently, and took it. More than the words he would speak, that exchange was telling. He was still human. He still cared, and though he could logically justify his actions and the actions of his people and the church, they did not sit well with him. The choices he had made were not easy, but he believed they were necessary. When Vera was done, I could see that if nothing else, Adrian understood the pain he had caused, and he did not enjoy it. That was the moment I decided working with him was worth a shot.

As the trust developed we discussed the origins of his crusade. It was illuminating. Like Vera, Adrian had had visions of the future. They pushed him to the conclusions he had made; and by the time we had finished talking it was clear to me that the visions he and Vera had experienced were not by accident. I suspected that they were the first seeds sewn by the Duke

I took the opportunity to redirect and get us moving in the right direction. Adrian's plan was not crazy, and I made a point to make sure everyone knew I thought that. But there were holes in it, and it was just as important that I made him aware of those as well. I said what I needed to, and I could see that he knew I was right. Then it was only a matter of him lending more insight, so we could take the pieces and build a better boat.

"You know, I never imagined I would be having this conversation," Adrian said. "I had made peace with the idea that I would be doing a little evil to serve a greater good. And that my penance for that would be an eternity of servitude in the name of what I had destroyed. Is that so wrong?"

"The conviction to do what is necessary is not something you should be ashamed of," I answered. "But you must understand that there are limits. No one has shoulders broad enough to carry the weight of the world."

"I never intended to carry the weight of the world. Just yours."

"By locking out those who could help you, you did," Vera said.

"One mistake is all it would take for your enemy to disrupt your plans," I said. "And with the enemy we now face, it would not be hard for him to force you into one."

"Tell me about him."

I paused for a moment. "I would not call him the king of demons, as there really is none. But he would be the closest you could find to having that title these days. He wields the power of persuasion like an extension of his hand, as evidenced by your visions. He has an infinite legion at his back and is a master tactician. Also, he's a serious asshole."

They all chuckled, and I couldn't help but grin myself.

"No, really," I said. "Fuck that guy."

"So, just for clarification," Adrian said, "we need to figure this out or the world is fucked, right?"

"Pretty much," I replied.

"Well, shit. How did we get to this point?"

I explained to Adrian what had happened after the church. How even though he thought he was guiding my hand, it was really the Duke who was guiding his. Adrian had been right—I was to be a tool to bring about the Tribulation. The information had been fed to him, spurring him into action which eventually resulted in him driving me into the Duke's trap, just as he had planned.

"Fuck! I swear I didn't know," Adrian said.

"I want to tell you that it's okay," I said. "But this is a big fucking problem. The good news is I think I know what his plan is."

I explained what I knew and let it percolate in their minds for a moment.

"I think I have an idea," Adrian said.

"Let's hear it."

"First, we need to explain what I had hoped to do, and how it works."

"Go on."

"Obviously you know what a soul is. But do you really know *what* a soul is? At a fundamental level?"

I shook my head.

"I do," Adrian said.

"Everything is energy—everything. At a basic level, even matter."

"Yeah, yeah, we know that. Go on."

"Okay, well, not all energy is the same. Yes, it's still energy, but there are differences in every kind of energy—that's how we can tell them apart. Specifically, every type of energy has its own distinct vibration or wavelength. Let's use magnetism as an example. Magnetism is magnetism—there is no magnetism plus one or minus one. It's just magnetism, no matter the situation is; it is what it is. If its vibration changes it ceases to be magnetism and becomes something else. The same concept exists for all forms of energy."

"Again, we already know that. Every soul is different because of its distinct vibration," Adrian said.

"Okay, good. Well, that vibration pattern is what we call a 'signature.' But that's not the only thing that makes it unique."

"This is what you called the Quintessence earlier, right?"

"Yes. The signature is only one of several different things that make up the full profile of something. You're made the same way as any of us. But you're different; you're not a soul. You're something else. You have power, influence, longevity, and substance far beyond any normal spiritual entity."

"Not *any*," I interjected.

"Well, yes. There's you and the other six."

"How do you even know they exist?" I asked, excited to hear the reasoning.

"It's just math. Energy coalesces, I'm sure you know."

"Yeah, and . . .?"

"You and the others are the mathematical inevitability of what I call the 'Continuance.' I believe you are born from the coalescing of prime particles formed during the Big Bang. Persistent energy forged from the birth of our universe. I can't prove it. But the math says it's true. I think you and the others are fundamental forces that bind reality together. Maybe. . ."

"We call ourselves 'Eternal,'" I said.

"We will go with that then."

"And you were gonna kill me?"

"In my defense, I was going to replace you."

"Fine, so according to these algorithms, I was made by the universe—not God, right?" I looked at Vera, waiting for Adrian to prove what I had been saying from the beginning.

"Who's to say that it's not the same thing?" he said.

It was not the answer I was looking for, and I had taken us off topic.

"So, the other parts of this Quintessence you spoke about . . ."

"Right," Adrian said, excited to share his research. "The other parts that form it are the Output, the Constants, and the Rigor. When all four are unified they determine the parameters for how a soul behaves in nature."

"What do you mean 'behaves'?" Vera asked, now very interested in what she was hearing.

"Each of these items is different from soul to soul. The Output is how powerful it is. Kind of like a magnet. Magnets

248

can be of different strengths. Some magnets can barely cling to a fridge, and others bend the very fabric of space and time. It's how powerful a soul is. The Constants is how resistance it is to change. Nothing is immutable, but the higher its Constants, the less susceptible the vibration is to being altered. The Rigor is how precise it is. The more defined the pattern, the more likely it is to remain coalesced. Basically, it's how stable it is. Still with me?"

I wanted to say I understood, but it was getting complicated. I shook my head.

"Ana, pick up the dagger," Adrian said. She looked at him like he was an idiot. "I can't," she said.

"Why not?"

"I'll pass right through it."

"Right," he said. "Cyrus, pick up the dagger."

I reached out and took it from the table. Adrian smiled. "Why can you lift it and she can't?"

"Because I can exist in the physical realm," I said. "She doesn't."

"But really, it's all the same, remember? It's all energy. There's something about you that makes you different. Put the dagger down."

I did as he asked. Adrian walked over and waved his hand through it.

"Same thing, right?" he said.

"So?"

Adrian closed his eyes and focused. Again, he stretched out his hand, but this time his fingers wrapped around the blade and lifted it from the table. It was only for a second, but he did it. The sound of the stone against the metal rang out, and then there was nothing but silence.

"Rigor," Adrian said, a bit out of breath. "The dagger has a higher rigor than she does. So her energy dissipates to move around the object, then reforms."

"How did you do that?" Vera asked.

"Practice," he said.

It was beginning to make sense.

"So, the ladies are clearly exhausted, like they spent a night in hell. I look a little better, but not by much. It's because we're slowly dissipating into the universe. But you, you've been around for countless millennia, have gone through much worse than any of us, and look fresh out of a shower," Adrian said. "Why?"

"Constants," I said. "I resist the environment to a much higher degree."

"I don't think I need to give an example of you being more powerful, do I?"

I shook my head. The science of the soul. Every once in a while, mankind and its insatiable hunger for knowledge presented me with one of these moments. Inspiring and frightening at the same time. I looked at the ladies, expecting to see them scowls aimed at Adrian from his comment on their looks. Only Ana was. Vera was lost in wonder at what she had learned, the wheels of her scientific mind spinning away.

"So, the dagger isn't what we think it is," she said.

"Good," Adrian said. "What else?"

"Law of conservation of energy," she continued. "Energy can neither be created nor destroyed. Which means the Answer doesn't kill, because it can't kill, because you can't destroy energy."

"What can you do to it, though?" Adrian asked.

"Change it. But change it into what?" Vera replied.

"I know what," I said. The words came out of my mouth without a thought, because I knew. Maybe I had always known.

"Hexen," I said.

"The shadow things?" Vera asked.

"Yeah."

"But why? Why that change exactly? Most things disperse when undergoing change. Souls don't—why?"

"I have no idea," Adrian said. "I was hoping you two had a theory."

"Will," I said. "It's the missing piece to your Quintessence. A spirit has a will. It is sentient. That's what binds it all together—will."

"Okay, that kind of makes sense, but how do we prove it?" Adrian asked.

"It doesn't matter," I said. "You two can debate the science of this later. What does matter is if I'm right, and they are held together by will, we have a much more important question to answer.

"And what is that?" Adrian asked.

"How much of that will is still lucid?"

"Why does that matter?" Adrian asked.

"He wants to talk to them?" Vera asked.

"Bingo," I said. "And if I can, maybe more. I don't know yet."

I felt my thoughts begin to wander. I don't know how long I was silent for, lost in the cascade of images and ideas. It was like a puzzle in my mind, shifting and turning. All the information I had was coming together into a unified vision of how best to proceed. A plan, something so crazy it just might work. I had it—at least I hoped I did.

251

"I think I have an idea."

"That's good. What?" Adrian asked.

I turned to him. There was only one last blank I needed to fill in.

"There's something else," I said. "The door in your room, I saw it smashed when you were killed, and again at the site where Larry Kennedy was killed. How did it change? How was it remade?"

A small smile grew on his face. He had forgotten about it.

"It wasn't remade," he said. "The destruction was very real; it only appeared to be remade."

"How?" I asked. "And more than that, why?"

"Everything is energy," he said, his smile growing wider. "Even light, when you understand that you can play with all kinds of things."

"So, it was . . . an illusion?"

"Yep. Just light being projected the way we wanted it to be. It was actually the first thing I learned while I was . . ."

"Okay, got it," I interrupted. "Can you do it again?"

"Yeah, of course, why?"

The puzzle that had been slowly sorting itself in my head was complete when he gave me his confirmation.

"I think that will do," I said.

"Wait, it will do what?" Ana asked.

I ignored her and refocused on Adrian. "At the start of this, you said it was you who was to replace me should your plan succeed."

"That's correct. But obviously things have changed."

"How exactly would you have done it?"

"Where are you going with this?" Vera asked. She was concerned, and I didn't blame her.

Adrian hesitated.

"Why does it matter?" he asked.

"How would you do it?"

The three of them just looked at me.

"You're out of your mind," Ana said.

"Did we not just spend all night talking about how we're not going to kill you?" Adrian said.

"I never said you were. I just need to know you can do it."

"The science is sound. And I've done preliminary testing. With the data, and enough time, yeah, I can do it. Probably," Adrian said.

"How confident are you?"

There was a small tremble in his voice as he replied.

"Ninety . . . percent . . . ish. But until I run the numbers and do the tests I can't know for sure. Why? What are you thinking?"

"I'm just thinking the way you were thinking when you put this in motion."

"Okay, I'm lost. Is this or isn't this part of the plan?"

"Everything is part of the plan, Adrian. Including the things that aren't going for us."

"And now you're scaring us. What are you going to do?"

"Moment of truth, people," I said. "We're going to give the Duke exactly what he wants."

"Meaning?" Vera asked.

"Open the floodgates."

12

Sacrificing The Queen

The looks on the faces of the several dozen men and women gathered in the room were not of excitement or happiness. The idea that the fate of all mankind could very well rest on their shoulders had something to do with it, I suspected. They were silent and focused as Adrian explained to them their role in what was to come. When he was done, there was no cheering, no thunderous applause. It was not a battle speech.

People think that when a commander sends the troops out to face the enemy, that it should be inspiring. Maybe what Adrian said should have been inspiring for them. After all, the finish line was in sight. But it only works that way in the movies. There were very real stakes, and there was a very real possibility that everything we had worked so hard for would fall apart. We could fail, and life as we knew it on this world would end. That's a lot of pressure. I wouldn't have cheered, either.

"Did you get what you needed?" Vera asked as I walked into the room.

"Yes," I replied. "They're in. They will do what I ask and

then meet us on the field."

"Are you sure this is how you want to do it?" Vince asked.

"The wheels are already in motion. I just have one last stop to make," I replied.

"You're still going to try to make contact?" Adrian asked.

"I've already made it; it's just letting them know that it's time to get the show started. I'll meet you at the staging point at midnight. Is everything else done?"

"Yes, everything on our side is ready. Just waiting for you to set it off," Adrian said.

"Ramsey?" I asked.

"Vera and I will have everything ready when you arrive."

"Good," I said. "I guess I'll see you guys on the other side."

I don't know if they had planned it or not, but everyone lined up in front of me. Vince was the first in line. He reached out his hand. I took it. He squeezed before giving one solid shake.

"No matter how this turns out, I want you to know I don't regret any of it," he said before walking away.

Adrian was next, extending his hand just as Vince had done.

"I was wrong. Let's hope that it didn't cost us."

"Well, the plan doesn't work without you, so here's to hoping that you being wrong was exactly what you needed to be," I said.

They each made their way to me, saying their part and moving on to their tasks. Vera was last. She took my hand in hers and brought it to her cheek.

"Are you sure you're ready for this?" I asked.

"Absolutely not," she said, laughing a little as she did. "But this is more important than how ready I feel."

"It will be okay," I said.

"I know," she said. "That's not what I'm worried about."

"What then?" I asked.

She paused for a moment. "You know I still think it's funny how oblivious you are sometimes."

I didn't know what to say for a moment. When I opened my mouth to speak, she moved. She pressed against me and for a moment I didn't know how to react. As she kissed me I was helpless to do anything, and it was a good thing. I slipped into whatever it is that people feel in those moments and vanished. My eyes opened as she pulled away. Vince was at the door, looking at us with a small smile on his face.

"We need to go, it's not a short trip" he said to Vera.

"Yeah," she said. "I'm on my way."

She walked away from me without another word and out the door past Vince. He turned to follow her before I called to him. He walked over to me, the smile on his face growing larger with each step, until he was close enough that I thought he was going to kiss me himself.

"That was new for me," I said.

"Was it?"

"Yeah. How did I do?"

His smile was so wide it looked like it had eaten the rest of his face. He patted me on the back, still grinning ear to ear.

"This right here might be the coolest fucking thing ever," he said, and began walking toward the door.

"So that means good, right?"

My feet touched down softly at the place I never wanted to be: the site of my seal. I had avoided it for so long, but I couldn't any longer. It had been thousands of years since I had stood

256

on that spot. It was eerily familiar, but at the same time, my time away had made it foreign. My boots left distinct prints in the powdered limestone that swirled atop the stones around the monument at the center.

I was nervous, but also happy. The first part of my trip had been the success I needed it to be. The relief of knowing that I had garnered the support I needed gave me courage for what I needed to do next. I walked forward toward the artifact, glowing and humming, just a few yards away from me.

The power it emitted was tangible. The air around it was thick, and the energy it contained made it feel almost electric. This totem, made tens of thousands of years ago, was the last pillar of a great barrier forged to insulate mankind from that which was beyond the Veil. The ancient stone looked almost the same as it had when it was forged, a testament to the lengths people were willing to go. It was built to last forever, but it wouldn't because I was going to destroy it.

I thought about the stone before me, its long history. Humanity knew so little back then, but they had faith, and that faith led them to build things like this. Things that were real. Things that had power and importance, thought they did not fully understand the implications of doing so.

Today, mankind knows so much, but believes nothing that they cannot see with their own eyes. I don't know which type of ignorance is better. Each has its virtue, but neither can last forever. It was time for that ignorance to stop. By my hand this world would either be saved or damned. I didn't know which; I just knew that I couldn't sit and do nothing.

I paused for a moment as I looked at the wonderful work that had gone into the totem. For those who had believed in the old ways, it was the work of God himself—or herself, or themselves—however you look at it. It was something divine, and that made people feel safe. I appreciated it, though it was I who had given it power, and not those who had forged it.

The other seals had already been cast down at my request. This was all that remained of the old ways. The pieces were moving; there was nothing that could stop it now. Only one left. The majesty that it represented was about to be cast down, so a new age could begin. I couldn't help but question the act. As the stone crumbled so, too, would the barrier between the physical and the spiritual. I was forcing the hand of my enemy by paving the way for his victory.

As I pulled my hand back to strike, familiar words I hated so much came to mind.

And I saw when the Lamb opened one of the seals, and I heard, as it were the noise of thunder, one of the four beasts saying, "Come and see." And I looked and beheld a pale horse, and his name that sat on him was Death, and hell followed with him. And power was given unto them over the fourth part of the Earth, to kill with the sword, and with hunger, and with death, and all the beasts of the Earth.

The sound of thunder did come, but it was not a beast. It was my hand against the stone. A wave of energy erupted, and the effigy shattered like a pane of glass. Its countless splinters fell to the ground and scattered at my feet. As they did the air grew cold, and I could feel the Veil lifting as the power the seals once possessed dissipated. It was done—there was no turning back.

The hum of the massive neon sign that adorned the side of the building where my friends stood was the only sound in the still night. As I approached, everyone looked calm, almost too much so. They looked ready, which, if I'm honest, was a relief. The chessboard had been set, the opening moves made. Everything had led us to this, it was time for the endgame.

The last light of the sun began to fade behind the mountains in the distance. And as it did I could feel the anger stirring beneath my feet. I had struck the hornets' nest that would bring about the rise of hell on earth. But if I had my way, that would be the end of it. The writings of revelation would stop now. I would erase the rest of that sixth chapter. There would be no martyrs, no terror, no trumpets. It was here that I would draw the line in the sand.

We had picked this battlefield for a few very good reasons. The lights of ARC Industries' south campus gave us the best visibility and took us out of the way of the general populous. The buildings were gathered around a giant courtyard. There was only a narrow path between them. It was a feature we could use to bottleneck our foes, should we be faced with something overwhelming. It was a tactic mankind had used many times to engage superior forces. I was counting on things to go the way I'd hoped. If they did, we would not need to use the architecture to our advantage.

It was a little after midnight when it started. The ground quivered in anticipation of our enemy's arrival. At the end of the lot I could see the ground begin to buckle and bulge. The light of the fire rising from beneath it gave off that familiar orange glow that I had seen so many times. The material succumbed to the heat, and molten bits were cast out as the pillar of flame burst through it and rose into the night. I began walking toward it, ready for what it brought.

The Duke came out of the flames at a near sprint. He was on me almost immediately. His palm landed hard against my chest and then rose to my neck as he lifted me into the air and brought me down hard on my back. Everything slowed for a moment. I could see the broken chunks of asphalt flying into the air and the sides fold up around me from the force that had been used to push me into the ground. It hurt, but I was glad. He was angry enough to lash out (which meant that the advantage was already mine).

"You motherfucker!" he yelled. "What are you doing?"

"I got tired of waiting," I replied, as if it weren't a big deal. I heard the Duke yell and then felt his knuckles on my face—once, twice, and then I lost count. When he was finished, he shoved me down into the ground again and stepped away.

"You have no idea what you've done," the Duke said.

"I'm going to assume that reaction means you're angry," I said, trying to stand up. I caught another fist to the orbital bone and fell back into the hole.

"This was not how this was supposed to have happened," he continued, and began to look around. "Then again, it is a bit poetic that it would happen here. I'm sure you had some grand idea that starting early would in some way disrupt my plans. You're wrong—it won't. You forget: I own you. I decide how this goes."

"So, what do you want to do, then?" I asked.

"Don't think that because I need you, Grimm, that I will not rain hellfire down on your world."

"I thought that was the plan, but not just on my world—everyone's."

"You're smart, Grimm. Too smart. But you're not me. You

lack something very important."

"And what's that?"

"Vision," the Duke said. "You can't see past yourself, and there is so much more to this than just you. Though I appreciate that you figured out that I would use you to break your seal, you forgot something."

"Then tell me," I said.

"I find it better to show you," he said, brandishing his glittering smile.

The pillar of flame behind him intensified and from it out strode Jaina, Sai, and Vaughn. Just as I hoped they would. Remnants of fire and shadow marred their bodies. They bled fire and their once-majestic garments were tattered and scorched. Looks of resignation adorned their faces—that they had become what they hate.

"You see? I even have power over those of you who are endless; you are no different."

I acted surprised. I needed him to think that I didn't already know that he had them.

"Grab him," the Duke said.

My brother and sisters moved like I do. It was but an instant before they were within striking distance. I only knew it because of the images of cinder left behind in their wake. I felt the burn of their hands on me, and then the jolt of being hoisted out of the crater. They pushed me down to my knees before one of them grabbed my hair and jerked my head back, forcing me to face the Duke.

He walked toward me again and took another swing, striking me in the temple.

"I think it's time we end this, don't you?" he said.

He turned his back to me, looked at the pillar of fire, and

began to chant.

"Cadite super nos, et abscondite nos a facie sedentis super thronum et ab ira Agni. Quoniam venit dies magnus iræ ipsorum et quis poterit stare?"

I listened intently as he spoke. *Fall on us, and hide us from the face of him that sitteth on the throne, and from the wrath of the Lamb. For the great day of his wrath is come, and who shall be able to stand?* He repeated the Latin over and over. With each chant the flames grew in intensity and then suddenly stopped. The pause was only momentary. The flames rose from the pits of hell once again—this time red as blood, soaring into the night.

From it emerged the first of the great steeds, Ruin. Fire spouted from its eyes, nose, and mouth. Its hoof falls sank into the asphalt as the heat and weight turned it molten. It was beautiful, and absolutely terrifying. When it stopped, Vaughn released my hair and walked toward the creature. It reared up as he approached, then calmed. He placed his hand on its side. The link had been made, and they became one. In a burst of fire, he mounted it, and I could feel the power the two of them combined possessed.

The Duke continued his chant, and the flames morphed into a vibrant green. Then, just as before, out walked the beast, Scourge. From its rotting flesh oozed a putrid sludge that burned the ground like acid as it moved toward its master. Sai released my arm and shoved me down before walking to her steed and placing her hand upon it. Their powers fused and began to twist around them, calming as she mounted the beast.

Soon after, the climbing flames erupted once more. The chromatic shift this time was to purple. From the darkened fire came the third beast, Misery. Its skeletal frame moved unlike the others, as most of the muscle had withered and turned to dust. In its wake it left behind a toxic cloud of aerosolized flesh. My last captor, Jaina, released me and walked to her steed. As she mounted it, its legs buckled, and it looked as if it were about to fall over. She brought her hand down and touched it. Their power combined, and the weakness fled the horse, propping it upright.

The three mounted horsemen walked forward, putting themselves between me and the Duke. His chant continued, and with it the flame changed one last time—to a brilliant white. There was a burst of power when the final steed emerged from the flaming pillar. It was different from the others, untamed and rabid. The horse bucked and threw itself wildly until the Duke ended his chant and managed to calm it down.

"Despair," he said. "That which you have brought to so many people for so many years. Inadvertently, of course. Part of the job. But this time . . . this time it will be the vestige that carries you unto this world's doom. There's a bit of poetry in that, isn't there? Now get up."

I looked up at the smug son of a bitch and remained on my knees.

"I said get up," he commanded.

"No," I replied.

"You don't get it. You owe me a favor, or don't you remember?" the Duke asked. "Well, I'm calling it in. In accordance to your blood debt, I compel you to use your power to command the armies of hell and cleanse this world."

The rune on my hand lit up and tried to pull me to my feet. I struggled against it, and as I did, the power it held over me turned against me. The rune seared my flesh, growing hotter the more I struggled. But I refused it; I *had* to refuse it.

"Only the power of Death can command that steed, and I refuse," I said through the pain.

"You don't have the right to refuse."

"You're right, I don't. But I am," I said defiantly.

"There are consequences for your refusal and you know them very well. You will be forced to comply."

"Maybe, but not right now. You see, you may have a strong position on the board, but I'm the most powerful piece on it. And I'm removing myself from the game. And without me, your army is incomplete. And without that army, you can't win."

The Duke scoffed at my assertion. "You think I can't win? Against who? Them? You brought a few dozen people with you to stop the most powerful force this world will ever see. They wouldn't even stand a chance against me alone, much less the combined might of your brother and sisters."

"Are you willing to take that chance?" I asked.

The Duke paused. He was smart enough to consider that we had come prepared for him. And so, he did what I was counting on. He made the smart decision.

"Fine, we do this the hard way. Just remember, you asked for this."

"Fuck you," I replied.

"Cyrus Grimm," he said, "you have been found guilty of violating a sacred blood pact. Do you deny it?"

"Fuck you!" I said again.

"Then in accordance with ancient law, you shall be banished to the Pits and suffer the consequences of your treachery until you fulfill your oath."

As he became silent I felt a pulse of energy, and then it had me. It was as if a great hand had grabbed me. It pulled me toward the flaming pillar and then into it. I could feel the heat all over me as I was consumed by the flames. It was only for a moment, and then I felt myself falling. I struck the wet mud in the pit of my holding cell hard enough that I had to just lie for a second and let the daze wear off. I stood up and looked around to try to get my bearings. The spiked walls were too high to see over; only the burnt orange of the sky above me was visible. A burst of flame came from behind me. I turned to see the Duke.

"You do realize that your gesture, though noble, is pointless," he said. "Time is not the same in this place as you well know. A millennium here is but a few minutes on the surface. You will have suffered what you feel is millions of years, and you won't even have bought your friends a day. Don't do this, Grimm. It's a waste of both our time."

"It's the principle," I said.

"You know nothing of principle. You protect a world that hates you. For what reason? Because it's the right thing to do? From whose perspective?"

"Mine."

"Then you are a fool. You want to change too badly, to be like them. But they are insects—short-lived and tiny. You have done your job for longer than even I have existed. Everything that lives, dies, and yet you value life. I've known you for a very long time, and I'm telling you as a friend, this will not be worth it."

"As a friend, you say?" I replied. "You are going to burn a world that I have safeguarded for eons. And though you don't understand it, life is the only thing that makes that world special. Watching the souls that call it home become better is more important to me than your false friendship."

I expected an outburst of anger, but he only smiled.

"There will come a day when you'll wish you had been on the right side of me."

"I doubt it."

The Duke's lips curled as he turned away.

"Call out for mercy when you've had enough," he said. "Oh, and make sure it's loud enough. Because you might accidentally burn for a few thousand years too long if it's not."

There was another flash of flame, and he was gone.

Most prisoners relive their greatest failures in this place. But I think he had something special in mind for me. As the smoke from his departure cleared, I could see the mud of the cell begin to bubble and sway. The bubbles popped, and from them I could smell the methane. It took only a few seconds and then the gas ignited. There was nothing but fire and pain. I tried to resist, but it was too much, and I emptied my lungs into the agony of my prison. I could not bear it, but I had to.

I did my best to isolate my mind from the constant onslaught of the flames. I did this by focusing on what I already knew. The Duke had pointed it out, with quite a bit of enjoyment. But he didn't catch it, so I made it my anchor. I listened to him say it in my mind over and over. Through the pain I couldn't help but smile each time he said it.

"Time is not the same in this place."

I don't know how many times I played the words in my head. I don't know how long I used them to withstand the flames. It may have been a week, a year, a thousand. I just kept playing it in my mind over and over. *Time is not the same*

266

in this place.

The Duke had said I couldn't see past myself. In thinking that, he had made his second mistake. I was not buying time for those on earth. I was buying time for my brethren, the remaining Eternals.

The agony of my endless burning was interrupted by the force of careening steel against my chest. The blow sent me flying across the cell and into the wall on the other side. When I looked up the flames had dissipated. The steel that had struck me had come from the cage as it was ripped open. In the gap it left stood Oman, Aiden, and Wynn.

I tried to push the chunk of mangled steel off of me, but I was weak, much more than I thought I would be. Aiden ran toward me and removed the wreckage that had me pinned before helping me to my feet.

"You all right?" he asked.

I nodded. "How long have I been here?" I asked.

"The better part of six hundred years," Wynn replied as she walked toward us.

"Better part?" I asked.

"All right, worst part. It's good to see you, Cyrus."

"You, too. All of you. You have no idea."

"We can guess," Oman said. "As nice as it would be to catch up, we need to move on."

"We should have plenty of time," I said.

"No, we don't," Oman retorted. "Just because you're a stubborn son of a bitch doesn't mean we have all eternity."

"The Duke said it would take a thousand years to pass just a few minutes on the other side," I said.

"That's right, but you've already lasted a century longer than anyone I've ever heard of down here. He knows you're a pain in the ass, and he knows how hardheaded you are. But eventually he's going to want to see how things are going."

I realized that Oman was right. He mentioned millions of years, but he was just giving an example. That didn't mean he expected me to last that long. I nodded in agreement.

"How far have you guys gotten?" I asked.

"A little less than half," Wynn said.

"I guess I have good luck."

"Damn right, you do," Aiden said. "It should go faster once you're rested."

"Good. How many are willing to stand with us?"

"Almost all of them," Oman said. "At this rate, assuming we release everyone that's imprisoned in his Pits, we should have comparable numbers to his legion."

I felt a huge wave of relief. The plan was going exactly as I'd wanted up to this point. But it was far from over. We still had a very long way to go.

The sound of shattering steel rang out for what would be the last time on this trip into the Pits. The soul flailed in the corner, screaming. His pain was over now. It was only a question of whether or not he was willing to join us. The answer was just as it had been for so many others: yes.

My voice carried on the burning winds of the underworld. It echoed among the ocean of countless unknown faces. It was a battle cry, a call to war against he who had brought them so much misery and torment. I wanted nothing more than to end their suffering and help them move on. But this was not the time or place for that. I promised all of them that their time for peace would come. But before that moment, they would have a chance to take revenge against those who had done them wrong. And though I felt like I was manipulating their anger for my own purposes, they had all made the choice to stand with me.

The millions marched behind us across the desolation toward our destination: a portal—one that would carry their might to the surface. Men and women of every race, creed, and age were united as one against a common enemy. The Duke thought that he and his horsemen were the greatest force the world would ever see. I couldn't wait to see his face when he realized what I was bringing to his door.

The landing where we would pass through the Veil and start the end war came into view. On the red ground was a pentagram large enough that we wouldn't even know it was there had we not been standing on the top of the mountain. The ground shook beneath the feet of my army. I turned and looked behind me as we descended into the valley. Like the pentagram, it was quite a sight to behold.

As we reached the edge of the circle I looked at my hand. The glowing rune inscribed on the back of my hand vanished. I had fulfilled my oath to the Duke for I was doing as he asked.

I would command the armies of hell and cleanse the world.

I would cleanse it of his filth and bring about the salvation of all those living on it.

There was a pillar of blue light at the center of the mammoth symbol. Oman, Aiden, and Wynn all slapped me on the back before I began to walk toward it. It began to spread over the entire symbol as I approached. It was then that the words of the good book came into my mind once more. Words that for so long I had hated. But for the first time I felt proud about the passage. I had good men and women at my back willing to sacrifice the peace of their passing to stand with me, the man they call Death.

The blue spread over me, and I was lifted into the air. As I moved toward the burnt orange sky I felt myself begin to shift form. My vision faded as the white light took me and hurled me to the surface. As it did, I couldn't help but smile as the words from the book played the line one last time in my mind.

"And hell followed with him."

13

And Hell Followed With Him

The burning orange sky faded away into the blackness of the cosmos overhead. The night was clear and calm, with only the hum of neon upon the evening air. I felt like I was floating for a brief second before my feet landed softly on the dirt of the courtyard, right in the middle of a faintly glowing blue circle. I raised my eyes and looked around. A collective sigh of relief adorned the faces of my friends as I appeared in front of them. The lone exception was Vince, whose chanting had drawn me up in the first place. The look of relief was replaced quickly with concern as the group's attention returned to the adversaries behind me.

There were no words from that direction, but I could feel the anger in the Duke's stare trying to burn a hole through me. I raised my hand where the rune had been, so he could see it. I expected to hear some kind of garish retort from him, but no words came. Instead there was only the sound of boots on the asphalt rushing toward me. The sound of his steps muffled as he entered the courtyard, and then came the sound of cutting air.

The ring of the clashing steel bounced between the buildings. He pressed his blade against my darkened hand as hard as he could. Tiny sparks flicked off the sword's edge from the friction. I closed my fingers around his blade and moved my head away from the edge. I twisted it to the side and stood to face him. The steel began to turn red from the immense pressure being applied to it as the Duke pressed it into my hand. I jerked the blade to one side and then reversed direction quickly. A sharp crack rang out as the metal gave way and snapped.

The sudden loss of resistance caused the demon lord to lose his balance. He fell toward me as he struggled to regain his footing, leaving him exposed. My free hand turned black as the night as it formed into a blade. I swiped with it. The force of it lifted him off the ground and pushed him away from me. He stumbled backward as he landed before scrambling back into an upright position.

A puff of black smoke and embers swirled around the Duke as he began his retreat. I could see a small spark of orange in the distance from where he had rushed at me—his destination. I pressed forward toward the spark. I was between the buildings before the black smoke left behind had even vanished. He appeared again but a few yards before me as I was in full sprint.

I readied myself to strike again but I didn't get the chance. Our forward advance was halted by what felt like a wall. As the shock of my sudden stop faded, I looked out. The edge of my right hand had been caught by a glaive. I followed it back to Jaina's hand. I looked at her and could see that the shield she carried was resting flush with my ribs. The wall I had hit. She had protected her master *but did not strike at me.*

The moment felt infinite as I realized they couldn't fight the power the steeds held over them.

The sound of grinding steel snapped me out of it as she jabbed her glaive toward me. I deflected it to the side and vaulted backward to safety. Jaina returned to the side of the Duke. He was down on one knee, clutching at where I had struck him. The wound I had dealt was significant, though he would recover quickly. He knew that I was not to be trifled with. The tatters of his once-pristine suit hung down over the wound. It had been cleaved almost in half, along with its wearer. His black blood poured out across the ground, hissing as it pooled on the ground and steaming like acid. I could see his broken form—the bone, sinew, and muscle had already started reaching out and combining back together.

The Duke caught his breath and gritted his teeth in pain.

"Bring him to me," he said, struggling.

Vaughn, Jaina, and Sai hesitated, doing their best to fight the power of the horsemen. But I could see they wouldn't be able to hold it off for long. There was a brief moment when I thought I could advance and strike at their master, but the three of them moved on me as I did.

I slipped beneath the long reach of Sai's spear as she swung it wide at me. Vaughn came from the left with his two short swords. He leaped at me with a cross slash. I dodged to my right and deflected the blows. I felt the crash of Jaina's shield on my back as she moved in from the right. I spun and rolled away from her, only to find Sai's spear waiting for me.

Everything was moving so fast and yet so slow. I caught my footing right as she jabbed at me. I moved up my hand in instinct of the coming spear. I turned my head away from the spear's point as it glided along my forearm and grazed my cheek. I felt the slight sting as it broke the top layer of skin and continued on past me.

The momentum of Sai's lunge had carried her forward. As my sight refocused I saw the opening. I spun around to avoid the spear and swept. My leg met hers and lifted her off the ground. She landed hard on her shoulder before rolling onto her back. I brought my hand down toward her, but it was met by the edge of Vaughn's sword.

He swung at me with his free blade. I moved to the side and then leaped away from him. He followed and launched a flurry of quick strikes. I cast each of them to the side in a shower of sparks as I backed away from the other two. We moved almost in unison, the millennia of familiarity transforming into a dance of steel and fire. He made a mistake before I did, and I caught him in it. He overextended on a thrust and gave me the chance to move around him.

I caught the guard of his blade and cast it to the ground away from him. I deflected his retaliation strike and moved in close. I drove my shoulder into his chest and lifted him off the ground before driving him down onto his back. His other blade jostled free from his hand, and I kicked it to the side before striking at him. As before, my attack never landed. The force of the swinging shield caught me in the ribs and peeled me away from the downed horseman.

I tumbled through the air and spun around to land on my feet. I saw Jaina lift Vaughn to his feet. He scooped up his blades, and they rushed toward me. I planted my feet and readied for their assault. It was then that I realized I had been fighting three, not two. I swiveled my head to try to find Sai. I saw the glint of the spear's head from the glow of the neon out of the corner of my eye.

I felt the sting of the spear in my side before I could move. I turned toward my attacker and wrapped my fingers around the shaft of the spear and held it, so it couldn't pierce further. Then I saw that that would not be needed. There was a look of remorse on Sai's face as she stared at the entry wound caused by her weapon.

"I'm sorry," she said as she yanked on the staff.

I felt a sting once more as the spearhead left my side. As it did, Sai moved away from me and toward Vaughn and Jaina. I expected them to come at me in unison, but instead they retreated back toward the Duke. He was almost healed. He stood up as the horsemen came to his side. As he rose I saw the last pieces of severed flesh connect and reform.

I removed my hand from the wound on my side so that it would do the same. Strangely, it did not. I looked at the blood on my hand and then at the incision. Something was wrong. Then I heard the Duke's laughs.

"Oh, Cyrus, that was good. I'll give you that. I expected resistance—hell, I wasn't even really that surprised that you refused to honor our agreement. But that's where you have a problem. The smart move when you escaped would have been to run and not come back."

"You knew I would return," I replied. "I had to."

"Of course, I knew. Order is the enemy of chaos. You wouldn't be you if you didn't come back and fight. And that's why this is so amusing. No matter what, I knew that you would eventually be mine. Either your will would break, and you would be willing in your servitude, or you would find a way out of the Pits and try to come and stop me. So very predictable."

"Guess you have me figured out," I said.

"Actually, yes, I do. I'm sure you expect us to replay the same scenario from earlier, where I commanded you to honor our agreement. But we're not going to do that. I don't know how you did it, but I can see by the absence of your mark that you've cheated the system."

"I did nothing more than what you've asked of me."

"Not a very good liar, Grimm. But that doesn't matter. You see this?" he asked.

The Duke pointed at the spear that had just been pulled from my side. Sai moved toward him and held it out for him to take. He wrapped his fingers around it and brought the tip to his face. He made a long, deep inhale of the warm blood on it.

"This spear is something I spent a great deal of time and energy finding. It's very special, as you can see," he said, pointing to my still-unhealed wound. "So are the swords, and the glaive; but it seems that this is the one you will get to hear about.

"As you are well aware, normal weapons leave no lasting damage to those from behind the Veil. You see, this was the spear that pierced the body of Christ. The spear that killed God. Fitting, don't you think?"

"It's just a spear," I said. "It's the wielder that gives it power."

"That's no fun," the Duke replied. "Correct, but no fun."

"This is going somewhere, right?"

The Duke's brows crumpled at my mockery.

"The power of the Horsemen is that of destruction. Something I made sure they knew how to use. That's what really makes this spear special. You see, aside from having the obvious side effect of diminishing your regenerative powers, it has this little thing," he said, pointing to the tip.

"This is, well, a blade. And blades, as you know, cause wounds, which bleed."

"Your point?" I asked, becoming impatient.

"You ruined my suit, spilled my blood. And so, I took yours."

The Duke ran his hand along the blade, collecting as much of my blood as he could. He sniffed it again and then licked some of it off his hand.

"Mmmmm, bitter. So much 'you' inside it."

As soon as I realized what he was doing I broke into a sprint. I moved like a beam of light across the asphalt to stop him, but it was too late. He stretched out his bloody hand and placed it upon the horse of Despair, completing the link. I felt the pulse of the steed's power latch on to me. I felt like the whole world was shaking beneath me as the horse pulled at me, draining my power. As my strength flowed out of me and into the horse, my legs buckled. A moment later, I felt myself falling.

The mix of granulated stone and tar dug into my face as I slid across the ground and past my enemy. I couldn't see it, but I felt the channel flowing between myself and Despair. It was like an endless siphon attached to me, and every moment it stayed attached, it drew more of me into itself. It wouldn't be long before he would have his fourth Horseman.

The pale horse reared back and brandished my power. Once more the earth opened up and the column of flame rose into the night. From that central point, orange cracks began to radiate across the ground. The world trembled as they spread, like it was breaking apart. Pieces of the world began to splinter off and fall into the depth, releasing the flames that struggled to reach the surface.

The first demonic claw jutted out from the now-gaping

cracks and dug into the ground. It looked as though space was warping around it as it struggled to move through the Veil. Then came another set of claws, then more—one after another emerged from the flame until there were too many to count.

I couldn't wait any longer. With what little energy I had left I yelled into the black of the night.

"Now!"

I looked out between the trampling claws and saw the streaking rounds fired from Adrian's people. I rolled over and began to crawl. I didn't get far. My breath was taken as I felt the thud of a boot on my back. I couldn't even turn my head to see who it was, but I knew. I was sure the son of a bitch was smiling as he did it.

"You see, Grimm, sometimes you just have to accept that you've lost. It won't be much longer until you're too weak to resist. And when you are, you will do as I say. Until that time, you get to lie here and watch your friends die at the feet of my legion."

I tried to press against him, but I was fading, and it was only getting worse. I felt something. Maybe it was anger at his taunt, or fear. I don't know. But the last bit I had left moved into my limbs and I gave one last burst of myself. The Duke stumbled away from me, and I kicked the ground. The force sent me sliding across the asphalt and into the middle of the swarming demons.

The sound of whizzing bullets and demon screams was all around me. I clawed at the ground between them, making my way toward the hail of incoming gunfire. In one collective wail the group of hell spawn around me fell to ashes. I felt the tug on my torso as I was lifted from the ground. Prescott dragged me away from the coming swarm toward where our people had dug in. Our small group, for now at least, was holding its own.

They pulled me around the side of the building, away from the main group. To my relief, Vince was still chanting, standing by the blue ring which I had risen through. It had begun to fill out and emblazon the same symbology that was in the basement of The Velvet Orchid. He was stoic, standing before it. His eyes were rolled back as he chanted the ancient words over and over. The pale blue had grown brighter and now almost matched the color of the neon sign overhead. The glow had spread through the lines in the circle, but he still had a way to go before it would be finished.

I turned to Prescott. "Where's Vera?"

"She and Ramsey are still making the final prep," he replied.

"And the others?"

Before he could answer Ana arrived at my side.

"We can't hold on much longer," she said. "How long do we need?"

"Long enough for him to finish," I said, motioning toward Vince. "I'm sorry."

I had expected to be able to keep the fight going and buy time for Vince to finish. But in that state, I was less than useless. I was using resources that should be used to hold back our enemy.

"Can we do anything to help you?" Ana asked.

I shook my head.

"All my power is being drained. I would need something to draw from just to get me back on my feet."

I winced as she reached down and touched the still-bleeding hole in my ribs.

"Get it for me," she yelled at Prescott. He ran off and returned shortly with the dagger.

She held out her hand in front of him. "Do it," she said.

"No," I said weakly.

Prescott hesitated.

"Do it!" she yelled at him.

I tried to lift my hand to stop them, but I didn't have enough strength. I could see the silhouette of the blade as it pulled away from her hand. She plunged her now-glowing palm against my wound. My body latched on to her and began to pull. Her face started to grow thin as my body soaked up the spiritual energy she was forcing into it. I tried to pull away, but Prescott grabbed me and held me down. All the brightness faded out of her as she poured herself into me.

"Tell Adrian I love him," Ana said. Her face had become nothing more than a skull. But she continued. I watched as the light went out in her eyes and the remnants of her soul collapsed and sank into the ground. She was gone. But her sacrifice had bought us some time. I was nowhere near full strength, but I could move, and I could fight. Prescott helped me to my feet, his eyes red and swollen.

"Stick to the plan," I said. He nodded and wiped away his sadness as best he could.

I rounded the building and looked out over the battlefield. The demons had breached the first line of soldiers we had brought. They now poured from the flaming cracks like water from a broken water main. I could see in the distance the Duke and the Horsemen had not engaged yet. But the legion was like a flood; they would force their way into the courtyard soon. It was getting to the point where we needed to fall back. I turned and looked around the corner to examine Vince's progress; he wasn't ready.

I ran toward what had devolved into a massive melee. I felt slow and sluggish, but my hands still hardened and cut like steel. I began carving my way to the center line where Adrian and the others were doing their best to hold off the onslaught. I broke into the gap that the group had made and gave the order to fall back into the campus courtyard. We had almost rounded the corner when the ground quaked. The shock was so violent that it forced everything to stop.

The world was silent for a moment until I heard the Duke begin to laugh. There was another jolt, then silence once again.

"This might just be my favorite part," he said before the third shock. One of the cracks began to widen rapidly and a part of the ground fell in, revealing a colossal opening in the earth. I knew what was coming. I just wondered how many. The first to slither to the surface was Serran. The fury she no doubt had been holding on to since our last encounter burned in her eyes. If she was here, then the others would not be far behind. I was right. Hexas, Azazel, Vargaz, and Ashtaroth emerged from the pit shortly after. The demons that surrounded us peeled away and ran back behind their masters.

"Fuck," I whispered to myself. I thought quickly and opened my mouth to speak but was interrupted by the Duke.

"He is weak!" he yelled out to them. "And I believe you have a score you would like to settle with him."

I turned back to Adrian and the group and waved my hand, so they would back up. The group reformed its ranks, and I joined them. We began to retreat into the courtyard as the group of greater demons pushed through the swarm toward us. We were moving well as a group, but it didn't last. Ashtaroth broke into a gallop toward us, trampling the demons that separated us from him. At the sight of his charge the lines broke once again, and it became a free-for-all as they ran to safety. I had to buy them time to get away, so I held my ground.

Ashtaroth brought down his massive arm in one mighty swing. I crossed my arms and met it as it descended. The force caused me to collapse to one knee and sink into the asphalt. Everything felt slow around me. I could see the broken pieces of blacktop floating in the air as the ground beneath me sundered.

Ashtaroth swung again with his other hand. I rolled to the side, narrowly avoiding it. Before I could regain my footing, I felt a thud on my chest as Hexas drove his shoulder into me and continued his charge. We collided with the side of the building, and the entire structure shook. Shards of broken concrete and glass rained down as I centered myself. The wall distorted slightly from the impact. A moment later the shimmer settled. I had hoped that none but me saw it. No one in the enemy army reacted, good.

The demon swung. I jerked my head to the side to avoid his claw, and slid past him, casting him to the side, away from the building. The other three were advancing on me quickly. I needed to make some space and keep them away from the structures.

I rushed toward them as if to meet them head-on. Right before we clashed I slammed down my boot and jumped as high as I could over their heads. As I landed I didn't get more than a few steps before seeing the massive arm of Ashtaroth coming at me from the side. It was too late to avoid it. I did my best to protect myself and took the blow. It sent me flying forty feet across the lot. I repositioned as best I could while airborne and rolled as I hit the asphalt, tumbling a few times before emerging upright. But I had addressed my immediate concern, we were well clear of the buildings.

As I stood up, I saw that I was completely surrounded by lesser demons. But they remained stationary; they dared not interfere with the hunt of the greater demons, the same ones that were now between me and the courtyard. I looked behind me to make sure the Duke and the horsemen were not entering the fray. They stood motionless with the swarm of lesser demons around them. If I wasn't running on a half tank I could have probably just powered through them. I was burning through the power given to me—power that was still draining into the pale horse. It didn't matter if I was fighting or standing; I was getting weaker by the second.

I thought quickly about my adversaries and how best to exploit them. I thought about my experiences dealing with them in the past as they launched their attack. Azazel made it to me first, and I parried a few of his swipes before taking one of my own. I grazed his torso, and he backed up just as Vargaz and Hexas arrived. Serran and Ashtaroth would be on me in a moment, so I would need to be in a good position to engage them. I resisted the urge to retreat to a place with better footing. I needed to do some damage (and quickly) while I still had the capacity to do so. I held my ground against the smaller demons and waited.

The lumbering swing of the big guy could be seen coming a mile away. I waited until the last moment before giving a quick swipe of my hand into Hexas's chest and, rolling away, knocking him into the mighty strike's path. The massive fist came down and shook the earth. I heard the sound of crushing bone and flesh as it pulverized the demon I had cast beneath it. I leaped onto Ashtaroth's arm and jammed my hands into it. Ashtaroth roared in pain and pulled his arm back.

I released and used the momentum of its retraction to hurl myself up toward his face. I drove my fist into his skull and pulled it out quickly. He swiped at his face as I jumped down and clawed into his back to slow my descent. I pushed off and rolled away toward more open space to await their next advance. I could hear the sound of bone popping back into place as Hexas began to recover. Serran's strength was her mind, and, though she was close enough to strike, she refrained and moved away from me to direct the action of the others.

Vargaz and Azazel came at me from different sides, but they were uncoordinated. I caught the first attack and grabbed Vargaz's arm, swinging him around and slamming him into Azazel. They slid across the ground and rolled to a halt between the buildings that led to the courtyard. I didn't want them there, and it must have shown in my reaction.

Serran turned toward them and saw what I didn't want her to. She realized she had a potential pressure point and told them to advance into the courtyard. I rushed toward them, but they had too much of a head start. Adrian saw them, and those he had brought who were still alive began to line up again. They opened fire at the two charging demons, their glowing rounds carving right through them. From my position they appeared to power through the oncoming fire. It wasn't going to be enough. I needed to give them something more important to focus on.

I changed direction and drew my hand back before lunging. I drove my hand into Serran's chest, and she gave out a deafening scream, instinctually calling out for help. I turned my head to see the two charging demons turn away from Adrian and the rest and head back to try to save their master. I lifted Serran into the air and drove her into the ground. I cocked my other hand back and brought it down toward her neck. It stopped a few inches shy of its target, interrupted by the still-mangled claw of Hexas. I retracted my hand from the demon queen and spun it around to swing at her savior, but the blow never made it.

I didn't see Ashtaroth's hand until it dropped me. I skidded across the ground before coming to a halt as his other hand pinned me to the asphalt. His fingers wrapped around me and he lifted and slammed me back into the ground repeatedly. I felt every part of me become limp as my bones broke and flesh tore. As my body weakened, all the strength I had went with it. Everything I had left—everything Ana had given me—was gone. I couldn't do anything but lie there as the five greater demons congregated around me. I could hear them discussing what to do, though I was so weak I could not make out the details. I felt myself being lifted, and then the pain started. I couldn't even scream as they dug into me. I don't know how long I hung there taking their punishment.

As I struggled to keep my eyes open, all I could see were the silhouettes of the Duke and the Horsemen coming toward me.

"That's enough," he yelled. "Put him down."

My back hit the ground with a thud. My exposed bones ground against the asphalt as I rolled into a resting position. I could feel my body putting itself back together. I wailed in agony as my bones began to pop and reconnect. It lessened as I began to mend. My arm was functional, so I rolled over and

285

looked toward the courtyard. I started pulling myself toward them to see better. It was slow, and my breaths were shallow. My lungs burned from the still-broken ribs pressing up as I dragged them across the ground. I did my best to ascend the slope of the crater that had been made where Ashtaroth had slammed me repeatedly on the ground. It was the hardest thing I could remember doing.

"Oh please, Grimm," the Duke said. "You'll never make it. And even if we let you, they can't save you. Hell, *you* can't even save you."

I tried to speak, but only muffled, broken words oozed out.

"I'm sorry," the Duke chuckled, "speak up."

I waited until I was almost to the top to try again. The same muffled words came out as I reached the lip of the crater and looked out toward my companions. I felt the edges of my lips begin to curl. As they did, the Duke's sadistic laugh halted and turned into a grunt of anger. His boot caught my broken ribs. The force of his kick flipped me onto my back. I tried to spit out a cry of pain, but only a groan came.

I felt my mouth begin to widen again as I looked up into the blackness of the night sky. I choked up the first laugh and felt my ribs begin to reset themselves.

"What's so fucking funny?" the Duke asked. I looked up at him. His eyes were burning with the fury from his lack of understanding.

I tried again to spit out what I had said as I was crawling up the side of the crater. But my chest cavity was still too damaged to produce anything more than a whisper. I looked at him again, and he knew that I actually wanted him to hear what I had to say. The fire faded from his eyes as he leaned down next to me.

AND HELL FOLLOWED WITH HIM

I pushed out the words once more, so he could hear them. "Check," I said.

He grabbed me by the throat and squeezed. I could feel my vision fading as his fingers tightened.

"What am I missing?" he demanded as he slammed me once more into the ground.

I pulled up my hand and turned it, so he could see once again that there was no rune on it.

He began to connect the dots as he thought back to his earlier comment about it not mattering how I had removed it.

"What did you do?" he screamed. "Tell me!"

I struggled to get out the words, but I wanted them to have as much impact as possible. So, I swallowed and forced them out.

"Being human gave me something . . . something special."

"What?"

"Vision," I said. I reached my hand to his face and tilted his chin up, so he could see my friends. "Chapter six, verse eight," I continued.

I could see the passage flash through his mind as the numbers fetched the words that went with them. His eyes widened.

The last of the glowing blue lines at Vince's feet made their connection, and, as they did, a burst of air emanated from the center of the courtyard. The shockwave almost knocked them all down, and I began laughing once again. A look of bewilderment crossed his face as he struggled to wrap his head around how he had missed it. His look of confusion was then replaced with blind rage. He drew the remnants of his broken sword and thrust it toward me.

Just as quickly as he had lunged so, too, was he cast to the side. His bones crushed audibly as Oman's mace peeled him out of the air and sent him crashing back to earth in a twisted heap of bone and flesh.

Before the Duke had even hit the ground, Aiden and Wynn were standing over me. They each grabbed an arm and pulled me away from the demons. They deposited me by the now-open portal before leaping back into the fray. The blue glow of the million souls flooding from the gate filled the night.

I looked up from where I lay and saw the legion flooding past me. They all held out their hands as they passed over me. I felt the first touch breathe life back into me, then another, and another. As the freed souls of men and women ran past toward the army of demons they each gave me a small part of themselves.

I felt the remaining pieces of my broken body fall back into their proper places, and I sprung to my feet. I could feel the power coursing through me as I watched my adversaries retreat. Oman, Aiden, and Wynn fell back and arrived at my side. They, too, laid hands on me and gave some of themselves. I felt like I was glowing. We readied ourselves and pressed forward to meet the demons.

The Duke, his Horsemen, and the greater evils had re-grouped as well, and were pressing forward with their swarm. You could feel the world shake as the two forces met. The Horsemen split off from the Duke; and Oman, Aiden, and Wynn did the same to engage them, while the Duke and the other five greater demons were cutting their way toward the courtyard, and me.

A slight grin spread over my face as I replayed it all in my mind. I had told the Duke that I had done as he'd said. And though I had not prepared for him to use my blood to complete the link with Despair, I had still done what I needed to: bought Vince time. Now there was but one thing left of the Duke's command to follow through on. I was to cleanse this world, and I would do just that. But it would not be in the way he had imagined it.

I would cleanse this world of the evil that had been unleashed upon it. By any means necessary.

14

Paying the Price

The sound of the clashing forces roared through the night, filling the air with naught but the sound of war. Everything bottle-necked between the buildings, creating small proxy battles and making way for more troops to press through. I pressed against the hordes of demons while the other Eternals drew the attention of the Horsemen. I fought my way to the front and began to strike down the demons at the point of attack. There was a swell at the bottleneck, and then, with a push, the faded blue glow of the souls we had liberated pushed back the fire into the parking lot. We were winning.

As we pressed the main force back toward the spiraling pillar of flame from which they'd emerged, the conflict of the Eternals moved away from the larger group. I could see my brethren battling in the distant corners of the field, sending waves of power hurtling into the night. I surveyed the battles quickly to ensure no one was in dire need of assistance before turning my attention back to the greater demons who had begun to plow through the ocean of blue in an attempt to push us back.

Everything felt faster, sharper, and more potent as I turned to face the coming enemy. The asphalt buckled under the sheer force exerted when I pushed off it. I moved quicker than I ever had as the power of a thousand souls coursed through me. I carved through the demons in massive swaths as I advanced toward the greater demons.

The roar of battle was pierced by the sound of clashing steel as my hands met the hardened scales of Ashtaroth. The massive demon's legs buckled under the force of my strike, and he collapsed to the ground. A shockwave erupted; its force cast down all of the lesser spirits in the immediate vicinity, friend and foe alike. A moment later the arm of the downed demon came raining down toward me. Unlike before, I now had the strength to challenge him.

I caught the swinging blade with an open palm and dug my fingers into it. The thick, bony matter crumbled like dried dirt and fell through my fingers as I clenched. The largest of my foes wailed in pain. I jerked him to the side before bringing down my other hand across his forearm. The spray of his black blood hit me in the face as his arm detached and fell to the ground beside me.

He reared up in agony and exposed himself. I surveyed his underbelly for my next point of attack, but I didn't get the chance to move. A joint attack from Hexas and Vargaz pulled my attention, and I darted to the side to avoid them. They quickly changed direction and lunged forward in pursuit. I dodged and parried the flurry of incoming attacks while backing away from the other advancing demons, trying to force one of them into a mistake.

Vargaz presented one first. I dodged to the side from his attack, and he overextended in his follow-up, which threw him off balance. I made a quick parry of Hexas's claw and redirected him away from my other adversary. I caught Vargaz's errant claw with my left hand and gave a stout yank in the direction he was already tumbling toward. His demonic feet left the ground. Once he was airborne I could do with him as I saw fit. I redirected my pull and cast him downward. He crashed headfirst into the asphalt and skidded a good ten feet. I knew my window to strike would be short and decided to play it safe.

I left the fallen demon and turned my attention to Hexas, who had turned and began to move in again. I halted my retreat and advanced toward him. He swung at me with the long bone protrusions he used as weapons. I slipped under the first one and then raised my hand to catch the second. I met it with my blade-hand, and it came to a dead stop. The black of my fingers turned pink again as they softened, and I wrapped my fingers around the bone. I moved under it before giving a quick swipe with my free hand. It struck the wrist of the demon, causing the hand and long bone spike I was holding to fall free of the arm.

Hexas wailed and then took another swing with his remaining arm. I caught it, too, and then cocked my leg back to strike. I felt the demon's leg bones crumble from the force of my kick. Both his feet lifted into the air and he fell backward. I followed through with my kick and spun around. Using the momentum, I brought down the spike that was still in my hand. It passed through the demon's left eye and out the back of his skull before continuing a solid twelve inches through the asphalt and into the ground.

The force of the spike hitting him snapped his neck before he even hit the ground, nearly pulling his head off as it dragged the rest of him with it. His body fell limp. I held on for a moment to make sure he would not move again. The roar of combat passed as the sound of fire met my ears, and the body of Hexas beneath me filled with a million cracks and began to turn to ash.

One down.

From the corner of my eye I saw that Vargaz had gotten to his knees and had almost risen. I released the crumbling bone spike and bolted toward him, ready to press the advantage before he could fully recover. I pulled my hand back and lunged forward. But I did not meet the soft flesh I had expected. The loud crash of metal rang out as my hand met the remaining massive arm of Ashtaroth. He swung it at me, and I rode the momentum of it and leaped backward and out of the fray.

The remaining greater demons gathered on him and then rushed at me together. I scanned the incoming attack and noticed that they were one short: the Demon Lord himself.

I turned around to see that the Duke had split off from the others and was cutting his way through the courtyard toward Vince and the portal. The realization of his intent cascaded into my mind. I dug my foot into the ground and changed direction to try to stop him. Every worst-case scenario played in my mind as I struggled to make my way to him before he could reach Vince and close the gate.

The sight of the Duke discarding the swaths of blue souls and breaking into a sprint made everything else stand still. I heard the echo of my voice as I yelled out to my friend to flee. He looked at me and then at the charging demon. I broke free of the crowd just as the Duke drew his broken sword. I moved faster than the demon, but his lead was too great.

The blue glow of the gate faded as Vince leaped away from the whizzing blade and landed hard on the ground. He rolled away as quickly as he could, barely escaping the broken blade as it crashed down again. Vince scrambled to his feet and away from the Duke, joining the group of armed personnel behind his position.

The last of the souls that had come through the portal before it closed moved past me, and I rushed toward the Duke. The sound of gunshots rang out as the troops opened fire on their assailant. He swatted away the glowing rounds that were on target with his broken sword and turned his attention to them. They tried to back up, but he was too fast, and before they could move to safety he was on top of them. I wanted to help, but as Vince hobbled away, I saw the wound on his chest and realized he had not made it away cleanly. Prescott emerged from the group and carried Vince on his shoulder, away from the group.

The sound of screams and cleaved flesh coming from those who had drawn the Duke away made my heart sink. Logically, I should have been helping them, but my friend was more important. I threw myself under Vince's other shoulder, and Prescott and I moved him through the courtyard into cover.

The blood poured from the gash in Vince's side. It was definitely bad, but on closer inspection no organs had been ruptured. Prescott drew his knife and cut into the hanging cloth of Vince's shirt. He pressed the liberated material on the open wound. Vince groaned in protest and pressed hard on the cloth.

"That's fucking Japanese silk, asshole," Vince said, tugging the collar of his ruined raiment.

"Good. It's expensively saving your life," Prescott replied as he began to cut more cloth from the shirt.

He looked at me as he pulled the dressing from Vince's garb. His eyes said it was under control. I nodded and turned back toward the battle. I could see that Adrian was making his way toward us as I left the two of them to address the wound.

The last sound of steel against bone rang out and with it the screams fell silent. The team we had brought was gone. The Duke's white suit was now red, and as he turned toward me I could see the corners of his mouth turn up. He turned toward me and pointed his riven blade at me, a challenge.

We met at the center of the courtyard where the faint outline of the portal had been scorched into the ground. The sound of his broken blade ringing out as it met my hand was piercing. He swung again, and I deflected it before launching my own strike. As we clashed it felt as if he was getting stronger and stronger. I made a parry of his lunge and felt the slight resistance of his flesh give as the blade passed through it. I had nicked his thigh, and he rolled away before emerging on his feet again.

I turned toward him and saw why the fight was slowly starting to swing in his favor. The once-mighty army of tortured souls had met the Duke's legion and been stifled. Without me at the front, Serran, Azazel, Vargaz, and Ashtaroth had cut down much of my army. What was left continued to fight, but the Duke had done what he needed to do. He had closed the portal. It was only a matter of time before those we had freed were overwhelmed by sheer numbers. With each one that fell, a little more of the energy they had given me faded. The realization must have shown on my face as the Duke's smirk widened and he once more leaped toward me.

Each successive swing grew more difficult to block or

deflect. Before long I felt like I was moving in slow motion again. I summoned everything I had left and unleashed it. I spun and brought down my arm. I felt the edge of the sword catch it and then give way. The Duke's elbow buckled, and he could do nothing but push the attack to the side, exposing himself. My hand landed hard on the ground. I used the momentum and swung my leg. My boot hit him square on the chest and sent him skidding on his back toward the fight that his army was winning.

He got back to his feet and watched me struggle to find stable footing. He knew I was spent and decided to leave me and engage the remnants of our forces. I felt a tug on my arm and stumbled toward it. Prescott supported me as we made our way back to where I had left Vince. I fell into a seated position next to him.

"You look like shit," Vince said, his face pale from blood loss.

I was breathing heavily and struggled to spit out words.

"We're not in a good place," I said.

"Really? I thought it was going fine."

Everyone wanted to be positive, but we needed to do something drastic, and soon.

"We need to do it now," I said. "Are they ready?"

"Doubt it," Adrian said. "Only one way to find out."

I nodded. Prescott reached for his hip and pressed the button. The beep and crack of his radio was harsh, but the sound of Vera's voice coming from the other side made it better.

"What the hell do you want?" she asked. "We're busy."

"Things aren't going so well out here. We need to start now," Prescott said.

"I can fucking see that from up here. We're going as fast as we can."

"Well, you need to be finished now!" Prescott yelled back.

"It's not possible, Nate," Ramsey said from the background. "You have to buy us more time."

"I don't care how you fucking do it, Gerry, but it needs to be ready now!"

"It's not going to happen, end of story!" Ramsey said.

The fighting was drowned out as I saw the gears spinning in Adrian's mind.

"Shut up!" I yelled.

Everyone halted and the others on this side were able to see what I saw. Adrian snatched the radio out of Prescott's hand and again the harsh beep and crack pierced the air.

"Vera, what if we reroute the system through the existing power grid? Would that be enough?"

"Stand by," she replied. The silence was murder as we waited. "It should work, but we're going to lose the other system."

"That's fine," I said. "Just make sure it counts."

"If we do this, they'll know we're here," Ramsey protested. "We're only going to get one shot at this."

I could hear Aaron and Marx in the background.

"You better hurry the hell up," Aaron said. "I already think they do."

"We'll make sure it's good down here," I replied. "Just get it ready."

I lifted myself up and surveyed the battle. Oman, Wynn, and Aiden had rallied and pushed the demons out of the courtyard entirely. We needed a tactical retreat, but I didn't know how to do it and not make it look suspicious. Luckily for me, someone else did. I felt the pull on my clothes as Vince used me to stand up. None of us said a word, but we all had the same idea. Adrian and Prescott helped Vince and I to the center of the courtyard. Maybe it was just hope coming from within, but I could feel the power rising through the ground as Vince started chanting again.

The etching on the ground sparked back to life and the blue glow grew brighter and brighter as the lines began to light up once more, tracing the shape of the pentagram. It did exactly what I hoped it would. I watched as the Duke and his greater demons saw it and surged toward us. The line that had formed between the buildings broke and the remaining souls began falling back. I heard the Duke give an order and the Horsemen broke from their fights with the Eternals and met the demons in the center for what he hoped would be their final push.

The Eternals appeared at our side and prepared to push back. I grabbed Oman's arm to stop them from advancing.

"The portal won't be open in time," he said. "We have to push them back."

"No," I said. "Let them push, just funnel them here."

Oman nodded and motioned to Aiden and Wynn. They hit the demons from the side as I had asked and pushed them close together. As they did it pushed the remnants of the freed souls back into us, and I felt myself recharging from the souls around me. There weren't many left, but as I felt the strength move back into my hands I knew it would be enough—it had to be. I strode forward into the fray and was met swiftly by the others.

The Duke was at the front of his legion, with the Horsemen right behind. His pride was tangibly hanging in the air above him. He wanted to be the tip of the spear that would bring him victory; which was exactly where I wanted him. He took the first swing, and I moved into it. My palm met his blade hand and stopped it cold. I squeezed and twisted, snapping his wrist and sending his broken sword to the ground. I yanked and threw my hips. The Duke sailed over my shoulder, and I slammed him into the ground by his broken arm. I swung at him, making sure it was slow enough that he would dodge it. He rolled out of the way and pointed at me with his good hand.

The Horsemen obeyed his command and converged on me. I slipped past the attacks and backed up into the glowing blue of the souls that still remained. They pushed in further along with the demons. Oman, Aiden, and Wynn played the defense game with me. Pulling their punches but maintaining their threat. I saw the Duke reset his wrist and scoop up his sword before pushing back to the front. He was furious, which was good. I engaged again, continuing to draw him closer to Vince and the reforming portal. It almost looked like a dance as we methodically drew them in.

Then it ended.

I heard the yell of pain from behind me to the left. I deflected an incoming sword swipe and threw and swung before looking to see what had happened. Wynn had caught Sai's spear right above her collarbone. Aiden cast aside his attacker and attempted to aid her. He landed the first blow using his cesti against Sai's ribs and then swung another, hitting her between the shoulder blades. Sai slid across the ground and stopped, not far from the Duke and me.

Wynn pulled out the spear and brought it down, snapping it across her knee. She gathered herself and rushed out toward Sai, slamming the broken spear into the ground. Sai rolled away and snatched the remnants of her spear, and the two reengaged. I looked at Aiden, who was trying to hold the line and reengage Jaina, but the damage was done. The demons had broken the line, and Hexas and Azazel had pushed through.

I threw one last swing to freeze the Duke in place, and broke contact to head off the two errant demons. The sound of gunshots hit my ears, and I saw Hexas stumble and fall as Prescott unloaded his sidearm into the demon's chest. The mag dropped, and I saw Prescott start to pull another from his belt. But it wouldn't be fast enough. The spring clicked, and he thumbed the slide release. The bullet chambered, but Azazel was already on him. The demon swung, and Prescott fell backward. He began firing into the demon, who was still swinging.

I broke free from the pack and reached the two just as Azazel was winding up for what would have been the death strike. My hand met his arm between the elbow and shoulder, sending it to the ground. He turned and swiped at me. I caught it with my left hand and then brought my right arm down diagonally at his neck. The first strike made it only halfway through his chest. I cocked back and swung again. I released his arm and it, along with his head and half torso, slid off his bottom half and fell to the ground. I drove my foot through his skull to stop his screeching, and then I felt it.

The sting of the steel in my back was excruciating. I looked down and saw the broken end of a sword sticking out of my chest. At first, I tried to pull myself off of it, but then realized my feet weren't on the ground. The muffled sound of people crying out reached my ears. I looked up and saw that it was from those gathered around the glowing blue circle, which was now only a few feet in front of me. I breathed deeply and yelled out as loud as I could, "Now!"

There was nothing for a moment, and then I felt the air begin to hum. Ramsey and Vera had done it. I looked at the buildings around us as the power drained and was redirected into the system that Ramsey and Vera had built. As it did, the buildings that surrounded the courtyard looked like melting wax fading away in short bursts as the projectors lost their juice, revealing the truth beneath. The facade of the ARC Industries campus vanished, revealing the real location of our fight: Memphis, Egypt. Though I couldn't see it, I liked to think that absolute confusion was written on the Duke's face.

A flash of blinding light hit us. We were being bathed in the light of the Answer. The rays of it felt like the surface of the sun. In unison everything the light touched began to wail in agony. I felt my feet hit the ground and collapsed beneath the searing light just as everything else did. I rolled over and clawed at the ground toward Vince, who shook with pain. Our gazes met, and his shaking hand went to his pocket. He knew what I needed. The stone blade fell to the ground next to him, and he turned his attention back to the agony that was consuming him. I clawed my way to it and wrapped my fingers around it before heading back.

The Duke was weakened, but he wasn't incapacitated. He was slowly climbing to his feet, and from there he would work his way out of the spotlight. I grabbed his ankle just as he got upright and swept it from under him, dropping him to his knees. He turned and grabbed my shirt before cracking me in the jaw with his elbow. He stood up again and lifted me with him. From that spot I could see the demons and souls writhing on the ground around us.

The Duke drove his forehead into my nose. I felt blood

spurt down over my lips. He reached around my back and wrapped his fingers around the handle of the sword that was still sticking from my chest. I felt like I was fading in the light as he held me there. With what little strength I had, I jabbed the dagger into his ribs. He did little more than flinch. He hit me again, and I retaliated with another jab of the blade.

Then another.

I continued to stab repeatedly with the same result as the first.

I could feel myself standing at the edge of unconsciousness. Then I woke up. The burning subsided and the light faded as the power grid started to collapse. Everything grew silent except my labored breathing and his chuckle.

"Oh, that was good," the Duke said smugly. "You built a high-powered light with the power of your precious dagger. It was decent idea, if it had worked."

"Who's saying it didn't?" I retorted, matching his smug smile with one of my own. Everything went white as he crushed my nose with his forehead again.

"Please," he said, "just admit you didn't think this all the way through. And Egypt? Who gives a shit?"

"Maybe you should," I replied, consequently catching another head butt. I continued, "Oh, come on. You've been watching. This was all you remember. You saw everything. You knew I would be there in Adrian's bedroom. You knew what he would do. All of this was by your design."

"So?"

"So, something happened after he died. Something you can't control."

The Duke thought about that night for a moment. "The remnants. So what? They're weak, driven by instinct."

"Are you sure?"

"Am I sure? I'm absolutely positive. They are nothing more than parasites. They feed on wounded souls, nothing more."

"Exactly," I said.

He looked at the dagger in my hand, and the realization of where he was standing hit him. I thrust the dagger up as hard as I could. It passed through the bottom of his chin and up into his head. He went limp and we fell forward. The hilt of his broken sword hit square on the ground and propped me up. The full weight of his body landed on me and the blade protruding from my chest pierced him as well.

The Duke looked at me and struggled as the swirl of black grew beneath us. The Hexen rose from the ground, drawn up from the ancient tombs that rested beneath our feet. Just as I had asked them to the night we had planned this. I lost myself to the memory as the darkness swirled around us.

It was almost on this very spot that Joe had passed. His soul, like all those lost here, had been fed on by the Hexen, until he, too, was like them. Though they did not speak, they listened. They heard me as I asked them to aid us in this fight should the need arise. It was silent agreement, but as the shadows amid the dark stared back at me I knew they understood.

I was brought back to the present as the hands of the Hexen slid into the Duke and began to tear at him. He couldn't scream from the blade I had forced through his jaw, but his dead black eyes darted back and forth as he bled on me. He even looked at me for help. He convulsed and struggled, but it was like a swarm of flies on honey.

"Take him," I said when I had seen enough of his suffering.

I felt the jerk as they pulled him toward the entrance of the tomb where the glowing waters would live up to their namesake and prove to be the final *Answer* to the Demon Lord's evil. I could feel the pressure of the blade as I was being dragged across the ground along with him. But it didn't hurt anymore. I felt the fingers begin to tear into me as they carried us into the tomb and down into its heart. The floor opened up, releasing the light into the room. As they dragged us down toward the glowing pools, it all felt worth it.

The Hexen would lower the Duke into the water and he would be no more. They would unknowingly send me with him. And it would be over. The light of the central chamber was calming, so I closed my eyes and waited for the end. I thought, perhaps, I would drift away into nothing. The scattered particles of my existence cast to the furthest reaches of the universe. There would be no pain, no happiness, no sadness, no fear, no hate, no love.

Just nothing.

I was comforted by that, but it never came.

I opened my eyes to witness the black hands of the Hexen setting me down gently on the ground. They moved away from me, and then, just as they had arrived, they disappeared in a torrent of shadow. I could look around, but I couldn't move. I could see that the other six Eternals stood at one another's sides, free. Their debts had been cleared. They could once again become who they were.

It felt like gravity increased as the six summoned their power. I could see the vague outlines of the horses. The power waned, and, as it did, the silhouettes twisted and contorted as the steeds of the apocalypse were pulled into the earth and cast back into the nether. As each horse descended, so, too, did a portion of the demon army that now stood frozen in place. Even the greater demons had stopped, just monuments to evil now. Just as quickly as the demons had risen from the earth, so were they cast back into it.

The steeds were gone, save one—mine. The army of demons tethered to it remained motionless as my friends helped me to my feet. I tried to stand but everything was jelly. I couldn't even hold myself up. They walked me slowly to the steed called Despair. It was almost over; just this one thing remained. I tried to lift my hand, so I could banish it like the others, but I had nothing left. I worried what would happen if I touched it. I tried a few more times, but with each try I grew even weaker.

I looked for Vera. I scanned everyone's face in search of hers. She was the only one who showed what all of us already knew: I was too damaged to recover. The wounds inflicted by the evil and light from the Answer had done so much more than weakened me. I turned my gaze away from her and looked down. I denied it for a moment, until I saw. My body was broken and torn far worse than I'd thought. I accepted it. It must have shown on my face because Vera burst into tears. She knew what was next.

"It's okay," I said. "We always knew that this was a possibility. We planned for it."

"That's not what's going to happen," she said. "You're going to be fine."

"I'm not. And that's okay," I said. "This is the way it has to be."

"Please don't. Please don't go."

"It's okay. You taught me what it is to be human. You showed me why I was more than just the garbage man. Why what

I did meant something. I got a chance to save you, to save everyone, and I wouldn't trade that for anything."

"There has to be another way," she said.

"There isn't," I replied. "There must always be death."

I used what little energy I had left to lift my hand to her chin. Our lips met, and what was left of me passed through them into her. As my power flowed into her I let go. Like sand in the wind, my form faded and was gone. Cyrus Grimm was dead.

15

Restoring Order

I looked through my new eyes—her eyes—and saw what was left of me vanish into nothing. I think of it now and remember her soul taking on mine. It was jarring, really. I was gone, but my memories remained. In that moment she knew me—or should I say, I knew him. We are one and the same now. Cyrus Grimm is gone, but so is Vera Essalte.

Everything flashed back into my mind. The discussion we'd had about what we would do if the plan didn't work. Adrian had been insistent that it was he who would take up the mantle of Death. But Cyrus insisted it was me. As his memories melted into me I saw it from an entirely different angle. He loved me, though he didn't quite know what that meant. He wanted so much more for me than to be like every other soul—to pass on, to be made new, and be reborn. He knew that if that happened that everything we shared would be lost. He didn't want me to go when this was over. And if he should fall, he wanted to make sure that I was safe.

I could see myself stepping into the chamber and going through the process that would make me like him. I felt his relief as the white light flooded over me and made me something more. I was only the backup, should things not go right. A lesson he had learned from Adrian. But for him, this was the most important thing in the world. Knowing how he felt—though he never said it—hurt more than anything I had ever gone through. The man called Death was now with me, though he never could be.

I—we—wanted to speak to the others and explain what was happening. But that needed to wait. Though the worst case had not happened. This was not the result we had hoped for, and there was still work to be done. I was nervous that I would not be able to be what he was (had been). Even with his life racing through my mind. I had all his power, his memories, and his skills. But as I walked toward the pale horse, all I could think about was if I would make him proud. The steps were almost in slow motion. I could feel him with me, but at the same time there was still a hole in my heart.

The mighty steed reared up and then settled down as I approached. The power that had been drained from Cyrus was fraying off it. The power hovered in the air like ribbons of bright-green silk. I stepped into them, and as they touched me I felt them connect to the deepest part of my being and latch on. The link between Death and the steed had been reforged. I was bound to his will and he was bound to mine.

The remaining army of latent demons stirred around us. I laid my hand on Despair's withered flesh. I waited for it to pull at me, but the link had already been made. I was in control of both it and the army of demons that stood idly all around us. I expected it to be unmistakably evil, but that's not what I felt. I couldn't put my finger on it at the time, but as I think back I would have to say that it was nothing more than the rest. A pawn made to play a role in a game it didn't understand.

The Eternals did their best to coach me through it—to be gentle but firm. The power coursed through me and into my hand. I wasn't sure if it was pain or fear that shone in the beast's eyes, but it reared again as I ended the ritual. Its form began to twist. The sound of breaking bones rang out as its skeletal frame collapsed in on itself and sank back into the depths. When it was gone, the demons shattered and fell to ash.

The sun broke over the horizon and light flooded onto the sand where we stood. So much had been lost, and yet so much had been saved. We cleaned up everything as best we could. The Eternals and I sealed the tomb so that no one would ever be able to abuse the power that it held. Adrian and I made sure that all the research we had done was also destroyed. Every loose end was tied, and every mistake buried. It was over, but it didn't feel that way. Something seemed out of place with the world.

After a time, I visited those who had been present through it all. Vince recovered from his wounds and eventually sold the club and moved away from the city. When I last saw him, he said that he had felt Joe's spirit talking to him. Maybe he had; maybe the Hexen that remained of his friend had found a way. I can't say for certain. He pledged he would find him and help him move on. I wanted to help, but I could only wish him the best in his search.

Prescott was eventually tracked down by the police and charged with manslaughter and various counts of conspiracy.

He cooperated fully with the authorities, directing them through the investigation and eventually leading them to the burned-out remains of the actions we had done to save everyone. I don't know if they ever closed the case, but by the time the proceedings were over, Prescott got off with time already served. He took some time for himself to spend with his daughter before eventually becoming a security contractor for the federal government. Last I heard, his daughter was going to graduate high school and had been accepted into Princeton.

Ramsey returned to ARC and did his part to make sure no one would find anything. He was eventually tasked with revamping the security systems for the entire company, a job which he gladly did. There hadn't been a security breach since. He was promoted to head of cyber security and did his job well for several years. At least until he was caught playing video games at work and was terminated. Prescott got him an interview as a white-hat hacker in the same federal agency he works at. His second interview is next Tuesday.

Detectives Marx and Aaron went on the run from me for some time. The idea of them moving on and losing who they were was not something that sat right with them. I didn't even realize they were absent until they came looking for me. The world had taken its toll on their souls, and they were exhausted when they arrived. They had begun their transformation into shadows. By that time, they were ready to move on. They still exist in the ether, waiting to be reborn and try again. They have good hearts, so I know in their next lives they will be good men or women. I just hope their hygiene will have improved the next time they walk the earth.

And then there's Adrian. He had wanted so badly to make

a difference in the world that he had inadvertently put it on a collision course with destruction. When Cyrus was gone I couldn't help but blame him. So many lives had been lost, including mine, because of his actions. I knew in my heart that he had been used, just like everyone else. But his brilliance had ultimately put all the wheels in motion. Unlike the detectives, he wanted to move on from the start. But I didn't let him. Instead I let him fade and twist into one of the shadows. I watched him wander for a long time, thinking it was punishment for what he had done. It was wrong, and I should have never done it.

Eventually, I took what was left of him to the other Eternals. But there was nothing to be done. I could have taken what was left and put it back into the life stream to be broken down and used by the universe to reinforce other souls. But I didn't. If I did, then he would be gone forever. He deserved better than that. Instead I left him to wander eternity as a withered soul. A reminder to myself that I owe every soul more than what I gave him.

Every time I see him, I hate myself for what I've done. Cyrus would have never let it happen, regardless of any personal feelings. When I watch his memories, I know that. Were he able to speak to me, he would have told me to save Adrian. But I didn't, and it haunts me. I couldn't forgive him when, really, there should have been nothing in me but forgiveness for him. Adrian will never again walk the earth and give to it his brilliance. I did a disservice to humanity and to the memory of the man I replaced.

The world moved on, and so did I. I thought a lot about Cyrus in the time that passed since the events. But I always chalked it up to memories, his or mine. Sometimes I was just lonely, and having him with me, even just in thought, was enough. I took on his role and performed it as best I could, pulling on his memories and experiences to make me better at it. I moved across the world and helped the departed move on. It was nerve-racking at first, but every time I stood with someone I just asked myself, *What would he have done?*

After a time, I fell into my new job and everything was normal. But there was something I just couldn't shake. That same feeling that something was out of place never went away. One day something came to me. I thought it was just a remnant at first. Another memory of Cyrus had left with me, rising up. But then it spoke. It wasn't a memory—it was a voice, a calling. I realized then that it was something much more.

The memory of his passing flashed in front of me, as if I was there again. I watched as he disappeared into the wind, the last part of him moving into me. Everything I felt was real. I didn't imagine it; it had happened. I felt myself connect with him again and I realized that he really had moved into me. He was here. Not just the memories, but all of him.

Time passed, and, as it did, he and I became more and more connected. We couldn't talk, but we could feel each other. I never told him I knew he loved me. But I could feel that he knew. I didn't feel alone anymore. I had already become proficient at it, but as the connection grew stronger he taught me how to do my job, his job. I began to see the little things that he saw, the idiosyncrasies that made each soul unique, special.

Humanity was beautiful. As I began to see it as he did, it

made me realize that even though he had said curiosity was the driving force that put this story in motion, it wasn't. He revered humanity in its flawed, uneven existence. They were his to protect, and he was willing to go as far as he needed for that purpose. He could have run at any moment, saved himself, and safeguarded the souls left in the ruins of the world. It was a mistake for him to do what he had done. But it was also what made him so special. He was gone, but he had saved them. They would never know how much he cared for them.

You might be asking yourself: That's it? That's how it ends? No happy ending? The boy doesn't get the girl? Sadly, no, because that's not the truth of the universe. Cyrus doesn't believe in God. Unlike him, I do. He keeps telling me that the idea of God is too perfect to exist in the real world. The real world is messy, jagged, and unstable. And more often than not, people are left with just broken pieces with which they must do the best they can. It's not glamorous, and it's not fulfilling. It's just life.

I don't think he's cynical, though. I just think that he's been around for a long time and has never experienced God as I did when I was alive. He didn't ever get to experience something so special that it made him believe that it could only have happened that way if there was some larger design.

I agree with him on some points. The world is absolutely messy, jagged, and unstable. But that's what makes it wonderful. There are so many things that cannot be explained. So many things he didn't know, in spite of his vast knowledge. So many eons spent wandering this little blue world and still he knew only a fraction of what it held.

Which brings me to you.

I want to thank you for listening to my story, his story. I cannot express how important it was to me that you hear it. I've played it over and over again in my mind in anticipation of telling it. Which takes me back to the beginning. As I told you then, I've been looking for you for a very long time.

Fact of the matter is, Cyrus never had the chance to believe in God. He never got to see the beauty that I see. I see that now. You see, sometimes, on very rare occasions, everything aligns perfectly in a way that doesn't seem possible. Humanity calls these things miracles. Moments like those are the reason that I believe in God.

I understand that with enough variables, these events are just statistical certainties that in the absolute chaos of the universe will eventually happen. There is no choice but for them to occur every once in a while. The anomalies are perfectly normal. And because of their limited knowledge, humanity places special significance in these things. It is the way the universe works. I know they happen, because I know they have to. And because of that, there has been one anomaly in particular that I have been waiting for.

You see, energy is everything, and everything is energy. Energy can neither be created nor destroyed. We know this. We also know that everything is different. The little idiosyncrasies that make each soul unique. All things have their own very specific wavelength. From a stone, to a soul, to the very primal forces that bind our world together. They are unwavering, unending, eternal.

Eternal. I like that word. We have used it to describe things that will always be. Things like Truth, Justice, Grace, Karma, Will, Wisdom, and Order. You'll recognize the names, I think.

They are the Eternals of our little story. And they are the guardians of this world. Because, you see, everything is energy, even them. And as we know, energy can neither be created not destroyed.

You see, I wanted to find you—you specifically. Because I knew that whether it was the will of God or just the infinite chaos of the universe spitting out that inevitable anomaly, you would eventually happen.

I didn't want just anyone to hear this story; I wanted *you* to. I wanted you to know who you once were. I wanted you to know that sometimes everything falls perfectly into place, and things that shouldn't be possible, are. I wanted to tell you that I love you. I wanted you to know that before you were this, you had made a profound impact not just on me, but on the world.

In a few moments, I'm going to kiss you. When I do, the remains that passed into me when you died—all the power, memories, and skills, everything that I have carried for so long waiting for you—will be yours again. The universe will have made things right, and you will be whole, once more the Aspect of Order.

Where we go from there, I don't know. I just want you to understand that whatever happens, I love you. And just as you have always been with me, I will always be with you. Now I want you to take my hands and repeat after me.

"My name is Cyrus Grimm, but you know me better as Death."

Printed in Great Britain
by Amazon